D1591239

THE LIGHT REFLECTED

THE
PROVINCETOWN
SERIES

Will Freshwater

WILL FRESHWATER

The Light Reflected
Copyright © 2022 Will Freshwater

This is a work of fiction. Names, characters, places, and incidents either are the product of author imagination or are used fictitiously, and any resemblance to actual persons, living or dead, business establishments, events, or locales is entirely coincidental.

Cover Design: L.C. Chase at lcchase.com/customcovers.html

ISBN: 979-8-9868995-2-7
Digital ISBN: 979-8-9868995-3-4

Printed in the United States of America

First Edition: September 2022

Visit Will's webpage: willfreshwater.com

THE LIGHT REFLECTED

THE
PROVINCETOWN
SERIES

WILL FRESHWATER

For Lynn

ACKNOWLEDGMENTS

It took eight long years to bring this story out of my head and onto the page. With each new chapter, I battled the dreaded "Sophomore Slump"—the fear and uncertainty of producing a successful second novel after *Favorite Son*. Somewhere along the way, I stopped worrying about whether the writing was good enough for publication and pushed forward. Ethan Hawke once said: "Happiness is in the doing, not getting what you want." Guided by that precept, I focused on the work and trusted that the process would be its own reward. In the end, I was not disappointed.

I often warn my friends that anything clever they say will probably turn up somewhere in my writing. Grateful for their trust, I want to give a huge shout out to all the wonderful people who provided inspiration along the way, including Lissa Bailey, Ben Murphy, J.D. Bowers, C.J. Mapletoft, Brian Cusick, Jeffrey Clouser, and Patrick Saparito. A special thank you to L.C. Chase for the cover design and formatting.

This novel would never have been possible without the love and support of Maggie Cadman. Although Maggie passed away suddenly in 2016, her keen insights and thoughtful guidance continue to guide me.

I also need to acknowledge the brilliant and incomparable Dr. Lynn DellaPietra. Lynn was two-parts editor and one-part therapist as we methodically worked together for the better part of a year. She also continues to be the inspiration for one of my favorite recurring characters in *The Provincetown Series*! In addition to talking through the story arc and content editing, her humor and wit helped me find my bliss again in writing. Thank you for your enduring friendship and unconditional support. You are my mirror and my Muse.

In *Favorite Son* I wrote: "Having a spare anything is generally a good idea...." A second DellaPietra on the project seemed to good to be true, but despite a busy schedule, Cheryl generously gave me so much of her time and creative energy. Her professional judgment and spot-on feedback unquestionably improved the novel. I am forever in your debt.

And last, but most important, I want to thank my husband Stephen for believing in me when I doubted myself. Your work and sacrifices made it possible for me to finally fulfill my dream of becoming a full-time author. The journey hasn't always been easy, but I wouldn't want to walk the road with anyone else.

TABLE OF
CONTENTS

# PROLOGUE

E VEN THOUGH the food at Spiritus Pizza was unremarkable, the place was a tourist favorite. The benches out front were the best spot in Provincetown to waste time people watching. Late at night, after the bars had closed, hordes of gay men would hurry there for one last chance to either hook up or console themselves with pizza. Despite the passing decades, the no-frills décor of the place was pretty much the same. There were no other customers inside, but one of the ovens was open, and a glob of dough was waiting on the counter. Peter had just begun perusing the menu when the kitchen door flew open and a man emerged wiping his hands with a wad of paper towels.

"Hey, sorry to keep you waiting. You're the first customer I've had all night."

Peter intentionally avoided making eye contact with the handsome guy standing in front of him. Still raw from his encounter with Paul, he was in no mood for games. The man was tall—well over six feet—and wore a plain gray T-shirt that accentuated his impressive physique. With short blond hair and chiseled features, he looked Scandinavian, but his skin was too dark. Leaning over the counter, the man's piercing blue eyes were like wandering hands.

"So, what looks good?"

That question was about as loaded as a pizza with the works. The guy's lascivious grin was bad enough, but such an obvious double entendre was too much on an empty stomach. This guy was a player who'd break lots of hearts come summer. Anyone else would have been flattered by the attention, but Peter was only craving food.

"Just a couple slices. Whatever's ready."

"Coming right up. By the way, my name's Max."

"I'm Peter."

Ding. Ding. Ding. The oven timer signaled the end of the first round.

In one fluid motion, Max slid a wooden peel beneath the bubbling pizza and transferred it onto a round, aluminum tray. With surgical precision, he made three cuts with a wheel and pulled the pieces apart.

"For here?"

"To go."

Peter was digging through his wallet for some cash when Max reached across the counter and grabbed his wrist.

"Don't worry about it. Dinner's on me. I was going to throw most of this into the trash anyway."

"Thanks," Peter said, stuffing a five-dollar bill into the empty tip jar. "See you around."

"Definitely."

In the heat of summer, a little flirty banter and some free pizza would have been enough to seal the deal. Stunted by winter, those same pickup lines sounded cheesy and stale. Helpless, Max watched as Peter grabbed his order and headed straight for the door. The arctic blast that snuck in behind him was even chillier than his disposition. Max shivered and moved the rest of the fresh pie from the counter to the warming shelf. Rejection stung worse than frostbite, but the crisp night air was a welcomed relief from the heat of the ovens.

Whooooooosh.

Max emptied his lungs in one long, unbroken breath as he used the hem of his tee to wipe his face. The prospect of some random play had been enough to get his heart pumping, but sweat without physical exertion was just an anatomic reflex. Like morning wood or a wet dream, it didn't count.

Tentative fingertips tested ridges and valleys of muscle as Max tucked his shirt back into his jeans and checked out his reflection in the stainless-steel backsplash. Even after months of hibernation, the image staring back at him looked ripped. Still, the floor-to-ceiling mirrors at the gym would be less forgiving. It would have been easy for Max to use short days and shitty weather as an excuse to blow most of his meager paychecks on bad takeout and beer, but pizza was

Kryptonite and the only six-pack that mattered was the one money couldn't buy.

The secret to staying jacked was finding the right motivation. Tonight, Fate had intervened. Max pulled on the waistband of his Jockey shorts and adjusted the obvious bulge in his pants to confirm what he already knew. Peter had piqued his interest.

Shirt or skins. Catcher or pitcher. Wide receiver or tight end.

In Provincetown, sex was a contact sport where players changed positions as often as uniforms. A stout few might skulk around past Labor Day and force the game into overtime, but there was always an invisible clock ticking down the final minutes to the buzzer. Fans were interested in variety, not prowess. Even the most seasoned starter got cut when the coach called up fresh talent. At thirty, Max was expected to surrender his spot as team captain and take a seat on the bench. Fortunately, what he lacked in youth, he made up for in experience. Rookies with more swagger and better moves were always blitzing the quarterback, but tonight the field had been wide open. Given the odds and his hometown advantage, Max should have had enough game to score.

"Whatever!"

Spitting out the bitter interjection, he snatched a damp rag from the sink and got back to work. The butcher-block counter separating the kitchen from the dining room looked clean, but years of spilled soda and splattered pizza grease left it perpetually sticky to the touch. Come summer, the newest batch of part-timers would waste the better part of a shift scrubbing the surface with harsh chemicals. It wouldn't do any good. Some stains were too deep.

After a few perfunctory wipes, Max gave up and turned his attention to the GE Coca-Cola Telechron clock hanging on the wall.

"Damn."

Like the last day of school or the night before Christmas, time seemed to slow the more you wanted it to pass. Summer days were longer, but the twelve-hour shifts flew by in a blur of glances and grins. Winter was another story. Minutes felt like hours when there was nothing and no one to do. Max closed his eyes and tried to imagine how good it would feel to have someone waiting for him at home. Come June there'd be an endless stream of guys begging for a table at

Spiritus and a turn in his bed. Tonight was a different story. The empty dining room was a metaphor for his stalled life.

It was *definitely* time to call it a night. The boss wouldn't mind if her only full-time employee bent the rules and checked out early. After all, it wasn't like anyone else was about to come strolling in.

Closing up the pizza shop meant trudging through a mental list of mundane tasks. Luckily, Max had spent the better part of his childhood using his imagination to spin sea grass into gold. The certainty that he'd never get to visit Disneyworld or meet Mickey Mouse drove a shy boy to make his own "Magic Kingdom" on the narrow ribbon of sand that separated the town from the harbor. Driftwood and clamshells were poor substitutes for mouse ears and plush, stuffed toys, but doing without taught him how to make almost anything into a game.

Twisting one arm behind his back, Max untied the strings of his apron and swept it over his broad shoulders.

"It's a bird! It's a plane! It's Seaman."

The salty pun didn't fit with the image of a wholesome superhero, but with a chiseled physique and booming voice, he more than looked the part.

Using preternatural speed, the unmasked caped crusader darted through the room upending chairs and sweeping the floor. It seemed like a waste of time to put on a show without an audience, but when it came to performing, Max knew practice makes perfect. In less time than it took to belt out the opening chords to "Superman's Theme," he'd bused the tables and gathered up an armful of half-empty condiment jars. Off-season was all about take-out, so replenishing the garlic powder and grated cheese was mostly just for show. Max could've skipped this task and moved on, but he'd made it a rule never to deviate from his usual routine. Besides, the mindless repetition gave him a chance to sketch out the adult-rated frames of a comic-book rematch with his new nemesis "Captain Frigid."

Freezer. Ovens. Grill.

With practiced efficiency, he went through the motions, checking each station to make sure the oversized appliances were locked down for the night. All work and no play were making Max a dull boy. Even off-season, he'd always managed to "get a little behind in his work," but it had been almost a month since his last hookup and his balls were turning bluer by the day. As soon as his shift was over, Max would dislodge the rusted ten-speed chained to the fence and pedal up Commercial Street to the Moors. With any luck, there'd be someone remotely doable prowling the dunes.

"No way, Maxie. You are not *that* desperate."

For once, the voice in his head was right. Sooner or later, Peter would find his way back to Spiritus. Two slices wouldn't sate his hunger. Even if the local fare wasn't up to his usual standards, he'd eventually realize the old adage about sex and pizza is true: When it's good, it's really good. When it's bad, it's still pretty good.

Guys who played hard-to-get were like winters in Provincetown. No matter how bleak the forecast, the sun would eventually reappear. Every now and then, the heat from a casual encounter would burn hot enough to melt the layer of permafrost around Max's heart. A one-night stand might stretch into a whole weekend, but the warmth from those romances was fleeting.

Bumping and grinding with strangers kept Max from freezing to death, but the only honest relationship he'd had in the past decade was with himself. Time was supposed to heal all wounds, yet the light of one summer lingered, more vivid and painful when he stopped to remember how much had been lost.

CHAPTER 1

Ten years earlier....

"STAYING OR GOING?"

Max had heard Gus ask the question enough times to know he really didn't care how the customer answered. After years of practice, Gus could wrap a slice in foil as fast as he could plate it. Busy assembling pizzas and making change, the old man behind the counter could never have guessed how accurately he'd summed up the internal debate young Max had been struggling with for days.

"Going."

The answer seemed like a no-brainer. Over the past few weeks, waves of visitors had ebbed and flowed up the congested, one-way streets. The cycling moon influenced the tides, but it was Mother Nature who decided the volume of weekend tourists. Sunshine guaranteed a full ferry of day-trippers. A cold, dreary day meant another wasted afternoon watching *Star Wars: The Phantom Menace* at the only movie theater in town. After suffering through a long winter that had annexed most of spring, Max Balais was ready for summer.

Locals knew better than to waste their money on the overpriced pizza during high season, but it didn't cost anything to sit on the wooden benches out front and people watch. East or West End, it didn't matter where you were staying. Sooner or later, every guy in Provincetown would wander past on his way to somewhere else.

Like the fleet of fishing vessels that came and went with the tides, the afternoon ferry had returned from Boston with the daily catch. Sporting neon tank tops and techno-colored shorts, schools of men flittered up and down the narrow sidewalks. Cruising for guys was as easy as fishing in a tidal pool. All you had to do was throw out a line and wait. Before long, an eager minnow would swim over to nibble at the tastiest, dangling worm. The real question was what to do with a big fish once you had him on the hook.

These were the same faces that lingered in the blue glow of the video screens at Luxor in Boston's Back Bay. Even so, everyone acted like they were meeting for the first time. Judging by the buoyant laughter and bare skin, the crowd had left their inhibitions back in the city with the rest of their clothes. The air reeked of duplicity and CK One, but the smell made Max's stomach growl with anticipation.

Bears. Daddies. Twinks.

Commercial Street offered a carnal buffet to satisfy even the most voracious appetite. Each hot dish that strutted by was another savory course to be enjoyed. Max was hungry, starving even, but the cracked digital watch on his wrist warned that his shift at the pier was only a few hours away. If time was money, he couldn't afford a snack. Still, it didn't cost anything to look at the menu.

Five. Three. Seven.

The scoring system Max used to rate boys was shamefully subjective and inexact. Everybody dreamed of meeting that perfect guy, but there was no point giving a single prospect too much attention since he'd inevitably disappear and get swapped out with someone new at the end of the rental week. But when it came to sex, it was less about finding "Mr. Right" and more like settling for "Mr. Right Now." Max made it a point never to window shop for things he couldn't afford to buy, but one high-ticket number stood out. Long on top and shaved tight on the sides, his flaming tuft of red hair was the perfect metaphor. He was smoking hot.

Ten.

Defying summer, the ginger was winter pale. All the shirtless guys around him were busy soaking up rays, but his alabaster skin seemed untouched by the sun. Despite the warm weather, he wore pressed chinos and an unbuttoned linen oxford with the sleeves cuffed up to the elbow. The noticeable track of blue veins snaking up his arms was like a secret treasure map. Tall and lean, his casual expression and natural movement made it clear how comfortable he was with his body. Almost to prove the point, he casually opened his shirt and raked his fingers through a patch of auburn peach fuzz below his belly button.

Discordant chords of conversation and laughter synchronized into the hum of a Siren. Fear of rejection was more effective than beeswax to blunt the song's empty promises, but the bonds that had once tethered Max to his insecurities were gone. Even if it meant getting his hopes dashed on the rocks, he had to follow the ginger's happy trail to find out whether "X" really marked the spot.

Max raked away the visor of blond bangs obscuring his vision and emptied his lungs.

Be cool.

Max repeated the mantra under his breath again and shook his hair back onto his face. Shoulders slumped and jaw slacked, he effortlessly affected a look that conveyed indifference. It was only the glint in his eyes that gave him away.

A guy who scored above an "eight" was considered relationship material, but boyfriends were like handcuffs. Fooling around with them was fun, especially in bed, but Max wasn't about to waste his last summer in Provincetown walking around with both hands tied behind his back. Truth be told, he'd probably spend most of his free time with just one guy. Still, only a fool would fall for the first pretty face when there was likely to be someone better—even hotter— waiting around the corner.

It was hard to think about leaving Provincetown, but Berklee College of Music had one of the Brass Performance programs in the country and Max was determined to get in and finally start working on his undergraduate degree. Only three years had passed since high school graduation, but he still remembered the exact moment when he realized his college plans would have to wait. No matter how many double shifts his mom worked at the diner, she still needed a second full-time income to make ends meet. Although Max accepted the heavy burdens that came along with the titles of "older brother" and "man of the house," he never gave up on his dreams.

Max had spent the past three summers performing in front of Town Hall while tourists tossed spare change into the velvet-lined case at his feet. Street performers never pulled in much money, but playing for a crowd made him feel like a real musician. Even though he was older than the average applicant, Berklee's admissions committee would be impressed when he blasted out an original composition at his audition. The real challenge was convincing his mom and sister that studying music wasn't a colossal waste of time.

"Yo, Blowhard! You want to give me a hand?"

"Right away." Max answered sarcastically as he surrendered his corner of the bench to the next waiting patron and tossed his untouched pizza crusts into the trash. "Just let me power up my DeLorean and jump back in time to last weekend when I spent my *only* day off waiting for you to breeze into town."

The return of the Cavanaughs to Provincetown was like the July 4th parade – an anticipated event that heralded the official start of the season. Max couldn't recall the particulars of how they'd first met, but Danny Cavanaugh had been his best friend for as long as he could remember.

"Sorry about the change in plans," Danny said. "I sent you an e-mail."

"Well, that explains why I never heard from you," Max said, staring off at some distant point on the horizon. "The high school library is closed for summer. I haven't been able to check my AOL account for weeks."

He could have added that his family couldn't afford a computer, but there was no reason to suddenly become "Captain Obvious" when the truth was as clear as the holes in his Reeboks.

Danny dropped his oversized duffle bags onto the sidewalk and pulled Max in for a bone-crushing hug.

It had been more than six months since they'd last seen each other, and time had changed them both. Danny's clunky Buddy Holly glasses were gone, and the lower half of his face was masked beneath an impressive five-o'clock shadow. Brooding eyes and dark scruff suited his dour Irish temperament, but the unkempt appearance made him look older than his twenty-one years. In striking contrast, Max looked like he'd been swimming laps in the Fountain of Youth. With his father's dark skin and his mother's Scandinavian features, people often mistook him for a teenager. A baby face came in handy for picking up tips, not guys. Doormen and bouncers were hard-core about checking IDs, so any twink inside a bar was fair game. But out in public, even the most voracious daddy lost his appetite for a tasty, cream-filled snack if there was a chance he'd get busted for corrupting a minor. Long nights pumping iron at the gym had given Max the body of a man. But inside, where it really counted, he still felt like a kid wearing his dad's Sunday suit.

"So, spill Cavanaugh. What have you been up to since graduation?"

While Danny complained about the internship applications and interviews at architectural firms that had forced him to postpone the start of his summer vacation, Max scanned the crowd. Commercial Street was teeming with tourists, but it was easy enough to spot his ginger in the sea of bleached blonds and dark brunettes. Balanced atop the metal handrail that separated the sidewalk from the street, he looked like a medieval gargoyle come to life.

Back in the real world, Danny rambled on. Apparently, the monthly stipend he'd been planning to use to finance his next great adventure had been cut off in May. The generous severance check hidden in his graduation card was more than Max would earn all summer, but the message from Danny's parents was unequivocal—having fun was no longer his full-time job. Ironically, he only had until Labor Day to decide what he wanted to do with the rest of his life. Come September, the Cavanaughs would close up the house in Provincetown and return to Boston. Unless Danny could find a way to turn one of his hobbies into a paying vocation, he'd have to move back home. Living under his parent's roof was hardly a prison sentence, but being a Cavanaugh ensured a life of privilege, not leisure. Danny's father would undoubtedly commit him to a period of indentured servitude working at the family foundation in exchange for free room and board.

Politically connected and well endowed, the Cavanaugh Foundation had done more than the mayor or town council had done to protect the dwindling list of historic Provincetown properties from a wave of developers who were determined to turn the quiet fishing village into the next Fire Island. Everyone expected Danny to follow in his father's footsteps, but the apple had not fallen close to the tree. Begrudgingly, he'd given up a few of his precious summers doing manual labor on a couple of the smaller renovation projects. But it was one thing to work with his hands on a construction crew and another to be chained to a desk managing bureaucracy. A job that tied him up in red tape would be a nightmare. —

Blinded by the sheen from his golden ticket, Danny couldn't see the envy in his best friend's eyes. Max would have given his left nut to trade places and step into an easy six-figure job. Instead, he was about to crash into a mountain of debt. It would take twenty years of playing weddings and bar mitzvahs to pay off all the student loans that would finance his music degree, but in the end it would be worth it. Risking everything wasn't a scary proposition when you had nothing to lose.

Rock Bottom.

That was a solid foundation he could build on. It also happened to be a great name for a gay porn star.

Max was just about to give Danny grief for complaining about his first-world problems when the ginger turned and flashed him a killer smile. Suddenly, the tension in the air was as thick as the meat in a lobster tail and twice as juicy.

Be cool.

The weekend was still young. No self-respecting player would show his hand so early in the game. Still, it was the chance Max had been waiting for to make a lasting first impression.

It was time to put the muscles hiding under his clothes to work. Opting for brawn over brains, he grabbed both of Danny's overstuffed bags and turned to go.

"Whoa, He-Man! You sure you don't want some help?"

"No, bro. I'm good." Max said, positioning each heavy duffle so the weight was evenly distributed across his back. Looming tall like a modern-day Atlas, he paused as conditioned glutes and quads engaged to stabilize his core. Even without looking, he knew the pose had achieved the desired effect.

"Let's roll."

The feeling that drove him forward was more primal and urgent than lust. This scene, or one like it, had played out every season for as long as Max could remember. It was the same street in the same town he had lived in all his life. Even so, the current of adrenaline coursing through his veins confirmed what he already knew.

This was the summer everything would change.

CHAPTER 2

D ANNY'S FADED Red Sox T-shirt looked like it had been spray-painted onto his chest and the beach clothes he'd bummed around in last season were a size too tight. Fortunately, there was a new summer wardrobe waiting inside the Filene's Basement bags at his feet. Although Danny bristled at the thought of buying stuff with his parents' credit card, it was time to replace the things he'd outgrown. Just for fun, he took a deep breath and felt the soft cotton straining at the seams. His first instinct was to re-enact a scene from *The Incredible Hulk* and tear the shirt from his back in a feigned fit of rage, but Max had already called dibs on all his hand-me-downs.

Like most of their working-class neighbors, the Balais family needed to earn enough during the short summer months to carry them through winter. Max and his sister Josie lived with their mom in a small two-bedroom apartment off Commercial Street. The landlord could have made twice as much converting the place to a weekly rental, but he had a soft spot for the struggling widow and her kids. Even though there was always food on the table and a roof over their heads, Danny knew money was perpetually tight.

"Looks like this is your lucky day."

Without saying more, he peeled off the coveted jersey and tossed it to his friend. Max discarded the year-old *Rolling Stone* he'd been reading and undid the buttons of his shirt. From across the room, Danny could see the threadbare elbows and the indelible ring-around-the-collar. Normally, he'd have pretended not to notice, but it was hard to look away when there was a half-naked guy standing next to his unmade bed.

"Damn, buddy. I hope you've got a permit for those guns."

Grinning sheepishly, Max assumed a classic pose and flexed his biceps. It wasn't like him to show off, especially when it came to his body, but he was stoked to finally have someone notice his transformation. The fact that it was Danny Cavanaugh who was giving him props made his success even sweeter.

"I started working out six months ago. The gym on Bradford was pretty much the only place open all winter. One of the regulars showed me how to use the free weights and new Nautilus machines. He thinks I'm a natural. The toughest part of packing on muscle has been eating enough protein to keep it up."

"Since when have you had trouble keeping it up?"

Max quickly pulled his new shirt over his head to hide the fact he was blushing. Last summer, he would've been ready with a quick comeback. After all, he and Danny had grown up trading sexual innuendo like baseball cards. A playful counterpunch would have restored the balance of the conversation, but the common language they'd always spoken suddenly sounded foreign. Crooning from inside an over-sized boombox, Michael Stipe filled the awkward silence with his soulful lyrics.

Everybody hurts.

Max couldn't have said it better. Sharing a secret usually brought people closer. Sometimes, it had the opposite effect. Now, more than ever, he needed to keep a safe distance from his best friend and avoid a replay of the epic mistake he'd made on New Year's Eve. It was one thing for Danny to be unaware of Max's unrequited feelings and another for him to consciously reject them. Suffering through high school under the weight of a massive crush had been hard. The rest, growing up different in a small town, had been easy. All Max had to do was hide in plain sight.

The same thirty-five teenagers had suffered through four long years at the only high school in town. Since there were more boys than girls in their class, dating was a game of musical chairs. Anyone who didn't move fast enough was left standing alone. Ironically, Max wouldn't have had it any other way. "Lack of opportunity" was the perfect defense to the charge that he didn't have a girlfriend. It also meant there were usually a couple of guys willing to bend the rules when it came to fooling around. Once their hormones kicked in, his over stimulated classmates were like sailors at sea. Desperate for relief, they'd inevitably wander into the dunes at Herring Cove for a quick roll in the sand. All Max had to do was play it cool and promise not to tell.

The old high school on Winslow Street looked like the Hollywood set from *Back to the Future*. There was even a massive broken clock over the entrance to remind students they were stuck in time.

Unfortunately, a couple of his best customers came down with a case of buyer's remorse and outed him to the senior class. A blow-by-blow account of what really went down would have evened the score, but Max didn't rat anyone out. Not once. Not ever. And he never confirmed or denied the rumors. It was one thing for his classmates to know his truth and another for him to start living it.

Growing up in Provincetown, a place where same-sex couples outnumbered their straight counterparts two-to-one, made gay the new normal. But having so many role models was more of a curse than a blessing when you didn't look the part. Every buff guy strutting up Commercial Street on his way to the A-House or Tea Dance was just another painful reminder of all the ways Max didn't fit in. Like runway models, the city boys seemed to relish the attention that followed them wherever they went. Max had spent most of his junior year standing in front of the mirror, imagining what it would feel like to be in the spotlight, wearing stylish clothes that accentuated a killer body. He may have been born gay, but conforming to the lifestyle was a choice. More than anything, Max wanted to find his place and finally fit in, but it was hard to embrace a culture that celebrated objectification when you felt like the best part of yourself was hidden inside.

At some point, he'd decided to avoid the notoriety that would follow his "big coming out"; being the only kid in school without a dad was distinction enough. Sexual orientation was as innate as eye color, but like the cool kids who wore tinted contact lenses, it was easier to hide what you couldn't change.

Max had perfected the art of responding to, without actually answering, questions about his love life. Casual conversations with his sister about pretty girls or hot guys were clues he left untouched. The buoyancy of sunny days and starry nights made it possible to float through summer days with Danny without having the inevitable heart-to-heart, but after a few too many eggnogs one Christmas, Max spilled his guts. Mumbling between gulps of his frothy drink, he'd finally spoken the dreaded word out loud.

Gay.

The wave of euphoria that crested with his confession broke and rolled back when Danny returned to Dartmouth College. Max tried to channel his existential angst about college into music and workouts, but all those repressed feelings were like an iceberg set adrift. Although he could see the tip of the glacier, there was no way to know what was lurking beneath the surface of the water. Even in the heat of summer, Max still felt a cold shiver remembering the titanic mistake he'd made after Christmas that had nearly sunk a friendship.

THE CAVANAUGHS' New Year's Eve party made the holidays almost bearable. Despite the looming apocalyptic prediction of "Y2K," the tempo of the evening was surprisingly upbeat. The music blaring from the Harmon Kardon stereo encouraged a roomful of guests to "party like it's 1999." Written by Prince back in the 1980s, the lyrics finally fit the occasion. The end of the millennium was less than an hour away and everyone was ready to leave the 20th century behind. Sulking alone in a corner with his rum-spiked Diet Coke, Max made a silent resolution. This would be the year he'd finally break away. With good looks and talent, he was going to do for the trumpet what Kenny G had done for the sax.

The dream of his future at Berklee was as bright as the crystal ball looming over Times Square, but Max still needed to find a way to supplement the anemic paycheck he was currently earning bagging groceries at the local A&P. Nearly all the businesses on Commercial Street were closed for winter, so finding a second job wouldn't be easy. Luckily, he was plugged into one of the most influential families in town. Mrs. Cavanaugh had spent most of the Thanksgiving holiday lobbying her neighbors to hire Danny's friend as their winter caretaker. Thanks to her recommendation, Max was going to get paid to babysit empty houses and flush unused toilets. Unfortunately, it looked as though she had demanded a *quid pro quo* from her son in exchange for the favor.

Doling out handshakes and refilling glasses on the other side of the living room, Danny looked visibly uncomfortable in tasseled loafers and cashmere blazer. Even though the New Year was only a half-hour away, his tolerance for mingling and polite conversation was wearing thin. As the Cavanaughs' eldest son, Danny was expected to help entertain the Boston Brahmins who'd made the long pilgrimage out to Provincetown. In truth, he preferred spending time with locals and tradesmen than hobnobbing with his own class. A few hours playing the double agent was a small price to pay for the freedom Danny enjoyed, but lurking somewhere among the socialites and gentlefolk was a femme fatale who was determined to accessorize his spiffy disguise with a matching ball and chain.

Christie McLean had just been accepted to Smith, but she had already shifted her focus from matriculation to matrimony. Subscribing to the theory that most girls met their future husbands in college, she was as serious as a second-semester senior when it came to finding her match. On paper, a buxom blonde with money to burn should been a winning trifecta for romance. In real life, the combination of those qualities only served to prove the timeless adage that beauty is only skin-deep.

Like the annual infestation of greenhead flies, Christie arrived in Provincetown each June, ready to unleash a summer of torture on a town full of eligible bachelors. Swatting at her was useless. Once Christie's razor-sharp mandibles were in, it was hard to get the bleeding to stop. No one knew for sure whether there was any truth to the rumor that the McLeans were distant relatives of the Cavanaughs, but it was painfully clear she had an insatiable appetite for Danny's blue blood.

Max didn't need to look at his watch to know it was close to midnight. Christie had already applied a fresh coat of Bonne Bell Lip Smacker. Still stinging from a poorly executed maneuver with mistletoe at Christmas, she was hell-bent on making sure the most kissable boy at the party was within range when the clock struck twelve. There was no point trying to shake her loose. Every time Danny looked over his shoulder, her over-glossed lips were smiling back at him. With less than fifteen minutes to midnight, time was running out. Luckily, his trusted wingman had a plan.

With light feet and a steady hand, Max detoured Danny around a cluster of guests and out of the crowded room. For a red-hot minute they were kids again, forging shortcuts through backyards and alleyways to avoid the human gridlock on Commercial Street. Evading a lovesick schoolgirl was a joke, not a crisis, but the mettle of their friendship had been forged in the heat of such moments. Even with a respectable head start, Christie would eventually catch up. There was only one room in the house where the snooty debutante would never think to look.

Buzzed on liquor and adrenaline, the two handsome fugitives scuttled past the empty dining room and through the butler's pantry. Despite the expansive size of the house, the timeworn axiom was true: The real party was always in the kitchen.

The caterers and waiters were too busy preparing trays of exotic hors d'oeuvres to notice the pair of young interlopers trespassing in their domain. Balancing tiny balls of caviar on quarter-sized wafers of Melba toast took patience and precision. A lesser man would have headed straight for the nearest exit, but Danny Cavanaugh wasn't about to let Christie's misplaced infatuation ruin a perfectly good party. It was time to stop playing defense and give the wily seductress a taste of her own medicine. Stopping at the sink, he snatched a bottle of Dom Perignon from a bucket of melting ice and whispered something to the bartender. With all the background noise and chaos, it was hard to tell whether his message had been received, but with only a few minutes left on the clock, it was time to throw a Hail Mary pass.

Max and Danny had just slipped out the back door when Christie suddenly appeared, wearing a look that could only be described as desperation. With about as much style as a prom dress from Sears, she shoved and pushed her way past the hired help who were too slow to get out of her way. Christie wasn't exactly the sharpest tool in the shed, but even the dullest hoe would have noticed there was only one way out of the kitchen. Once the huntress had her prey cornered out on the terrace, she'd undoubtedly send Max inside to fetch her purse or some other unneeded item. Danny had never shown any interest in his "kissing cousin," but the blood in his veins was red, not blue.

Christie was willing to bet that alone in the dark with a pretty girl, his hormones would kick in. All she had to do was smile and let nature take its course.

Just when it seemed all hope was lost, a hero swooped in to save the day. Randy Turner was a gold-star gay who couldn't even think straight, but after years spent watching guys hit on each other, the veteran bartender had mastered the art of the pickup. Following Danny's shorthand instructions, he grabbed a sparkling flute of champagne from a silver tray and strategically positioned himself in front of the back door. By the look of it, he was about to find out what happens when an unstoppable force meets and immovable object.

The dark backdrop of the unlit deck had turned the kitchen window into a one-way mirror. Holding his breath, Danny watched as Randy's dark eyes and full lips stopped Christie cold in her tracks. A proper young lady would never compromise her reputation by canoodling with the help, but it was too late to waste time playing hard to get. Throwing caution to the wind, she downed the champagne in one gulp and stepped forward to claim her consolation prize. Ironically, she was going to get her kiss after all. Too bad it would come from a queen, not a prince. The magic of the fairy tale would fade at midnight, but that was more than enough time for Danny and Max to make their escape.

SITTING ON TOP of the house like a top hat, the cedar-shingled cupola was the perfect hideaway. For as long as anyone could remember, the unfinished space had only been used for storage. But after a long weekend in November that had felt like a month, Danny had gotten the idea to transform it into his "Fortress of Solitude." Downstairs, his bedroom was palatial compared to the cinderblock box he shared with two roommates back at school, but too much attention from his doting mom made him feel like he was under house arrest. The big house on Telegraph Hill might as well have been Alcatraz and nothing short of a pardon from the governor would save Danny from a life sentence working at the Foundation. Still, if he could figure out a way to get the town council to grant their conservation petition at the hearing in August, he just might be able to earn an early parole for good behavior.

With practiced stealth, Danny led Max up the winding metal staircase and stepped out onto the deck. The view from the top of the house was a revelation. Stretching out in every direction, the surface of the ocean reflected the twinkle of a sky full of stars. The light from moon was bright, but it offered no warmth. Shivering against the cold, Danny grabbed a heavy blanket off the cot in his partially furnished room while Max dragged two wooden lounge chairs over to the ledge.

"Here. This should help."

Max pulled a corner of the pea-green army blanket around his shoulder as the sounds of big band music wafted up from the party below. The staccato clicks of his teeth chattered in time with the tempo as he scooted his chair closer to Danny to conserve body heat.

"I think we've earned a drink."

Danny hurried to peel the foil off the Dom Perignon before his fingers went numb. Wedging the bottle securely between his legs, he undid the wire cage and applied steady pressure to the cork with both thumbs.

POP!

The pressure that had been steadily building all night climaxed in a deluge of bubbly champagne. Instinctively, Max buried his face in Danny's lap and wrapped his lips around the neck of the bottle to catch the spurt.

"Easy, stud," Danny whispered as he playfully shoved his friend away. "There's plenty to go around."

To make his point, he raised the bottle to his mouth and drank.

Max wasn't sure if it was all the rum and cokes or a buzz from adrenaline, but what few inhibitions he had left were starting to slip. Each rhythmic pulse of Danny's Adam's apple triggered a corresponding pang of lust.

Hands. Lips. Neck.

Like the 31 scoops at Baskin-Robbins, each part of the male anatomy was another flavor he wanted to try. Max had spent almost half his life pretending his sexual appetite was bland and vanilla. Now that the truth was out, there was no reason not to indulge his carnal cravings. He was too inexperienced to know whether the swirl of feeling was infatuation or lust, but one thing was painfully clear: Max was craving a sample of "Some Young Guy." Imagining how many warm, wet licks it would take to finish off a double scoop, he closed his eyes and held his breath.

"By the way," Danny said, playfully nudging Max with his elbow. "I saw you checking out the bartender downstairs."

WHOOOOSH.

The heavy exhale created a cloud of fog that momentarily obscured the flush on Max's face. As usual, he hadn't fooled anyone with his "Mister Cool" act. It was time to come clean about the dirty thoughts swirling in his head. Without thinking, he wrapped his frozen hand around the bottle wedged between Danny's legs and tugged it free. Using the back of his sleeve to wipe away any traces of backwash, Max took a long drink and waited for the liquid courage to kick in.

"I was that obvious?"

"It's kind of like Clark Kent hiding behind those geeky glasses. Don't worry, Superman, your secret's safe with me."

Max felt an uncomfortable spasm in his diaphragm as Coca Cola mixed with the French champagne. The burp that followed wasn't the only thing that left a bitter taste in his mouth. It seemed like a cruel joke that Christie McLean was about to ring in the New Year with a hot gay guy while Max was stuck on the roof with his straight best friend. The fact that Danny was sexier than Randy made it even more tragic. Right place. Right time. Wrong guy. It was the same sad story of his life.

Ten!

The white noise from the party below shifted. Tuned to the right frequency, a chorus of jubilant voices counted down the last seconds of the millennium.

Nine...Eight...Seven...

Tomorrow, Danny would shove his freshly laundered clothes into a duffle bag and head back to school.

Six...Five...Four...

Max was about to get left behind again with nothing but regrets and PG-rated memories of yet another wasted night.

Three...Two...One...

It was time to stop being so mild mannered and start leaping tall buildings. If Max wanted his story to change, he'd have to grab the pen and write his own happy ending.

HAPPY NEW YEAR!

Kissing a guy is a lot like body surfing. You spend most of the time waiting for the right wave to come along – one that you can throw yourself into and ride all the way to shore. When it finally happens, it's thrilling and terrifying at the same time. You're totally present, reveling in the moment, even though everything that's happening is beyond your control. All you can do is hold your breath and wait. The whole experience only lasts a few seconds, but the rush of adrenaline leaves you breathless, wanting more.

"Wow."

"Seriously."

"That was like kissing my sister."

"Except Josie uses more tongue."

The spontaneous laughter that followed blended in with the soundtrack of the party below. The palpable heat between Max and Danny was hot enough to melt the ice on Shank Painter Pond, but acknowledging the obvious chemistry would only make a bad situation worse. Fortunately, the comedic nature of their friendship made it possible to turn an epic mistake into a punch line. Time and distance would cool the memory of the kiss. By the time summer rolled around, the story of New Year's Eve would be something they'd joke about over beers. Besides, it wasn't the first time they'd indulged in a little, harmless experimentation. Luckily, those amateur attempts at sex had been written off as just another teenage rite of passage. It would take more than swapping spit to end their friendship.

"EARTH TO Blowhard? Do you read me?"

"I need to bolt," Max said, snapping awake and noticing the time. "I'm going to be late."

Locals had three options for earning a steady paycheck: serve food, work the tourist traps, or gut fish. Since Max's mom and his sister Josie had the first two jobs covered, he drew the short straw.

No one could say whether or not *La Benedita* was truly blessed as its Portuguese name implied, but her captain had promised to grace Max with a generous bonus if he stayed on until Labor Day. Assuming he got into Berklee, he'd have to miss freshman orientation, but the extra cash would cover the cost of his textbooks.

"Stop back when your shift is over?"

"Definitely."

"Later."

Normally, Danny would've walked Max back into town, but he was itching to unpack and mark his turf. It had taken most of the long Christmas break to convince his parents to let him move into the cupola, and he was determined to settle in before they changed their minds. A one-room studio wasn't the same as having his own place, but it was better than bunking with his family downstairs. Now more than ever, he needed privacy.

It was summer in Provincetown and Danny was ready to play.

CHAPTER 3

WHOEVER THOUGHT *Flock of Seagulls* was a cool name for a band never worked on a pier. Wings spread and beaks agape, a legion of feathered demons demanded tribute. Max ignored the screech of plaintive cries and scraped the bloody remnants from his cutting board into the chum bucket. As captain of a trawler, Jasper Avellar had many rules, but the most important was about birds, not fish: Never feed the gulls.

The daily catch had been good, and spirits on *La Benedita* were high. As usual, the more experienced crewmembers were busy cleaning cod while the rookies paid their dues hosing out the bait wells and swabbing the deck. The T-shirt Max had just inherited from Danny was already stiff with salt water and stink. After four summers at sea, he'd grown accustomed to the semi-permanent layer of sweat and brine that coated his skin. Days were long and the work was hard, but Jasper was one of the most respected captains in the fleet. Vacancies on his boat were coveted and few. Anyone lucky enough to secure a spot on his crew worked hard knowing there were ten other guys waiting to take his place.

Dead eyes stared up at a cloudless sky.

Although the fish lying on the cutting board had tipped the scale at fifty pounds, the edible flesh on the beast was less than half its actual weight. It had taken a sharp hook and a strong line to drag the leviathan from the sea, but the defeat of such a noble creature was a cautionary tale about the dangers of swimming in unfamiliar waters.

With practiced precision, Max sliced off the cod's protruding cheeks and laid them on a clean sheet of parchment paper. Although small, the delicate meat was the tastiest part of the fish. Chefs at restaurants like Pepe's or The Red Inn were waiting for their daily delivery. Tonight, hungry tourists would pay city prices to dine on fresh seafood. It would have been nice to sample a few of those delicious dishes, but with his modest wages, Max could barely afford an appetizer.

The cries of the birds became more urgent as he slit open the cod's bloated belly and inched his notched blade up the length of its spine. Ironically, cleaning fish was a lot like playing the trumpet. It took a practiced technique and an innate sense of tempo to do it right. Slicing and dicing faster than the next guy, Max trimmed away the barbed edges and separated the meat from the skin. Once the fillets had been rinsed and deboned, he bedded them under a blanket of ice and affixed a lid to the top of the Styrofoam cooler.

"Angelo! Delivery."

At the sound of his name, one of the shirtless *guapos* on deck bucketed his mop and grabbed a clean polo from the makeshift clothesline that moored the ship to the wharf. Instead of putting it on, the young man draped it over his forearm like a fine linen napkin. All the delivery boys had to wear logoed shirts, but covering up such a beautiful body was like putting a Members Only jacket on Michelangelo's *David*. Max didn't bother repeating his usual mantra to stay cool. Half naked or fully clothed, there was no way to chill out when Angelo was around.

"Hey, *oi*" Jasper called out, slipping in and out of English as the most stylish member of his crew sauntered by. "Did you finish washing *o convés*?"

Provincetown High only taught Spanish and French, but Max had picked up enough Portuguese to get by. Even without a literal translation, he'd heard his captain pose the question enough times to know what he was asking. The freshly scrubbed deck of *La Benedita* was glistening, but it was important to make sure the work had been done right. Angelo nodded a quick affirmation. Almost as an afterthought, he reluctantly pulled on his shirt and gestured for Max to pass him the cooler of fish.

The two young men were about the same height, but Max had at least twenty pounds of brawn on his *amigo*. It was one thing to dead lift something heavy and another to carry it all the way across town.

Angelo's sinewy muscles were more for show than go. Still, a hot guy strutting his stuff was *muy caliente*. Max's internal engine began to growl as he depressed any inhibitions and slipped his revving libido into gear. It was never a good idea to mix business and pleasure, but the afternoon shift was almost over and he was ready to roll.

"This one's really stuffed. You sure you can handle such a big package?"

Angelo wasn't much of a talker, but his smirk confirmed he was undaunted by Max's boasts. Arms locked and knees bent, he managed to take the whole load without breaking eye contact.

"Suit yourself."

Straining against the weight, Angelo purposely leaned forward and pressed the Styrofoam cooler into his crewmate's crotch. Max smiled and took a step back. Under different circumstances, the gesture would've provoked a friendlier response, but there was nothing he could do about it with Jasper looking on. Fraternizing at work was against the rules and Max needed his paycheck.

"*Apresse-se!*" the captain shouted in a deep, menacing voice. "The fish needs to be delivered to the restaurant right away. *Rápido!*"

Everyone knew what it meant when Jasper repeated himself, especially in Portuguese. Any other member of the crew would have headed straight for town, but the sight of Danny Cavanaugh walking up the pier in a tight tank top was enough to stop the Latin lothario dead in his tracks.

"*Olá amigo. Como's vai?*"

Ignoring his captain's orders, Angelo balanced the cooler on a wooden pile and listened as the handsome *gringo* spoke to him in his native tongue. The casual banter was a welcomed relief from the shouted orders and biting taunts that passed as conversation on the boat. It may have seemed out of character for a Cavanaugh to stop and chat with some random guy, but for whatever reason, Danny was always more affable with strangers than friends.

Max plunged his knife into the nearest fish and slit it open like a letter. Part of being a local was learning to accept the transient nature of the short summer season. Tourists came and went in a repeating loop that started and ended on Saturday afternoons. There was nothing wrong with making a new acquaintance, especially one who looked like Angelo, but Max wasn't about to open up his closest friendship for a platonic ménage a trois. Growing up without much made it twice as hard to share.

The afternoon shift was almost over, but there was still plenty of work left to do. With renewed determination, the crew carved through mounds of scales while laughter drifted through the air like the funk of red tide. Danny usually had a thing about waiting around for anyone, but by the sound of it, he'd found a pleasant distraction to help pass the time.

In an unusual display of force, Max tore a fillet right off the bone. Wide-eyed and animated, his best friend was getting a good buzz from all the love. Danny wasn't into guys, but flirting was like drinking. When you were thirsty for attention, it didn't matter who was pouring. By the look of it, Angelo was serving it up from the top shelf, but all he was going to get for his trouble was a firm handshake and a wicked case of blue balls. This come-on comedy routine would make for a good laugh on the long walk home. Still, the joke was getting old, fast. It was time for Max to deliver the punch line.

Consequences be damned, he tossed a handful of fish scraps into the air. Like a scene from *The Birds*, the flutter of wings and the cacophony of cries that followed were of cinematic proportions.

WHOOOOOOSH!!

Max felt his lungs constrict as a blast of cold water hit him like a wave. Instinctively, he put up both hands to protect his face from the manmade tsunami and turned toward the source. After a day in the sun, it felt good to be wet, but the crew's boisterous laughter made his skin burn with shame.

"Mister Balais!"

The heavily accented voice invoked Max's surname with the gravitas of a schoolteacher. Once he knew had everyone's attention, Jasper closed the nozzle and let the hose fall to the ground. Sometimes it took more than a stern look to keep his crew in check, especially at the end of a long day. Max had always impressed Jasper as a mature and responsible young man, but he was acting like a teenager that needed a refresher course in common sense.

"What have I said about the dirty *gaivotas*?"

"Never feed the gulls."

"When you get hot, you forget. The water, it cools you down. Now, you are OK? You are *bom* again?

"Yes, Captain. I'm good."

There was nothing more to say on the matter. Jasper was good about making a point and moving on. The Portuguese sailor was six-foot-four, with dark eyes and arms as thick as Angelo's legs. Despite his imposing stature, he chose to lead, not dominate, his men. That quality was, in part, what made him such a fine captain. It was also pretty damn sexy.

Luckily, the water sports had been enough to divert Danny's attention. Max scanned the horizon for some sign of Angelo, but his crewmate was gone. Lust was a powerful motivator. So was fear. After seeing Jasper in action, Angelo knew what would happen to him if the afternoon delivery was late.

"*Boa tarde capitão*. How was the haul today?"

"*Olá* Danny. The catch was good. Tell your mother I've saved the best fish for her."

"I'll do that. *Muito obrigado!*"

Danny casually slipped in and out of Portuguese like a native son. After a lazy semester studying architecture in Lisbon, his accent was nearly perfect. The easy way he got on with Jasper made Max feel even more tongue-tied. When it came to making small talk, Max had always subscribed to the seaman's adage that men and fish both get into trouble when they open their mouths.

"Mister Balais. I can see that you're anxious to spend time with your *melhor amigo*. Go. Enjoy what's left of the day."

Even though Jasper fished for a living, he was letting Max off the hook. Taking a cue from his captain, one of the rookies rushed forward to take his crewmate's place. Less proficient than Max and visibly unsure, he stepped up to the cutting board like he was about to perform surgery. The expensive fillet gloves would protect his hands from minor mishaps, but the blade was sharp enough to pierce the stainless steel woven into the fabric. Experience, not fancy gear, was the best defense against peril.

Even though he was a better seaman, Max didn't like the idea of another guy taking his job. Normally, he'd have stuck around to finish his shift, but the afternoon ferry had just docked and a platoon of new recruits was marching down the pier. The sound of casual conversation and laughter from the rank-and-file was a battle hymn that set his heart racing. After a long day working next to a shirtless squad, he was ready to enlist.

"*Graças capitão.*"

Max tried to mimic the subtle, sonorous tones of his father's native tongue. The words were right, but the accent sounded more Irish than Portuguese. Even so, his captain appreciated the effort and nodded in acknowledgement before turning his attention back to the rest of his crew.

"So, what do you feel like doing tonight?" Danny asked as Max led the way up the narrow metal gangplank that connected the jetty to the pier. "And please don't say pizza and a movie."

"So, I take it you've already seen the new *Star Wars* flick?"

"Twice, back in May, with the rest of the civilized world. Even Jar Jar Binks would think that suggestion was lame."

"O.K., I get it." Max said, suddenly feeling as provincial as the name of his town. "How about we grab a six-pack and check out 'The Fisherman' scrimmage at the high school?"

"Football and beer? Pass! That's way too straight, even for me. Come on. Pretend like you asked me out. How would you blow me away?"

Recasting a low-key Saturday night as an actual date didn't make things any easier. Max stared a hole into the sidewalk and waited for a burst of inspiration. There was a time, not so long ago, when these long summer days were like pennies in a jar. He worked and saved all year just so he could spend them with Danny. Along the way, they'd stumbled into a few grand adventures, but their shared history was mostly a collection of ordinary moments. Secretly, Max had always worried Danny would outgrow their friendship. Now, being together – just hanging out – wasn't enough.

"All right, Cavanaugh. P-Town may not be Boston, but I'll come up with something that'll curl your toes."

"Atta boy Balais!"

Anyone else would have pumped for more information, but Danny hated "Twenty Questions." That was a good thing since Max was short on answers.

"Let's head back to the house. My parents and brother are out on the boat, so we'll have the place all to ourselves. Unless we're going to a rave on the beach, you need to grab a shower."

Suddenly aware of his appearance, Max tried to rake a hand through his hair.

"Never going to happen." Danny said, palming his pal's head like a basketball. "Saltwater is stronger than Dep. You're going to need a serious 'lather-rinse-repeat' to get rid of that hair helmet."

Buoyed by the prospect of a night on the town, the two young men lunged into a sprint. Since Bradford was the most direct route back to Danny's house on Telegraph Hill, it was a surprise when Max cut left onto Commercial Street where tourists swarmed like mosquitoes in front of brightly lit storefronts. The main drag was abuzz with activity, but it felt as if everyone was moving in slow motion. Monday through Friday, the human gridlock on Commercial Street was almost tolerable. Come the weekend, the urge to start swatting was an itch that needed to be scratched.

What Danny lacked in brawn, he made up for in speed. Max knew from experience the only way to beat him in a footrace was to unlevel the playing field. Cars and people wouldn't stop an agile runner, but moving barriers were bound to at least slow him down. Navigating a human obstacle course meant hopping from the street to the sidewalk, twisting around lampposts, and gently moving shoulders and torsos out of their path. All that extra effort would inevitably break Danny's stride. Although he'd not been blessed with the Cavanaugh genes, Max knew how to get around anything standing in his way.

Powerful muscles propelled them further and faster, past the Coast Guard Station, and through the heart of the West End. All in, it took them less than six minutes to run the narrow mile that separated Telegraph Hill from the pier. Most of the route had been on level ground, but the steep incline of the last block left both young men gasping for breath.

Unable to speak as he sucked in air, Danny shoved Max toward the outdoor shower and ducked into the kitchen to score some beers. Like most of the affluent families who summered on the Cape, the Cavanaughs looked the other way when it came to their son's consumption of alcohol. Given Danny's penchant for challenging authority, it would have been a mistake for his parents to reinstate Prohibition in the beach house. Most young people fixated on what they couldn't have, so it made sense to encourage moderation, not abstinence. Danny and his mom had an unspoken agreement that she'd perpetually replenish the six-pack of expensive IPAs in the kitchen refrigerator as long as he stayed away from the hard liquor in the bar of his father's den.

The distant clink of beer bottles sounded like wind chimes as Max tugged off his T-shirt and squirmed out of his shorts. Beaming down from a cloudless sky, the heat of the sun was tempered by a breeze off the ocean. It felt good to be naked. It would feel even better to be clean.

Hot and heavy, a steady rain poured out of the rust-encrusted showerhead. Max pressed the palms of his hands against the wooden walls of the stall and adjusted his stance so the pounding spray hit him in just the right spot. Even though his skin was already pink from the heat, he turned the cold faucet down. The shower back at the apartment had terrible water pressure and the mildewed vinyl curtain made the tiny tub feel smaller. A long, hot soak without his sister nagging for her turn was a luxury he was determined to enjoy.

After ten uninterrupted minutes of wetted bliss, Max felt clean. The foamy puddle of water slinking down the drain had rinsed away the dirt and sweat, but his skin was still a dark mocha from long days working in the sun.

Blond hair. Blue eyes. Killer tan.

The guy staring back from the other side of the mirror looked more like a movie star than a beach bum. Maybe Max's luck *had* finally changed. Now, he just needed to work out the details of his non-existent plan for the night. There were plenty of bars and nightclubs in Provincetown, but anything trendy was geared toward a gay clientele. Given his laidback disposition, Max was pretty sure Danny wouldn't mind an all-male crowd. The mood would definitely be chill and he'd enjoy having the freedom to dance without crashing into the annoying eclipse of girls that were perpetually in his way. Picking a place was easy. The hard part would be getting in.

Ironically, Max had been born on Labor Day. That meant he wouldn't turn twenty-one until the last day of the season. Bouncers weren't rocket scientists, but anyone with half a brain could tell he was underage. Even with the muscles of a grown man, his baby face was a dead giveaway. Good vibes and bad lighting would improve his chances, but it would take a miracle to get them into any place worth going to on a Saturday night. Looking to the sky for divine inspiration, he was surprised to see Danny smiling down at him from the roof.

"Just checking to make sure you didn't drown. You ready for a beer?"

"Definitely."

"Heads up."

"Wait!"

Max only had a split second to get into position before Danny started to pour. It was hard to swallow the deluge of beer without choking, but after a series of long gulps and a belch, the bottle was empty. Even though he'd nearly drowned indulging his friend's twisted sense of humor, Max was used to these kinds of pranks. Like much of what passed between them, the impromptu drinking game was all part of the elaborate initiation he had to endure to gain entry into Danny's private club.

Wrapping a sun-bleached towel around his torso, Max scurried up the spiral staircase to the roof where Danny was waiting. Buzzed on beer and dizzy from the height, Max grabbed hold of the metal railing around the Widow's Walk and held on tight. He couldn't understand why Danny wanted to spend the whole summer camped out on the top of the house, but the view was worth the climb.

A blustery breeze had animated the tall grass blanketing the marsh. Hanging low on the horizon, a tangerine sun set the ocean on fire. There were a bunch of half-baked theories about how the water and sand played with the quality of light in Provincetown. No one could say for sure what made it so special, but adding alcohol to the mix amplified the effect.

Max popped open another beer and hobbled over to the open door of the cupola. Even the most grueling gym routine was nothing compared to his daily workout on *La Benedita*. After a long day heaving nets heavy with fish, he was ready to kick back and relax. Although he'd taken care of the Cavanaughs' house all winter, this was his first time back on the roof since New Year's Eve. The feeling of déjà vu was more intoxicating than the beer.

Million-dollar view aside, Danny's new digs left a lot to be desired. Mrs. Cavanaugh had sewn blue and white curtains for the windows, and Max had scavenged milk crates from the A&P to hold Danny's collection of architecture books, but even with a good cleaning, the room still smelled musty. It was hard to image why anyone would downsize from a comfy king to a rickety metal cot, but the prince of the house preferred to live like a pauper.

"Damn it!" Danny cursed under his breath as he shuffled through a shoebox full of CDs. "That little bastard nicked my new Santana."

Despite being a decade younger and vertically challenged, Sam Cavanaugh had overcome his fear of heights and raided his brother's music collection. There was an unwritten code in the house that gave each family member squatter's rights to anything not being used. It wasn't enough to just say an object was yours. To make property private, you had to brand the item and stake your claim. Danny grabbed a roll of masking tape and used a magic marker to write out "DANNY'S TUNES" in bold, black letters. Affixing the label to his boom box wouldn't keep Sam out of the room, but it would stop him from gradually moving his brother's things back downstairs.

Max never had a problem with his sister pilfering his stuff. It would have been nice to think it was because Josie respected his status as "man of the house." In truth, it was probably because he never had anything worth stealing.

"Dude. You're sporting *major* wood."

You couldn't tell from Danny's tone whether he was passing judgment or simply making an observation. Either way, the half-open bath towel girding Max's loins suddenly felt like a washcloth. Apparently, a cool breeze was all it took to give him a boner. Desperate to hide his burgeoning manhood, he grabbed his jeans off the floor and pulled them on. Unfortunately, the pressure of denim on flesh just made the problem worse.

"Do you need to take care of that before we head out?"

Even though his tone was playful, Danny's words felt strangely premeditated. He seemed bound and determined to make his gay best friend admit he was warm for his form. Max wasn't sure how he'd make it through a whole summer without cracking from the strain, but the overwhelming desire to conceal the "surprise party" raging in his pants gave him a bombshell idea.

"No time for fun and games. We need to get going."

Max hung his damp towel on a rusty hook and started sorting through a plastic laundry basket filled with last year's hand-me-downs. After discarding a half-dozen of the collared shirts, he tossed Danny a plain white Tee and kept a black one for himself.

"This is at least two sizes too small. I won't be able to breathe."

"Don't worry. Where we're going, you won't be wearing it long."

"Absolutely not," Danny said, hurling the shirt back into the hamper. "I'm down with the Boatslip or A-House, but the last time we snuck into Purgatory I spent the whole night getting mauled by a bear from Braintree while you sulked in the corner. There's no way I'm *ever* setting foot in that hellhole again."

Danny was being dramatic, but he had a point. Max had clearly overestimated his friend's receptivity to spending his whole night searching the menu for a dish he'd never find. Dragging a straight guy to a gay bar was like taking a vegetarian to a meat market. Unfortunately, there weren't any clubs in town that catered to his bland appetite. The only option on the table was to take Danny to a place where he could order off the menu. That would have been easy in Boston, where the hottest venues were all mixed. In Provincetown, however, their choices were limited. As usual, Max had to make do.

"So, let me make sure I've got this right. You want to go somewhere with good music and bad girls?"

"And there should probably be a few hot guys there, too...for you."

"Well, why didn't you say so?" Max said, smirking triumphantly as he squirmed into his T-shirt. "I know just the place."

CHAPTER 4

D ANNY CAVANAUGH was being watched. Across the room, red-lacquered lips sucked a pink cocktail dry through a thin, plastic straw and stiletto heels accentuated a pair of Rockette's legs perpetually frozen in a classic bevel pose. The gorgeous blond sitting at a booth in the corner was trying too hard to get noticed, striking poses that accentuated her best features. Unknowingly, Max had planned their big night out at the one place Danny had vowed to avoid all summer. He should have said something earlier or proposed an alternate venue but now the twin gravity wells of curiosity and desire were creating a powerful pull. What little space there was between Danny and the blond seemed to be getting smaller by the minute. Although they'd never met, an unspoken offer had already been made. All he had to do was acknowledge the flirtation with a smile to close the deal.

Danny pushed the drink in front of him away and reminded himself that arousal was an omen, not an invitation. After all, this was Provincetown. The evening would end with a whimper, not a bang. A fleeting summer romance could be forgiven, or at least overlooked, by the tight-knit community. But there was no way a Cavanaugh could get away with an anonymous hookup in a place where everybody knew his name.

Danny started to walk away from his high-top table, but he only made it as far as the bar. Pulling a tattered leather wallet from his back pocket, he signaled for service and tossed back the rest of his drink. Another round of liquid courage would drown out the voices in his head. But it would also embolden the little devil between his legs to sin. If he did, a hangover would be the least of his problems in the morning.

"JUST DO IT."

The marketing guru created Nike's trademark slogan to encourage achievement, not rationalize self-destruction. After a couple stiff drinks, it was hard to tell the difference. Danny was ready to stop thinking about the future and start sowing his wild oats. An impulsive decision to embrace his darker side would never hold up in the light of day. But tonight, in the shadows of a crowded bar, some meaningless sex felt like the only way to relieve the pressure that had been building all year. Making a mistake, even a big one, was better than doing nothing at all.

"Can I get a Planter's Punch?"

The bartender lifted a bottle of rum and raised an eyebrow to confirm the order. Danny leaned over the polished mahogany counter and gestured for the man to come closer. Anyone else would have just shouted over the roaring music, but a Cavanaugh never raised his voice to be heard.

"Make it two."

The hand signal that followed could have been confused for a peace sign, but the bartender knew his clientele: The fine young man standing in front of him was looking to borrow trouble.

The blond in the corner already had a cocktail, but Danny wasn't about to walk over empty-handed. Slapping a twenty on the bar, he double-fisted the peach-colored drinks and tried to think of an icebreaker that didn't sound like a cheap pick-up line.

"Perfect timing." Max said, helping himself to one of the plastic cups as he slipped a muscled arm around his friend's slumped shoulders.

Danny never expected to get cock-blocked by his own wingman, but he couldn't disagree with the assessment of the situation. If Max had stopped to use the restroom and shown up a minute later, he would have seen something that would've been hard to explain away. Like his little brother, Danny had sticky fingers. Back in the city, a few stolen nights in a stranger's bed had been enough. Now, in the heat of summer, he was turning into a romantic kleptomaniac who couldn't fight the urge to pick up something cheap he really didn't need. Sooner or later, Danny was going to get caught in the act.

"Later," he mumbled under his breath as he turned his back to the leggy blond and raised his glass for a toast.

"Bros before hoes."

"Dicks before chicks."

The laughter chaser that followed abruptly changed to a cough when Max took the first sip. Tourists thought Planter's Punch was just another fruity cocktail, but the bartender had filled the straw with Bacardi 151. Highly potent and infamously flammable, that first mini-shot was like swallowing a bolt of lightning.

"Thor, the God of Thunder, just shot his load down my throat."

"You wish."

Danny carefully lifted his straw above the water line and watched the rum drizzle out. Once the pure alcohol was safely diluted into the drink, he took a long sip and tried to forget how close he'd come to making an epic mistake.

"This place is packed."

Like houseboys and hair color, businesses in Provincetown changed with the seasons. Trendy clubs came and went, but there was one place that lived up to its name. Moored in a prime location on Commercial Street, The Crown & Anchor continued to reign as one of the most popular spots in town. Max and Danny had strategically decided to start the evening inside the crowded restaurant where the bartenders were too busy serving thirsty tourists to notice Danny passing drinks to his underage friend. The hotel, restaurant, and cabaret were all interconnected. Once inside the compound, patrons could easily move back and forth between venues. Max and Danny slipped out the side exit of the restaurant and merged with the line that had already formed to enter the nightclub. With any luck, they could just glom onto a large group of patrons and stroll right past the lone bouncer manning the door.

Traveling in gaggles that were tighter than their jeans, the gay cliques were far too uptight to invite a couple of hot strangers to join their intimate kikis. Danny probably could have sweet-talked his way into a group, but he was preoccupied with something back at the restaurant. A high-pitched squeal of laughter signaled the migration of a vulnerable herd of co-eds. Max caught Danny's eye and gave him a subtle nod. Focused on the party waiting just beyond the metal doors, the two girls at the back of the line seemed oblivious to the presence of the handsome escorts that had sidled up to them.

Ironically, a "hetero-pairing" doubled their chance for success. If the doorman was gay, he'd look right past two couples. If he turned out to be straight, the girls' miniskirts and crop tops would be a serious distraction.

Like sheep in wolves' clothing, the flock fell into line as each young lady retrieved her driver's license from a cordovan Etienne Aigner wallet. Unable to walk and chew gum at the same time, the guard had a simple, two-step process to check IDs. First, he made sure the one-inch photo matched the face of the person standing in front of him. Then, just to be sure, he'd check again to confirm the patron's date of birth. By the look of it, the bouncer was only carding the first few people in each group and just waving the rest right in.

Max counted the number of couples in front of them as droplets of sweat trickled down the small of his back. The plan was for Danny to provide cover while Max slipped through the open doors. The simple ruse would probably have worked, but just as the doorman looked up and made eye contact, the girl standing next to Danny reached back and yanked her friend to the front of the queue. Suddenly stag and next in line, Max was fresh out of luck.

"Don't worry," Danny whispered under his breath as he stepped back and took his place at his friend's side. "I got this."

Max swallowed hard and tried to be cool as he watched Danny casually surrender his ID. You could almost smell the smoke coming from the bouncer's ears as he studied the license and struggled to do simple math in his head. After a significant pause, he handed the laminated card back to Danny with one hand and reached for Max's ID with the other.

Repeating the process, the doorman studied the photo for what seemed like forever. Since his family didn't own a car, Max had waited until last summer to get his driver's license. Even though the picture was less than a year old, his new muscles and chiseled features created a dramatic before-and-after effect. When the bouncer finally looked up, the smile on his face confirmed he liked what he saw. The muscle at the door was "family." Suddenly, Danny knew what he needed to do to save the night. It was now or never.

Just as the bouncer was about to look down again to check the date of birth, Danny grabbed the back of Max's neck and pulled him in. Like the climax of a classic fairy tale, the kiss that followed had enough magic to do the trick. Distracted by the sight of two hot guys making out, the doorman lost the ability to add and subtract. Danny and Max kept at it until one of the patrons behind them started to complain about the wait. Visibly flustered and eager to get the line moving again, the guard handed Max back his ID and waved them through the open doors.

"Now *that* was a kiss."

"Anything less and we'd have been out on the sidewalk. You can thank me later."

"Definitely."

Max had messed around with enough guys to know when someone was really into it or merely going through the motions. It was probably just a case of wishful thinking, but he couldn't shake the feeling that his friendship with Danny, like the Planter's Punch, might be spiked.

Once inside the nightclub, Danny headed straight for the nearest open bottle while Max did a quick lap around the room. Most of the patrons were seated at bistro tables, staring at a silky, silver movie screen that doubled as a backdrop to the stage. Music videos had been around forever, but someone had artfully spliced together a montage of memorable sitcom scenes and classic movie vignettes. Since Max didn't have cable TV or the money to see all the latest and greatest films, most of the cultural references went right over his head. Even so, he still laughed along with the rest of the audience. As much as Max hated camp, fitting in with the gay tribe meant pretending to love the pithy quips doled out by icons and divas.

"Pssssst."

Somehow Danny's signal projected over the buzz of the crowd like the hiss of a dog whistle. Trained to respond to the call, Max scampered over to join him at a small table for two at the front of the house.

"We can't sit here. It's reserved."

"I can read, Killjoy," Danny said, snatching up the white VIP Only card and tearing it in two. Don't worry. I slipped the waiter a Benjamin when I ordered drinks. Just sit down and relax."

Max slid into the padded club chair and tried not to think about how many hours he had to work to earn a hundred bucks. Even though he'd have been happy standing in the back and pocketing the cash, it felt good to live like the other half for a change. The catwalk that jutted out from the stage ended less than a foot in front from their table. Tonight, he had a front-row seat for the best show in town.

The waiter barely had time to make it over with the first round before the music started and the houselights dimmed. Max was already drunk with anticipation, but Danny told the waiter to keep the drinks coming and discreetly passed him a fat wad of bills. The bright spot that appeared on the red velvet curtain told the audience just where to look.

"Ladies! Gentlemen! And those who travel in between..."

The disembodied voice that blared from the speakers paused to appreciate the enthusiastic round of catcalls and applause. It was hard to tell if the person speaking was a man or a woman. Given the impending performance, *that* was unquestionably the point.

"Tonight, our dazzling Court is here to tease and titillate your senses. Please join me in giving a regal welcome to The Ladies of the Crown."

The velvet curtain parted to reveal six silhouetted figures that were larger than life. Hiding beneath billowing gowns and tiered, powdered wigs that extended the scope of the illusion, the performers were dressed to impress.

"Wow!" Max said, clapping wildly as he admired the artistry of the tableau. "They look fantastic."

The showmanship was indeed impressive, but as far as Max was concerned, the most dazzling thing in the room was the glimmer in Danny's eyes. The performance had barely started, but he was already hooked. Max settled back into his chair and breathed a sigh of relief. The night was a success. Now, he could finally stop worrying and enjoy the show.

What are you looking at?

The question was more theatrical than rhetorical. Although the music was pre-recorded, the audience could almost feel Madonna calling out the audience of voyeurs leering from the shadows. Fingers snapped the tempo of the melody while a throbbing drum gave it a heartbeat. The same musical phrase repeated again, begging for a release. When it finally came, the singer and performers moaned together in delight.

Strike a pose.

Bathed in eerie pools of blue light, the illusionists on stage obeyed their invisible mistress's commands. Mechanically swiveling on sinuous joints, torsos bent and wooden arms swung into new positions. Each movement was perfectly choreographed. Like mannequins in a store window, the performers stood frozen as the deafening bass pulsed through the speakers.

Vogue.

The first whisper of the title lyric was an incantation, calling forth the physical manifestation of something intangible from an ethereal world. Repeated a second time, the same word was a call to action. Moving as one, the reanimated ensemble tore off their breakaway dresses and stepped forward into the center spot. Like orbiting disco balls, the glistening rhinestones encrusted in their corsets and bustiers set the room ablaze with a thousand flickering flames.

For five minutes and eighteen seconds Max watched a bevy of beauties work the catwalk in fishnet stockings and six-inch heels. The performers were lip-synching, but the exaggerated facial gestures and elaborate choreography made the show come alive. The song might be Madonna's, but each regal queen on the stage owned her performance.

Ladies! Gentlemen! And those who travel in between....

The illusion was so flawlessly executed it was impossible to tell which was which. Clapping with the beat of the music, the crowd hooted and cheered in all the right places. The energy of the song rose and fell with each verse, finally crashing into a finale that brought the audience to its feet.

One by one, each performer took a measure of praise before falling back in line as the true star of the show stepped forward to take her bows. Smiling demurely, Lady Angelique slowly rotated her hand in a royal wave and threw air kisses to a crowd of adoring fans.

"Well, fuck me." Danny said, slow clapping as he stared transfixed at the dazzling figure at center stage. "I guess you're not the only guy on the *La Benedita* who's been hiding a secret."

It took Max two beats longer than it should have to figure out what his friend meant by the remark. By then, it was too late.

"Oh, boys," Angelique said, calling to Max and Danny from the edge of the catwalk. "Would one of you chivalrous gentlemen rescue a damsel in distress? I'm afraid I may break something on these treacherous stairs."

"Like your neck?"

"Like a heel!"

"I am at your service," Danny said, stepping forward to offer his outstretched hand. "But I think we can all agree, you're hardly a damsel."

"And if we're being honest, I'd have to say that you're no gentleman," Angelique said, playfully slapping him on the shoulder with her closed fan. "But this Mister Sister is thirsty. I think I've earned a drink, *n'est pas*?"

Right on cue, the waiter appeared with an expensive bottle of champagne. Given the timing, he was either psychic or this was an overused shtick to get some poor sap to pick up the tab. The safe bet was on the latter.

"So, how's it hanging Angelo?" Max asked in an uncharacteristically sarcastic tone. He was trying to make a joke at his crewmate's expense. In truth, he was crazy-jealous of the guy for having the balls to flaunt his secret identity in front of a room full of people.

"That is a rude question, *maricon*. And you will address me as 'Angelique' when we're not at work."

"Actually, the name suits you," Danny said, pouring on the charm. "Since you look like you were sent from heaven."

"Now isn't that a sweet thing to say? Maybe I was wrong about you Mister Cavanaugh. I may have found myself a knight in shining armor after all."

Despite, or perhaps because of, their rocky start, Danny's compliment had gone straight to Angelique's head. Purring demurely as she sipped her champagne, it was hard to tell whether Danny was stroking a kitten or a poking a tiger. Either way, Max had a bad feeling he'd end up being the one who got scratched.

"How long have you been working here?"

"I've been *headlining* at the Crown & Anchor since Memorial Day. However, I've been collaborating with our musical director and choreographer since Christmas."

"Wow! That's a lot time to spend on a five-minute act."

"Well, did you see those clumsy missteps during the grand finale?"

"No," both men said, answering in unison.

"And. You. Never. Will."

It was clear that the onstage show was still playing out at the table. Flying high on the adrenaline of her performance, Angelique was ready for whatever gibes or jeers came her way.

"Everyone expects me to play the shy coquette. Y'all just write me off as just another pretty face. I've got to work twice as hard to prove I have a brain and I'm not afraid to use it."

"Oh, there's no denying you're smart and full of sass," Danny said, sliding into a southern drawl to match his opponent's noticeable accent. "Still, I can think of a better way to put that pretty mouth of yours to use."

"Darling, that sounds delicious," Angelique quipped in her most seductive voice. "But after such a robust performance, this *mamacita* is famished! I need a real meal, not an appetizer."

The heat of the exchange turned Max's face red. Danny often used sexual innuendo as bait for barbs, but he seemed more interested in getting a rise out of the drag queen than taking her down. Curiosity always had been the drug of choice for the Cavanaugh boys.

Angelique's cheekiness had clearly piqued Danny's interest; it was hard to tell where the illusion ended and the real infatuation began. Even so, there was one thing Max knew for sure: male or female, he wasn't going to hang around and watch his best friend flirt with his crewmate again. Two parts envy and one part lust, jealousy was a potent cocktail and he'd just been served a double.

"While you two try to figure out who has the biggest dick, I'll be in the restroom taking a leak."

It was ironic that a club that challenged mainstream norms about gender identity still had a ladies' room, but the long line snaking down the narrow hall confirmed how, appearances aside, there were still immutable differences between the sexes. Apologizing under his breath, Max endured the glaring looks as he passed by the queue of angry women starring a hole into the sign marked "Gulls" and slipped through the door for "Buoys".

Unlike the rest of the club, the men's room was empty.

A better man would have offered to let the waiting ladies use the vacant stalls, but discretion was the better part of valor. Thankful for a moment of privacy, Max sallied up to the stainless steel urinal and undid the button-fly of his 501s. The powerful stomach muscles hiding under his T-shirt were already straining against the rising tide. Adjusting his stance and taking aim, he exhaled as a wave of heat rose up from his feet and crested in his loins.

CRASH!

The flimsy pine door to the restroom flew open and the roar of the club spilled in. Stopped mid-stream, Max listened as the guy who'd interrupted nature's call stomped across the tiled floor in black leather boots.

Be cool.

Max repeated his mantra, but it was going to take more than a few words of reassurance to get things started again. His swollen bladder was doing its part, but the rest of his equipment was temporarily out of service. Time slowed and the silence in the room became more uncomfortable as the man unfastened his belt buckle and stepped up to the trough.

"You alright, mate?"

Although well intentioned, the stranger's question made a bad situation worse. Rather than give an honest answer, Max stared straight ahead and cleared his throat.

"I must not have to go."

That was a lie. The first of many he would tell the guy standing next to him. Truth be told, he felt like a water balloon ready to burst.

Pee shy.

The inability to urinate in public sounded like an innocuous condition, something akin to "puppy love" or "butterflies in your stomach." Any other gay man would have just parlayed his predicament into an adorable shtick about water sports and golden showers. Sadly, Max lacked the genetic cocktail that made it possible to be clever under duress.

Max was full of piss and vinegar when he played the trumpet, but he was tongue-tied when it came to converting thoughts into words. Fortunately, what he lacked in courage, he made up for in curiosity. With over-practiced stealth, he stole a quick glance at what was hanging from his neighbor's unzipped pants. Not since Moses had anyone ever been so surprised to see a burning bush.

"I'm Liam."

"Max."

Although they'd already engaged in some serious visual foreplay on Commercial Street, the ginger acted like they'd never laid eyes on each other. Max focused on his own dilemma and tried to finish up, but Liam's British accent and the heat from his open fly was enough to make him sweat.

These brief moments, the "in between" when anything was possible, were the most exciting part of meeting someone. Just outside, Danny was waiting for his buddy to return and continue their night out on the town. Ditching him and sneaking off with Liam would be a real dick move. Besides, even if Max wanted to take things to the next level, there was no place for them to go. Josie would come right home after work and Max couldn't imagine doing the morning walk of shame back from wherever Liam was staying. Maybe, just his once, he could stop over thinking things and be a little reckless?

Max was just about to suggest they head back to the bar and make his current condition worse with another drink, when Liam zipped up and walked away. Apparently, he was done waiting around to see if the grown man next to him could make water. Literally left with his dick in his hand, Max readjusted his stance and leaned forward. It looked like he wasn't going to get his rocks off anytime soon, but he was determined to satisfy at least one of his biological needs.

"Try thinking about Niagara Falls," Liam said, turning on one of the faucets and opening the restroom door. "It helps."

Max glanced over his shoulder and offered a few mumbled words of thanks, but his ginger was already gone. Disappointment mixed with relief as a warm stream began to flow. Talk about an icebreaker.

By the time Max finished and washed up, Danny was waiting for him in the narrow hallway. It was clear from the look on his face he'd noticed his friend's prolonged absence and connected the dots.

"So, which one of you came first?"

"I was just about to ask you the same question. Where's Angelo?

"You mean Angelique? The hell if I know or care."

Without saying more, Danny turned and signaled for his favorite waiter to close out his tab. The next show was about to begin and the crowd had easily doubled in size. The laidback vibe of the early evening had noticeably shifted. Alcohol and impatience were changing the well-mannered audience into something less predictable.

The more sensible patrons were heading out before things got out of hand, but Max wasn't about to cut and run without making at least one more pass at Liam. Scanning the crowd, he quickly spotted his red hair blazing like a roadside flare. With a vast sea of humanity between them, it would be nearly impossible to get close enough for proximity to trigger another random encounter. That meant one of them had to be bold enough to make the next move. Counting slowly under his breath, Max tried to look irresistible as he stepped into his ginger's line of sight.

There were at least a dozen suitors vying for Liam's attention, so it was less of a surprise and more of a foregone conclusion when the dazzling smile Max shot from across the room missed its mark. Even though he hadn't put his best foot forward in the restroom, Max had secretly hoped Fortune would intervene. Next time, he'd be more careful and make it clear he was looking for good luck, not bad.

The night was still young and so was Liam. Subscribing to the notion that when you double your pleasure, you double your fun, Liam locked eyes on Max as he walked over and offered Danny an outstretched hand.

Being a good wingman was about knowing how to read a room so you could open metaphorical doors for your friend. Loosely applying the concept of "guilt by association," Danny had turned up the Cavanaugh charm to make Max seem just as confident and cool. Unfortunately, the ruse had worked too well. It was one thing to compliment your buddy's best attributes and another to overpower them. Danny had succeeded in calling attention to the dynamic duo, but Liam had set his sights on the hero, not the sidekick. The action scene that was sure to follow would be epic. Luckily, the time it took for Liam to maneuver across the room had given Danny a chance to plot out a series of carefully choreographed moves from his playbook.

Step #1 – Introduce yourself first so your friend can learn someone's name.

"Hey there! I'm Danny and this is Max. What's your name?"

"I'm called Liam, but actually we've just met in the head."

"He was giving you head?" Danny asked with a playful smile as he put a hand to his hear and pretended to have misheard. The gesture made it clear he was twisting Liam's words to lighten the mood with a joke. "Cruising the restroom, Maxie? Classic!"

Step #2—You and your buddy are having a good time and you're inviting others to join the party.

"I wasn't trying to pick him up."

"You weren't?" Liam asked, inserting himself into the conversation with pouty lips that were begging to be kissed. "I'm crushed."

"The point my friend was *trying* to make," Danny quickly interjected, "Was how hard it is to really get to know someone in a place like this. Maybe you two could meet up later for a drink?"

"I usually close out the evenings at Purgatory. Maybe I'll see you boys there? First round is on me."

Step #3 – Know when to make an exit.

Something about the growl in Liam's tone made it clear he wasn't speaking figuratively. While Danny wasn't particularly jazzed by the idea of doing a body shot on a stranger's abs, it would definitely set things in motion with "Big Red." Still, he knew Max would never be bold enough to actually throw caution to the wind. Too many years of doing without had conditioned his friend to think that never getting what he wanted was a just a prolonged form of delayed gratification.

The first chords of the next show echoed through the speakers like a warning. Offering a quick wave good-bye, Danny grabbed Max by the shoulder and steered him toward the nearest exit. Outside the club, a team of second-string illusionists was hard at work on Commercial Street, passing out glossy advertisements to passing tourists.

"Hey, handsome! Leaving so soon?"

Reflexively, Max turned toward the voice, but he quickly realized the question had been directed at someone else. Up close, the leggy blond from the restaurant seemed larger than life. Danny managed a toothless grin. It would take more than a straw full of 151 to give him the courage to do more. Unable to move or speak, he transmitted a silent S.O.S. to his wingman.

"Come on Danny," Max said as he shoved his friend up the crowded sidewalk toward Spiritus. "Let's roll."

"Bye-bye, Danny Boy," the blond called out in a seductive voice that was an octave too deep. "Come back soon."

"O.K. Now *that* was a close call."

"Huh?" Danny asked, looking over his shoulder to steal another quick look back. "What do you mean?"

"*That, that, dude looks like a lady.*"

Max belted out the lyrics in his best Steven Tyler.

"You knew that was a guy in drag, right?"

"Of course," Danny said, stepping off the curb and onto the busy street. "You could see his Adam's Apple from across the room. Come on, let's jet back to your apartment. I know something we can do to make this a night you'll never forget."

CHAPTER 5

"**O**UCH! YOU'RE hurting me."

"Fidgeting is making it worse. Hold still."

"Danny, I'm serious. Don't push it in."

"Relax. Breathe."

The more Max tried to think about something else, the more acutely he felt the burning sensation. Every nerve in his body was focused on one spot.

"Are you sure you want me to stop?"

It was a fair question for Danny to ask, especially since Max had been looking forward to this rite of passage since puberty. Still, now that it was happening, he was having second thoughts.

Sweat. Spit. Semen.

Pleasure was a messy business that left a guilty stain. Pain was something altogether different. Clean and precise, every searing sensation was logged in a ledger that marked the slow, unbearable passage of time. Grasping his best friend's shoulders with both hands, Max nodded his assent. After all, he'd suffered more for less. Besides, a moment of discomfort was better than a summer of regret. It was now or never.

Danny tightened his grip and pushed harder.

POP!

It was hard to tell whether the sound was real or just inside his head, but the fiery heat was gone. Now, all Max felt was satisfaction.

"Well," Danny asked in a more subdued voice now that the worst was over. "Do you love it?"

"Very cool. I look just like Corey Hart in the 'Never Surrender' video."

Max's right lobe was as red as a tomato, but the earring had pierced the cartilage in just the right spot. Danny took a step back to admire his handy work.

"You'll look even cooler once you stop crying."

"You have no idea how much it hurt."

"It was just a little prick."

"Like you?"

Laughing as tears trickled down his cheeks, Max touched the gold stud in his right ear and winced. The tiny puncture wouldn't even count as a flesh wound, but the blood spilled and the curses uttered had infused the precious metal with a kind of magic. Every time Max saw the gilded talisman, he'd remember this night.

The safety pin hadn't done any real damage, but Max's plaintive yelps and Danny's cajoling sounded like something out of "Deliverance." Fortunately, no one was around to hear. Since Max's mom and sister were both still at work, it made sense to lance his lobe in their apartment instead of fumbling in the dark up in Danny's cupola. The alcohol in the Cavanaughs' liquor cabinet could have been used as anesthesia and antiseptic, but Sam would have ratted them out to Danny's parents before Max's ear was even numb with ice. There weren't any cold beers waiting in the old Frigidaire, but what the tiny apartment lacked in amenities, it made up for in heart.

Separated by a thrift-shop nightstand, twin beds pressed against the paneled walls, trying to squeeze a few more inches of square footage. Although Max and his sister shared the bigger room, there wasn't nearly enough space for two full-grown adults. Josie had claimed most of the closet and all of drawers the highboy dresser. Max didn't mind. Everything he owned fit in a cardboard box under his bed.

A slice of the coveted seascape slipped in from between the handmade curtains. The single window offered no cross breeze, but at least it faced the harbor. Being a waitress at an all-night diner meant Max's mom was mostly nocturnal. Lara Balais said it was easier to sleep through sunny days in a windowless room. In truth, she just wanted her kids to have the fresh air and a water view.

A cool ocean breeze almost made up for the lack of air conditioning, but Max had gone odor blind to the funky smells that came and went with the changing tides. After a long day at work, he was ready to kill the lights and crash. There was just one problem: Danny was sprawled across his kid-sized mattress. Josie's unmade bed was available but trespassing into her space would have violated their unwritten code. Suddenly, the crowded room felt smaller.

Despite its shortcomings, the modest apartment would seem like a palace compared to student housing at Berklee. Most of the freshmen lived in the dorms, but Max was planning to get a place off campus. High rents and low inventory meant he'd be sharing his apartment with a bunch of roommates.

"I've been checking the classifieds in Bay Windows and the Boston Globe. It looks like I'll be able to afford a pretty sweet pad."

"You're kidding, right?" Danny asked, opening his eyes and propping up his head with a lumpy pillow. "Those ads are for sublets. The city is lousy with students trying to get out of their leases and head home for the summer. Come fall, those same rents will double."

"Are you serious?"

"Sorry to burst your bubble. Anyway, aren't you getting a little ahead of yourself? Don't you still have to get accepted?"

"That's just a formality."

"Like good grades and SAT scores?"

"You don't understand how it works," Max explained, grabbing his trumpet and nervously fingering the valves. "It's all about the music. I just need to ace my audition next month."

"Speaking of blowing your horn, what's the story with you and that guy at the nightclub? Are you into him or what?"

"Why the sudden interest in my love life? Are you writing a book?"

"I'm just trying to figure out when you developed a taste for ginger."

"Probably about the same time you got a kink for drag."

The silence that followed was as loud as a number by the Boston Pops. Their usual banter had the right cadence and tone, but verbal sparring was like making music. No matter how good the performance, one sour note could ruin a perfect run.

"You have to get up early for work in the morning," Danny said, giving up his spot on the bed and heading for the door. "I should go and let you get some sleep."

"Sunday is my day off. Stay and we can watch 'Saturday Night Live.' That new chick, Tina Fey, is totally killing it on 'Weekend Update.'"

"Summer re-runs stink. Besides, the only channel that comes in clear on your crappy TV is PBS."

Sharpened to a point, the truth pierced deeper than a safety pin. Even with three paychecks coming in each month, cable TV was a splurge the Balais family couldn't afford. Still, Danny had broken a longstanding pact by calling it out. Maybe it was time for him to go after all.

"Later."

Max locked the deadbolt and listened to the sound of his friend's heavy footfall on the wooden steps. He felt bad about the way the night had ended, but there was no point chasing after someone who didn't want to be caught. A good, clean fight would have been the easiest way to work things out. Unfortunately, Danny preferred brooding to brawling. Max wasn't about to lie awake all night chewing on his words. There was only one other way he could think of to blow off steam. Luckily, the scrappy little pugilist between his legs was ready to go a few rounds.

Stumbling back into the bedroom, Max unbuttoned his shorts and slid a warm hand under the waistband of his tighty whities. Working in shifts meant someone was usually awake and stirring about the apartment. A few moments of *real* privacy, without the threat of his mom or sister walking in, was better than porn. Max grabbed the still-warm pillow wedged between the bed and the wall and pressed it to his face. Like canvas tents or burning leaves, Danny Cavanaugh had a smell that was hard to forget.

Max took a deep breath and closed his eyes. Despite years of practice, it was hard to concentrate on the matter at hand. Random thoughts and conflicting feelings were invading the space in his brain that was usually reserved for fantasies.

Provincetown. Danny. Boston.

Past, present, and future swirled together like paint on a canvas. The night had ended badly, but the evening wasn't a total loss. The boring summer palette of blues and grays now included hot pink and red. Angelique and Liam were vibrant characters who had already altered the otherwise predictable colors of the season. Max tried to bring the new image of his ginger into focus, but his inner eye was scratchy and dry. The rhythmic motion of his hand slowed and his grip released. Drifting between time and place, he pulled the pillow tighter into a hug and surrendered to sleep.

"HONEY, I'M home!"

The metallic clang of keys hitting the Formica kitchen counter was louder than an alarm clock. It was still too early for Lara to be finished with her shift at the diner. That meant Josie was back and looking for company.

"Hey, sis," Max said as he emerged from the bedroom and joined her in the kitchen. "How was work?"

"I quit."

"Seriously?"

"Seriously."

The story that was sure to follow would be a good one, but Josie's timing couldn't have been worse. Hawking T-shirts to tourists was a job, not a career, but Max needed his sister to take his place as breadwinner so he could go off to school. Even though their mom would never admit it, she needed another full-time paycheck to keep the family afloat. There was no way Max could leave in September if Josie was unemployed.

"My manager told me I had to start wearing the merchandise."

"What's wrong with that?

"He wanted me to wear a T-shirt with a picture of a donkey piñata on it."

"And?"

"It had the words 'I'D HIT THAT' printed in red letters across the chest."

"Wow," Max said, filling a foggy, plastic cup with tap water and drinking it to quell his growling stomach. "Is that sexist or racist?"

"Both. He's a total douchebag."

"So, now what?"

"Now, I get to spend what's left of my Saturday night hanging out with my big brother and his best friend. Where's Danny? Please tell me he's out getting us pizza?"

"I wish."

"He got bored?"

"He got pissed."

"That was going to be my next guess," Josie said, pulling out what was left of her share of a meatloaf from the refrigerator. Max had already devoured the day-old loaf of bread, but he'd left her the heels. Josie slathered the crusty slices with mayo and added a couple thick pieces of tomato to compensate for the thin sliver of meat in the middle. Cutting the sandwich in half, she took one wedge for herself and handed her brother the other.

"We were picking on each other and things went too far. I can't remember who started it, but we both said things we regret."

"Of course you did," Josie said between bites. "You're buddies. Go find him and make up. He's probably sulking down at Lewis Brothers. Unlike us, he can afford to drown his sorrows in butter pecan."

"You're right about the making up part, but not the ice cream. Danny is addicted to grease and carbs, not sugar. Anyway, Mom will be home soon. What are you going to tell her about the job?"

"That I'll find something better. And I will. Stop worrying about me and go fix things with your friend."

IT WAS just after midnight, but most of the sun-drunk tourists were asleep, dreaming of lobsters and rocky shores. Back in Boston, all the cool bars and alternative dance clubs were just getting started, but every reputable establishment in Provincetown was closed. Even though the A-House was open until one, its patrons were already starting to make their way to Spiritus. Half-starved and horny, strangers-turned-friends shared stories of failed hook-ups and bad romance as they wandered up Commercial Street for last call.

The guys loitering outside the pizza shop were hotter than a slice right out of the oven, but Max was there to find Danny, not cruise. Still, he couldn't help noticing how many guys were checking him out.

Glassy eyes, like wandering hands, checked out the muscles straining the seams of his T-shirt. Tall and lanky, Max had always felt like a sideshow freak with bad skin. Now, after a year of working out and a tub of Clearasil, he'd become the main attraction. Fortunately, he wasn't the only one putting on a show. Manspreading across more than his share of a wooden bench, Danny Cavanaugh stood out in the crowd.

The boys on Fire Island wore Gucci loafers to run out for milk at the Pantry, but the closest Provincetown came to couture was flip-flops. Still, Mrs. Cavanaugh made it a point each year to supplement her son's summer wardrobe with a few select items from Dunhill or Brooks Brothers. Danny hated putting on airs, but he always made an exception and dressed the part for his parent's July 4th gala. The rest of the summer he bummed around in frayed khakis and faded tees.

There weren't any fireworks or American flags up yet, but it looked as though Danny had decided to do a dress rehearsal. Decked in green linen shorts and a bright pink polo, he had upgraded from the Army/Navy surplus store to Ralph Lauren. Danny definitely blended in with the colony of WASPs buzzing around him, but seeing him prepped out was like watching Patty Hearst wear a beret and carry a rifle.

"Yo, bro."

Max felt his face blush as three different guys turned and responded to his call. Unfortunately, none of them was Danny. Even though he was only a few feet away, it wouldn't be easy to get his friend's attention.

Max's formidable height and girth made him a big fish in a little pond. The sidewalk was chummed with pheromones and sweat, but the circling sharks were wasting their time. Tonight, Max only had eyes for one guy. Somewhere, buried deep beneath the tendons and muscle, his heart was beating faster. The kiss back at the nightclub was more than a flash of heat lighting. Maybe it was time to finally admit the truth: getting into Berklee wasn't the only thing he'd been dreaming about.

Summoning as much swagger as he could manage, Max forged ahead and pushed his way through the human wall. The troops had closed ranks around their captain. Luckily, the two lieutenants flanking Danny were too busy debating politics to notice another chiseled body in a field of nameless grunts. Max had the advantage of surprise, but his enemies had the high ground. Determined not to retreat or surrender, he puffed up his chest and continued his frontal assault.

"Hey, Danny. What's up with the pony shirt?"

The question was meant as a joke, not a social commentary, but no one was laughing. Too late, he noticed all the other soldiers in the platoon were wearing the same uniform. When confronted by a superior force, the best strategy was to divide and conquer. When Danny finally looked up and made eye contact, Max was ready to spirit him back across enemy lines.

"Let's get out of here and head back to my place."

"Excuse me," a Nixon clone barked as he broke rank and stepped forward. "We're trying to have a private conversation. Go find someone else to take home tonight."

"Actually, I was talking to my friend, not you," Max said, dropping his voice an octave and flexing his muscles. "We have some unfinished business."

"No, we're good." Danny said, stretching his arms across the back of the bench to show he was staying put. "You guys all know each other, right?"

"Sorry, Balais," one of the other guards said, stepping forward and offering an outstretched hand. "I didn't recognize you. You've really changed since last summer – like one of those Charles Atlas before-and-after cartoons in the comic books."

"Thanks, Trey."

Jonathan Howard Taft III was one of the only guys in town who could give a compliment with one hand while he bitch-slapped you with the other. In New England, rich kids wore nicknames like accessories, but few of them were cool enough to pull off the affectation. A direct descendant of a U.S. president and a legitimate "third" in the Taft family, Trey definitely knew how to work the numbers that trailed after his name.

"Nice T-shirt, Max," Trey said in a voice just loud enough to alert the rest of the Republicans caucusing around him that he was about to make a point. "Hey, Cavanaugh. Didn't you used to wear one just like it back in Lisbon?"

Openly gay and undeniably handsome, Trey was the kind of guy you wanted to belt or bed. One good cut deserved another, but retaliating would confirm he'd hit a nerve with the obvious dig. With abs of steel, Max could handle a sucker punch for wearing Danny's hand-me-downs. Rich kids were usually callous, but they weren't often cruel. Trey and his minions would relent if they knew the true extent of the Balais family's financial problems, but that would only make things worse. The only thing Max hated more than ridicule was pity.

"I'm sorry about what I said earlier," Max said to Danny as he slowly backed away. "I wanted you to have a good time tonight, just not at my expense. I guess Angelo isn't the only one who knows how to dress up and put on a show."

Inspired by the illusionists at the Crown & Anchor, Max had tapped into his inner diva. He was done being an open book that Danny could read. Rather than stand around waiting for the next sarcastic question or veiled insult, Max turned and walked away. Getting in the last word wasn't the same as being right, but it still felt pretty good.

"HEY, REX! Wait up."

Max was still replaying the exchange with Danny in his head when he heard a voice calling from half a block away. Normally, he'd have just written it off as a case of mistaken identity or cloudy beer goggles, but even from a distance he recognized the guy strolling toward him up Commercial Street. The red hair was a dead giveaway.

"Are you daft? Didn't you hear me?"

"I heard you yelling after someone, but it wasn't me. My name is Max."

"Yes, of course you're called Max. With those dreamy blue eyes and lovely muscles. How could I forget?"

"Well, a popular guy like you has a lot of names to remember. How did you come up with Rex anyway?"

"Well, it rhymes with sex, so it was the first thing that came to mind when I thought of you."

"I guess I should be flattered. Heading home alone?"

"I certainly hope not."

Blue or gray, depending on the light, Liam's cloudy eyes were not the windows to his soul. Small twitches and minute changes to his expressions hinted at swirling currents hidden below the calm surface. The Y-shaped dimple in his chin was so deep that his blade couldn't shave it clean; strands of red whiskers in the center made the cleft look even more prominent. The rest of his features seemed a half-size too big for the rest of his face. But instead of creating a caricature, it only accentuated his natural beauty. The effect was a look that felt larger than life.

Max dug his hands into the pockets of his cargo shorts and discretely pinched his leg to make sure he wasn't dreaming. Just when it seemed like he'd struck out, Max was back up at bat. The hottest guy in Provincetown had just thrown him a hard, fast pitch right down the center. All Max had to do was keep his eye on the ball to hit a grand slam and score.

"Come on then." Max said, with a smirk that hid his unresolved feelings about Danny. "Let's go."

MAX. MAX. *Max.*

Liam might not be able to see the face of the man who was ravaging him on the dark patio outside his quaint New England cottage, but "Rex" was going to make sure Liam never forgot his name again.

The male body had eight erogenous zones and Max was determined to master them all. Years of self-study and various levels of sexual experimentation had left him with a better than average grasp of male anatomy. Even though he understood the basic mechanics, the more subtle nuances were still a mystery. Luckily, summer school was in session.

The guys Max had been with in high school were all about receiving pleasure, but none of his partners had been eager to reciprocate. Tonight, Max was going to get as good as he gave.

Lips. Tongue. Breath.

Kissing was like good conversation. For it to work, you had to keep things interesting and listen to what your partner had to say. Liam wasn't using words to communicate, but his lips were telling Max exactly what he needed to know. It was hard to resist the impulse to tear Liam's clothes off and devour his body. Hexed by darkness and nerves, the engorged buttons of his shirt were suddenly too big to slide through the tiny slits. The harder Max tried to undo one, the more arthritic his fingers seemed to become.

"Here, let me make this easier for you."

In one fluid motion, Liam slipped out of his shirt like a snake shedding its skin. Slithering closer, he grabbed the belt loops of Max's cargo shorts with his index fingers and pulled until their torsos were fused together. A forked tongue lapped at bare skin and sharp fangs penetrated the soft flesh of a shoulder. The bite wouldn't leave a mark, but it was hard enough to provoke a breathy hiss.

The momentary jolt of pain dispelled any lingering inhibitions. Danny loved to tease his friend about being a "blowhard." Tonight, Max was going to live up to that nickname. Without missing a beat, he slid a hand around Liam's slim waist and down the back of his chinos. There was a brief moment of hesitation. Grabbing Liam's ass like a trumpet, Max used his first and third fingers to part the firm cheeks and slid his middle digit inside. Just the right amount of pressure applied to his sweet spot made Liam sing.

"Bloody hell."

"Yeah?"

"Bugger me."

"Huh?"

Before Max had time to ask for a translation of the British slang, Liam was kneeling on a chaise lounge chair with his bum in the air. Max spit into his hand and covered himself with the slickness. Stepping forward, he pressed the head of his cock against the tight pucker of Liam's backside and pushed.

"Wait! Stop!!"

The urgency in Liam's voice shattered the romance of the moment.

"Shit. Did I hurt you?"

"Quite the contrary," Liam said reassuringly as he grabbed something from the pocket of his jeans and pressed it into Max's hand. "But you need to suit up before we start."

Max felt a mixture of embarrassment and relief as he tore open the foil wrapper and unrolled the condom. Wearing a rubber to screw was like skinny-dipping in a T-shirt. But barebacking was for fantasies and vintage porn. In real life, sex was always safe. That was harder to practice than preach.

There were a bunch of colloquial labels that were used to define Max's sexual orientation, but words couldn't describe how good it felt to finally act on his desires. Even though he'd been rolling around with guys since puberty, he'd never actually gone all the way. "Oral" and "anal" were both four-letter words but, in reality, the two forms of sex were as different as night and day. Ready, willing, and able, Liam was about to take what was left of Max's virginity. This was it. There was no turning back.

Fortunately, the short break in the action had done nothing to diminish the heat of the moment. In fact, the time-out had given Max a chance to mentally review the rudimentary choreography he'd spent years watching on the worn VHS tapes he snagged for almost nothing when the video store went DVD. On screen, the top talent was all about getting down to business, but there was undoubtedly a lot of "behind the scene" preparation for the bottom boys. Max didn't need a script or cue to know what was supposed to happen next: It was time for him to stop poking around and put his mouth where the money was. Lifting Liam up by the hips, Max burrowed his face into the heady crack of his ginger's bum.

"Oh!"

Rimming was another sexual experience he could now cross off his bucket list. As Max's warm, wet tongue poked and probed deeper, his free hand rhythmically pumped Liam's boner. Max couldn't help thinking about the semester he'd wasted trying to master the trombone.

Yes. Yes. Yes.

Max had seen a fair amount of action, but all of his previous encounters had taught him the wrong lessons. When sex was good, you wanted it to last. Unfortunately, a quick hookup had always been just that; finishing up fast, before you got caught or someone changed his mind.

A practiced thumb applied just the right amount of pressure to the vein running the length of Liam's shaft as Max's firm hand tightened and released its grip. Predictably, the combination and rhythm produced a volcanic response. Without warning, Liam gasped as a thick load erupted from his cock. The flow of bodily fluid that sprayed out onto the chair cushion was white, not red, but it was as hot as lava.

Max stepped back to admire the view. The sweet ass spread out in front of him was like a ripe peach, but he'd inexplicably lost his appetite. His virginity was still intact. A part of him couldn't help wondering whether the deed would live up to the hype. Unspent, but satisfied, Max peeled off the unused condom and tossed it into the bushes. At least cleanup wasn't going to be an issue.

"Thanks, bro. Catch you later."

"Wait. You're *not* going," Liam declared as he tried to stand on legs that had turned to rubber. "Come inside and have a rest. We can have another go again later."

Max hated the idea of waking up in a stranger's bed. The smart thing to do was to head home and toss off in the shower, but he was tired of playing it safe. Without thinking, he nodded in agreement.

Liam took his companion by the hand and led him through the darkened house to his bed. The cool, cotton sheets pulled the remaining heat from their naked bodies. The closest Max had ever come to spooning was with his pillow, but tonight he was willing to give anything a try.

"Sorry," Liam said, yawning in the middle of what was supposed to be a passionate kiss. "I'm knackered."

Max didn't need an English-to-English dictionary to know his ginger needed rest, not sex. It had been a long day and an even longer night. Wrapping a muscled arm around the warm body pressing up against him, Max closed his eyes and surrendered.

CHAPTER 6

HALF ASLEEP and suffering from a serious case of morning wood, Max hugged his pillow and listened for the usual morning sounds of Commercial Street. The grinding engine of a delivery truck was better than an alarm clock, but all he could hear was the lilting melody of wind chimes and the bass of the crashing surf. It was still early. Josie or his mom would come in and wake him soon enough. Sighing, he rolled over and gave thanks for a few more minutes of uninterrupted rest.

Max was just falling back into a deep sleep when the pillow he was holding heaved and rolled over to the other side of the bed. Suddenly, scenes from the evening before flashed in random sequence. The plot and characters were a little fuzzy, but the star of the show was still lying naked next to him in bed.

Max hadn't planned on spending the whole night with Liam, but a cool breeze off the bay made rest more appealing than sex. The plan had been to grab a long shag and a short nap on the king-sized bed. Unfortunately, his body had been ready for eight hours of sleep. He was out cold as soon his head hit the pillow.

The sun was already up and shining through the open windows. Sneaking away like a thief, Max retraced the short route back through the cottage and slipped out the back door onto the patio. He was almost to the pile of his clothes lying conspicuously at the foot of the lounge chair when it became clear he wasn't alone. Sitting around a cast-iron table, Liam's parents were enjoying morning tea and taking in the view.

"Oh, my," a woman exclaimed as she carefully placed her cup in its saucer and wiped her pursed lips clean. "Well, hell-o."

"Ah, shit." Max muttered under his breath as he struggled to figure out the protocol for meeting a trick's parents. "Good morning."

For his part, the woman's husband simply glanced up and offered a tight-lipped smile before retreating back into the safety of his morning paper. Apparently, a naked stranger standing in the courtyard didn't rate as news.

Max tried to cover himself with hands that were too small. More amused than shocked, the woman smiled and pointed to a terrycloth robe hanging on a hook next to the outdoor shower.

"Darling, why don't you cover up and introduce yourself while I pour you some tea? I think you could use a cuppa."

Max darted around the patio, trying to recall the sexual choreography of his late-night patio tryst with Liam. Like an X-rated scavenger hunt, he quickly gathered up his underwear, shorts, and T-shirt and stepped inside the outdoor shower stall to get dressed. As he pulled on his clothes, Max noticed a dark-haired teenager watching from the second-story window.

"Please don't mind Kyle. He's our youngest. Like most teenagers, he spends most of his free time sulking about in his room."

"Good morning, parental units," Liam proclaimed as he appeared, fully dressed, in the doorway. After receiving the customary nod from his father and smile from his mother, he walked straight over to Max and kissed him squarely on the lips.

"Hello, Lover. Sleep well?"

Too embarrassed to reply, Max nodded and tried not to let all the attention go to the little head poking up from between his legs. He was about to sit down on one of the lounge chairs when Liam's mother called out for him to stop.

"Not *there*, darling. The filthy birds have left white stains all over the cushions. I'm afraid we'll need a scrub brush and suds to get them clean."

"I'll take care of the mess," Liam answered with a smirk that suggested his mother was already in on the joke. Max got the impression that this scene, or one just like it, had played out before.

"I should get going."

"Already?" Liam's mother asked without even a hint of irony. "Won't you stay for a bite? I think we may even have some coffee in the kitchen."

Max was trying to be as unobtrusive as possible, but Liam's mother seemed determined to show her guest every courtesy. You could say a lot of things about the British, but they were courteous to a fault.

"Thank you, Mrs...." Max said, stopping mid-sentence when he realized he didn't know Liam's last name. "But I've really got to be going. I'm sorry to have ruined your breakfast."

"Ruined it? Why, not at all, my boy." Liam's father suddenly came to life at the suggestion that anything could spoil his morning. "I'm glad to see my son is making friends. I do hope you'll come again?"

Liam's mother echoed the sentiment of her husband's invitation, but Liam was ready with the perfect response.

"Yes, Max. I hope you'll come. Soon."

"Definitely."

Max coughed out a hasty goodbye as he slipped out the front gate. What he'd shared last night with Liam wasn't love, but it was lovely. Any residual anger he felt toward Danny had burned away in the heat of the morning. Besides, there was no way he was going to let a stupid fight keep him from telling his best friend about one of the hottest nights of his life.

A SLOW morning at the diner meant empty booths and shitty tips, but it also gave Lara Balais a chance to spend her break drinking coffee with her son. While Max tore through breakfast, his mom emptied the pockets of her stained apron and spread her tips on the table. Unfortunately, the stack of pancakes in front of Max was an inch higher than the mounds of quarters and dimes her late-night customers had left as a gratuity. At least his breakfast was on the house. Given how much he could eat, that perk alone was worth at least half-a-shift's worth of her minimum wages.

"Slow down. You're going to make yourself sick," Lara said, reaching across the table to steal a slice of bacon from her son's plate. "I don't know what you and Danny got up to last night, but you sure worked up an appetite."

Max chuckled to himself as he soaked up a puddle of syrup with a folded pancake and shoved it into his mouth. He wasn't about to give his mom a blow-by-blow of his one-night stand, but he also wasn't about to start lying to her either.

"Danny and I hung out for a bit, but I actually ended up crashing with my new friend, Liam. He's from England and has a wicked mane of red hair."

Even though he'd grown up in Provincetown, Max still had some traces of his father's Boston accent. It was too subtle for most people to notice, but Lara could hear her husband in her son's voice.

Miguel Balais had been dead ten years, long enough for time to backfill the space his life had once taken up in their small world. The first twenty-three years of his abbreviated life had been spent working on his family's farm in Chavez, hidden away in the province of Tras-os-Montes in the northeastern corner of Portugal. Starkly beautiful and isolated from the modern world that thrived along the coast, the harsh climate of his home was nine months of winter and three months of hell. Miguel spent most of his free time exploring the plateaus, rivers, and mountains of the region. Capturing fragments of the dramatic vistas and timeworn folklore in paint and canvas made it easier to imagine a day when he could leave it all behind to pursue another life.

When his chance finally came, Miguel grabbed a half-empty backpack loaded with his favorite paintbrushes and stole away on the first plane heading to America. The plan was to hunker down with a half a dozen other struggling artists in a loft in Soho, but after less than a week in the city that never sleeps, Miguel was exhausted. Using what little money was left in his pocket, he rented a car and drove a few hundred miles north, to the savage wilds of Connecticut. With the reluctant help of the cousin of an uncle's neighbor, Miguel managed to secure enough part-time jobs to finance a ramshackle apartment in New Haven. Yale University cast a long shadow, but mornings serving coffee and evenings bar backing at "Cahoots" still left him with a few hours to sleep and an afternoon of sunshine to paint by. The repetition of days and nights felt more like indentured servitude than creative license until the fateful night when a girl called Lara smiled at Miguel across a crowded room.

What happened next, the where and when, seemed less important once their separate lives blended into one. Over the course of a single semester, Lara dropped two business electives and started worked evenings at the library so her boyfriend could pursue his art. Always the observer of beauty, Miguel had already realized the obvious by the time his girlfriend refused champagne at his first big exhibit in Guilford. In the blink of an eye, the pronouns "I" and "me" abruptly changed to "us" and "we". For better and for worse, a baby on the way changed everything.

It took fortitude and a fair amount of stupidity for Lara to resist the temptation to turn to her affluent family for help. In the end, the unavoidable reality of a biological imperative forced her to trade the promise of her Ivy League degree for the gamble of a simpler life in Provincetown. Six months later, Max was born in a small hospital in Hyannis Port.

Most of Max's mental snapshots of his father had already yellowed. Still, he could remember sitting in this same booth, eating a mound of ketchup-soaked fries while his dad sketched on the back of a napkin.

Ink. Paint. Charcoal.

When money was too tight for supplies, Miguel would transfer the images swirling in his head onto whatever medium was at hand. The consummate artist, he once used his own blood to rouge the red lips of a woman who had gotten trapped inside one of his canvases. Max would've done just about anything to get his hands on one of his dad's paintings, but Lara had sold the entire collection to one of the smaller dealers in the East End. Despite the quantity and quality of his work, the proceeds weren't nearly enough to pay off all the medical bills Miguel's illness had left behind.

While Lara enjoyed the last few minutes of her break, Max bused his dishes and wiped down the table. He was just about to pour his mom a second cup of coffee and explain that Liam was something more than just a causal buddy when Josie walked into the diner. Wearing a matching uniform and apron, she looked more like Lara's sister than her daughter. She greeted a few of the regular customers with a painted-on smile, but Max could tell by the angry look on her face that she was ready to punch more than the time clock.

"Good morning, honey, I'll put on a fresh pot while you grab a bite."

Lara's break was officially over. Max knew that was his cue to get out of the way and let his family get back to work.

"Later."

If Josie heard her brother say goodbye, she didn't show it. Max knew his sister wasn't happy about working at the diner, but she was smart enough to understand what it meant for him to go away to school. Only one Balais was getting out of Provincetown. Josie had always made the best of her little life, but like the tiny bedroom she shared with Max, it sometimes felt like the 1.8 square miles of her world were slowly closing in.

Max didn't know what felt worse – a stomach full of carbs or a gut full of guilt. The pancakes and bacon could be purged with a good workout, but he needed to find a way to keep his family's kitty purring while he secured his own finances for school. He was already pulling double shifts on *La Benedita* to help his mom out with the rent. There was only one way a guy like Max could supplement an anemic income.

MAX TWISTED the lid off the plastic bottle and squirted out a couple drops of lube. Pushing intently, he fingered the valve until the stiffness gave way. The stubborn piston was tight from disuse, but a little playtime would loosen it right up. Max pressed his lips to the puckered opening and slipped the tip of his tongue into the metallic-tasting hole. He took a deep breath and felt his diaphragm expand with air.

Playing alone was one thing, but it was hard to get used to the idea of letting other people watch. Max's shoulders felt unnaturally stiff and a dozen voyeurs' eyes made his skin itch with anticipation. Most guys would have felt too self-conscious to perform in front of an audience, but he was a born exhibitionist. Hooking up with Liam again would make Max feel like a million bucks, but it wasn't going to pay the bills. If he wanted to score some fast cash, it was time to stop fooling around and get down to business.

Be cool.

The nerves would pass once he stopped thinking and just let go. Checking his stance and relaxing his hips, Max closed his eyes and pushed his whole body forward to blast one out.

An impressive crowd had gathered on the sidewalk outside City Hall to listen to the talented young musician play. The key to a really good set was picking the right mix of songs. As usual, the weekend audience was generous with applause and tips. Once the music stopped, a couple of guys hung back to flirt, but they quickly moved on to the next attraction once it became clear the hot trumpeter was interested in making music, not time.

Max tilted his horn forward and depressed the water key. After the steady stream of saliva draining from the horn slowed to a trickle, he blew into the mouthpiece to clear away any excess moisture. The velvet trumpet case at his feet was overflowing with paper money and coins. One twenty-minute set had brought in more cash than Max usually made in a day on *La Benedita*. He couldn't decide whether the unexpected windfall was because of his talent or new muscles. Either way, it didn't matter. There were times when he was tempted to quit his day job and just make music, but the summer season was much too short. Besides, playing gigs for his super would have turned something he loved to do into just one more way to make ends meet. Like actors waiting tables, hauling nets and gutting fish wasn't glamorous, but it was honest work and brought in a steady paycheck. As soon as Max got his first big break in Boston, he'd quit the part-time jobs. His trumpet was a golden goose that would keep laying eggs. Max was just about to start another set when he noticed a familiar reflection in the bell of his horn.

"Well, we meet again."

"Don't sound so surprised. This is a fishing village, not Paris."

"That explains why I haven't been able to find a decent croissant."

"The closest thing we've got to international cuisine would probably be French toast."

"Yes," Liam said, pulling at a loose thread on the sleeve of Max's tattered shirt. "The town, like your music, is charming, but provincial. I'm afraid you'll need more than natural talent to make it in the big city."

"So, I suppose you're going to tell me how to up my game by adding some urban flair to my show?"

"Naturally," Liam said without even a hint of condescension. "You need a sharper hook to bring in the crowd. Lucky for you, I've got just the ticket."

"Seriously? I'm all ears."

"No. You're all muscle. And that's precisely the point. If you really want to drive the crowd wild, you have to show some skin and give them the shirt off your back."

"What? No way. I could *never* play with a bunch of people staring at me in my shorts."

"Why not? A true artist knows the secret to a great performance is to always give the audience what they want."

"He's right," Danny said, appearing from out of nowhere with a Big Gulp of Dr. Pepper and Diet Coke he'd mixed up at the local convenience store. In a gesture that was hard to miss, he sauntered right past Liam and casually passed Max his favorite drink. "Strip down like the Chippendales and you'll really clean up."

Max didn't want the sugar or extra calories, but he took a long sip from the white plastic cup anyway. The caramel-colored syrup, like his friend's peace offering, was sweet, but it left a bad taste in his mouth.

"You don't think I'm good enough to get into Berklee."

"Bullshit," Danny said, stepping closer into Max's personal space. "You're good—really good—but Boston is a world-class city that's full of talented artists. Instead of chasing after a pipe dream, you should wake up and think about what will happen if you try and fail. The higher you climb, the harder you'll fall. Trust me, I know"

"I've seen your life up close, Cavanaugh. You *always* get what you want. I couldn't care less what you think about me or my music."

"We both know that's not true," Danny said, taking back his drink and casually tossing it into the trash. "That's why we're always at each other's throats. You're always looking for me to give you strokes."

"Whatever."

"Come on, Maxie. Let's not do this again. We need to talk, but not here or now. Meet me out at Race Point later? We can hike down to the lighthouse and watch the planes land at the airport."

"A sunset stroll on the beach," Liam said, shifting his gaze back and forth between Danny and Max. "Now *that* sounds terribly romantic. Is it a proper date or can anyone tag along?"

As usual, Max and Danny's timing was off. Like any good Brit, Liam was expressing his affection through the filter of mockery. It was one thing to tease a guy to get his attention, but Liam had struck a nerve by insinuating that Max and Danny were secretly crushing on each other. To his credit, he was only half wrong.

"The more the merrier," Danny quickly responded with a smile that warned Liam not to take the joke further. "I'll invite a couple of my other friends and we can make it a party."

"Sorry, I can't make it," Max said, breaking out of the huddle to do another set. "I need to practice."

"Bollocks. I'm hardly an expert, but your fingering technique during last night's performance was brilliant. You're already a master. Let's go out to the beach with your mate and have a good time."

Deep in his gut, Max knew that he'd regret giving in, but all work and no play had left him feeling like a dull boy. Come September, he'd spend every waking hour in class or practicing. This was his last chance to kick back and enjoy himself. The longest days of the year were still in front of them, but September would be here before he knew it. Too soon, the weather would turn, and before anyone had time to notice, summer would be over.

CHAPTER 7

MAX KNEW as soon as he pulled off the bike trail that Danny had made good on his threat to turn a quiet night at the beach into a full-fledged party. Neatly lined up in a row, a fleet of Range Rovers and two-seater convertibles made the parking lot at Race Point look like a luxury car dealership. Tomorrow, a crew of auto detailers would spend the morning hosing off sand and applying coats of Turtle Wax to restore a like-new shine. After all, what was the point of owning a status symbol if it didn't impress?

Locals knew better than to rely on cars to get around in Provincetown. Max's ten-speed was only gently used when he'd bought it from the rental shop on Bradford, but the salt air had already aged the metal frame. Layers of dried sand and rust on the chain made it twice as hard to pedal. The bike still got him where he needed to go, but despite the effort, it felt like he was going nowhere fast.

Liam fastened his own bike to a splintered, wooden fence while Max just let his fall to the ground. At this time of day, the beach was practically deserted. Besides, the only silver lining to owning a hunk of junk was never worrying about anyone stealing it.

Walking in single file, Max blazed a trail up the steep dune that separated the beach from the graveled parking lot. It made sense for him to take the lead, since he knew the way. Bringing up the rear would also give Liam a chance to enjoy the view. Up close, Max's posterior was hotter than the sun-scorched sand. After a year of leg and glute workouts, his calves looked like they'd swallowed a grapefruit and his tight rear end looked like it belonged on a Greek statue.

Mother Nature had endowed her favorite son with the physique of a god, but she seemed determined to prove he was at least half-mortal by putting his endurance to the test. The dune became a mythological creature, shifting its granular surface to discourage unwelcome interlopers from reaching the top. Like a gaping mouth, soft sand swallowed Max's sandaled feet whole, making each step more difficult. By the time he reached the summit, the climb and view had left him breathless.

The deep azure sky was melting into a swirl of color. It was well past eight, but the summer sun had decided to hang around for happy hour. Skipping across a fiery horizon, the evening ferry was carrying the last of the weekend tourists back to Boston. Although the local economy enjoyed a boost from these stragglers who'd stretched out their stay, Ben Franklin was right when he said that guests, like fish, stink after three days. Envy of the lucky passengers bouncing and bounding their way back to the city was usually enough to turn Max a seasick shade of green. Tonight, his lust was fueled by a passion that was stronger than his urge to wander.

Given his age and libido, the only thing he should've been thinking about was getting drunk at the party and laid by his date. But even the prospect of free booze and easy sex couldn't keep Max from ruminating on all the unspoken things he wanted to talk through with his best friend.

Danny or Liam.

It was anyone's guess whether the evening would end with a bang or a whimper, but at least Max was taking risks instead of watching all the action from the sideline. Even though his future was still foggy, there was one thing about his predicament that was crystal clear. For once, Max was right where he belonged.

Further down the shore where the water was breaking, the party was in full swing. Even though Danny didn't have his mother's natural talent for entertaining, he'd been to enough fraternity mixers to know that when it came to social intercourse, alcohol was an aphrodisiac. A large tin washtub, loaded with wine and spirits, was strategically placed in a tall tuft of sea grass. It wouldn't take long for the liquor to work its magic. Soon, inhibitions would drop and strangers would start acting like friends.

The soundtrack of the evening was already starting to change. Audible laughter and animated conversations were the kind of communal foreplay that would quickly turn-on the crowd. Inevitably, the rising tension would peak and someone would say or do something that crossed the line. Once the guests started screwing each other, the night would devolve into something less predictable and more entertaining. Max could hardly wait for the fun to begin.

Meanwhile, coed couples sheltered together for safety as Christie McLean tried to earn her title as hostess. Flitting back and forth between clusters of guests, she greeted Danny's friends with a smile that was sweeter, but less intoxicating, than the fruity concoctions swirling in her guests' plastic cups.

"What do you say we make an 'Irish Exit' and go have our own little party back at my place?"

The blond fuzz on Max's forearms stood on end as tiny bumps appeared on his skin. Liam's indecent proposal was enough to give him goose pimples, but Max quickly rubbed them away and shrugged off the suggestion. He wasn't about to slip away now and blow his chance to make things right with Danny.

With a single look, Liam knew he was losing his case. Luckily, he was as skilled as an English barrister when it came to handling another man's briefs. After checking to make sure the coast was clear, he stepped closer and slipped his hand down the front of Max's cargo shorts.

"What are you doing? Stop that right now. I mean it."

Given the ardent protestations, Liam was surprised when he found something hard to grab onto. A quick wank would've put them both in a more festive mood, but sex in a public place was a risky proposition. The other guests were standing close enough to feel the heat radiating from the skin-on-skin friction. All it would take was one wayward glance in the right direction. Still, it was the risk of getting caught that made the whole thing so hot.

Although Liam had felt the stirrings of real passion last night, he'd clearly failed to make a strong first impression on Max. Max seemed more interested in prattling with Danny than snogging, but Liam wasn't about to let a sure thing slip through his fingers again. Determined not to take no for an answer, he stepped even closer and tightened his grip. The audible moan from Max confirmed that Liam had matters well in hand.

"Max? Oh...Max?"

Balancing a wine spritzer in one hand while she used the other for balance, Christie McLean looked like a drunken sailor as she stumbled down the dune in a blue-and-white striped sweater. Despite her boisterous laughter and feigned pleas for help, the effect was more sad than comical. Luckily, she was too focused on choosing her next step to notice the only same-sex couple at the party stealing third base just a few feet away.

"Later."

Max choked out the word as he forcibly detached himself from Liam. Almost as an afterthought, he slid a muscled arm across his ginger's shoulder to send a subtle message: he was fast, not easy. Liam tried to hide his obvious disappointment, but by the time Christie managed to traverse the dune, the sexual tension had gone as flat as her espadrilles. As usual, her timing was perfect.

"You're finally here! Honestly Max, I didn't think you were *ever* going to come."

"I'm starting to have my doubts as well," Liam said as he dialed down his sex appeal from "smolder" to "charm" and extended his hand. "Better late than never."

"And you must be Liam," she said, grabbing onto him like the ground beneath her was about to give way again. "Danny mentioned Max might bring along a special friend. My, but your hand is *warm.*"

"Sorry about that. I was just showing Max how to give a proper 'West London Handshake' and we seem to have gotten a bit overheated."

"We'll have to get you a nice cocktail to cool you down."

"Darling, you've read my mind. I'm suddenly in the mood for something milky and sweet."

"Do you mean a White Russian?" Christie exclaimed as if she'd correctly answered a Jeopardy question. "We certainly have the vodka, but I'm afraid we don't have any heavy cream or coffee liqueur."

"Actually, I'm craving a velvety shot of "Suhm Yuhng Guhy.""

"Oh, now doesn't *that* drink sound exotic!"

"I haven't been able to get my hands on any all weekend," Liam said with a straight face as he grabbed an empty plastic cup and turned toward Max. "But if I get lucky, I'll get a load of it tonight."

"Well, do save me a taste. Although with my delicate palate, I'll probably end up spitting most of it out."

Bawdy humor sounded stupid and crass when only one side was in on the joke. Christie McLean wouldn't know a good double entendre if it slapped her across the face. Chuckling out loud, Max tuned out the rest of the conversation and amused himself thinking about how thrilled she'd be if Danny offered to give her a "pearl necklace."

"Max? I asked if you were enjoying the party?"

"You'll have to excuse our friend," Liam said, playfully nudging Max in the ribs as Christie filled his empty glass with an unnaturally pink liquid. "He doesn't seem to be in a very festive mood."

"I thought this was going to be a chill night. Who invited all these people?"

"Why, *I* did!" Christie exclaimed in a singsong voice that betrayed her delight at finally being asked. "Danny stopped by the house this afternoon and practically begged me to help with his party. Isn't it just marvelous?"

"You certainly do make a handsome couple," Liam said with an inflection that wasn't lost on Max. "Frankly, I can't imagine him with any other girl."

The haughty accent Christie was affecting was almost as annoying as Liam's real one. Both spoke English, but neither seemed to understand the other without a working stiff like Max to translate. Plain talk, just saying what you mean, seemed to be the primitive language of the masses.

"Well, speak of the devil and he shall appear," Christie said, sounding more like a Southern belle than a Northern blueblood. "Look, Danny. Max is finally here! And he brought along his *boyfriend*."

Christie had trouble spitting out the last word, but at least she'd made the effort. Danny stopped to refill his drink and took a long gulp before he stepped forward.

"I thought you had to practice?"

"I got tired of blowing my own horn."

"Glad you could *both* make it."

"A chance to hang out with you and your *girlfriend*? We wouldn't have missed it for the world."

Like a bratty kid in a crowded elevator, Max had just pushed all of Danny's buttons. Each verbal exchange was another stop on a different floor. A Cavanaugh always maintained his composure, especially under duress, but Danny's scowl made it clear he wasn't happy about being taken for a ride. Ready for a change of topic and company, he tossed back the rest of his drink and handed Max his empty cup.

"You should both grab another drink," Danny said, taking Christie by the hand and pulling her toward the nearest clique of guests. "Although from what I saw a few minutes ago, Liam's already had a stiff one."

Max felt his face blush with anger. Getting caught red-handed wasn't the happy ending he'd been hoping for, but a little alcohol would take the sting out of getting slut-shamed by his best friend. Even though it meant getting up an hour earlier to run off the empty calories he was about to consume, Max was willing to make the sacrifice.

The glass bottles in the tin washtub were still half-full, but it looked like the bar was only stocked with vodka and gin. Most of his friends had bought into the "Clear Craze" with fad drinks like Zima and Crystal Pepsi, but Max never trusted booze that could pass for water. Alcohol should look the way it made you feel – dark and muddled. Beer was out of the question since the word invoked images of love handles and swollen bellies. That only left wine—a beverage reserved for tipsy housewives and First Holy Communion. As usual, when it came to getting what he wanted, he was coming up high and dry.

Liam thanked Christie when she filled his plastic cup with pink punch, then discretely spilled it into the sand when she wasn't looking. Drawing Max into a tight huddle, he fished a leather flask out of his pocket and unscrewed the top.

"It's 20-year old Scotch from my father's stash."

"Won't he miss it?"

"Not likely," Liam said, tipping back the small canteen and taking a long swallow. "He's got a whole case of the stuff back at the house.

Besides, he goes through too much of it to notice when I nick a few fingers from the top."

Max mimicked Liam and threw back a shot. The liquor was as old as he was and just as strong. Instantly, the heat from the spirits spread to his extremities. After a few more sips, Max's mood started to level off. Insincere smiles and sightless stares didn't seem quite so annoying. It felt good to chill out and stop trying to manage situations that were beyond his control.

Ironically, the Scotch was having the opposite effect on Liam. Two fingers had emboldened him. "The more the merrier" was usually a polite response to the arrival of an uninvited guest. For him, it was a call to action. Liam was tired of waiting for someone else to get the party started. It was time for him to borrow some trouble and make his own fun.

"Master Cavanaugh," Liam called out in voice loud enough to silence the other guests. "Shall we liven things up with a friendly game of Truth or Dare?"

"Sure, I'm in. But only if you promise to drop the formalities and just call me 'Danny.'"

"Given how well we're about to get to know each other, we probably should be on a first-name basis. Is anyone else brave enough to join us in a game?"

For more than a decade, Max had been keeping a secret file on the moral missteps of Provincetown's social elite. Even though he would have loved to finally get the chance to ask a bunch of juicy questions and goad a couple of guys into doing something they'd enjoy but regret, the game would only be as good as the players. Trey didn't have the guts to admit he was really a "power bottom" and Christie wasn't about to flash her tits on command. Still, it would be a nice change of pace to hear Danny give some honest answers.

Most of the guests were liars or cowards. The few who did step forward to join in were either brash or brave. The rest of the onlookers formed a loose circle around the players and waited for the game to start. Everyone at the party had a different set of virtues, but they all had the same vice – they loved watching other people squirm.

"Truth."

Ready. Fire. Aim.

Danny was shooting off his mouth before he'd properly sized up the target. Since it had been his suggestion to play, Liam was well prepared to challenge the other players with embarrassing questions and humiliating dares. There was an inherent level of risk in going first, but Danny was betting the first round of the game would be painful, not fatal. His sterling reputation was like a suit of armor that would protect him from a few body blows. Liam would knock him down, but once Danny got back up, he'd be ready with a counterpunch. This was going to be a bloody duel, not a quick execution.

"I'm not going to go easy on you."

"I'm not afraid of a simple question."

"Maybe you should be?"

"Maybe you should stop talking smack and get on with it."

A collective snicker rose up from crowd. Looking on from outside the circle, Max felt like a sailor watching the sea before a storm. The red sky was an omen of the tempest that was bound to break.

"So, *Danny*," Liam began, spreading out his arms as a gesture of inclusion toward the waiting crowd. "How many people at this party do you know, shall we say, in the 'biblical sense'?"

"One."

"Only one lucky girl from this bevy of bathing beauties?"

"Who said it was a girl?"

Max had spent most of his life invisible, dreaming of the moment he'd finally get discovered and take his place at center stage. Tonight, his wish had finally come true. Too bad it was for all the wrong reasons. As far as the other guests were concerned, Danny could've been talking about someone back at school or any one of nameless tourists who invaded Provincetown each summer. Still, the smart money was on Max. Suddenly, the label of "best friend" felt like a blazing scarlet letter.

"I do like the cut of your jib, Danny," Liam exclaimed, slow clapping to show his delight. "But now I'm simply *dying* to know whether you prefer to enter a room through the front door or the back passage?"

"Let's just say I'm not into assholes like you," Danny said, stepping into Liam's personal space and looking him squarely in the eye. "I've already answered your question. Now, let's see if you're man enough to ask me for a dare."

"What would you have me do?" Liam quipped, stepping even closer until the men were almost bumping noses. "Shall I run into the water naked or do a shot of your cheap gin?"

"One good turn deserves another? I dare you to take Christie back into the dunes for a quick 'Seven Minutes in Heaven.'"

"I think we've had more than enough fun playing this game," Christie said, tugging forcefully at Danny's arm to pull him back into her world. "Max and Liam are probably tired of hanging out with all us boring, straight couples. You boys should go enjoy yourselves at the A-Hole or one of your dance clubs."

"I think you mean A-House," Max said under his breath to avoid calling any more attention to himself. He couldn't tell whether Christie was trying to make a joke or being intentionally offensive. Only Trey seemed to appreciate the how painfully comical the situation had become. Laughing freely, he grabbed three Peroni beers from the ice chest and stepped into the middle of the fray.

"Come on, boys. For once, Christie is right. This really isn't *our* scene."

"And who might you be?" Liam asked, ignoring the beer and taking another nip from his flask. The casual observer would've described his look as menacing, but Max had seen that sexy scowl before. His ginger was on the make.

"John Howard Taft, III. But everyone calls me Trey."

"That's dreadful. My great-uncle had a scrappy mutt called Trey. He was a dirty, little bugger who spent most of the day lounging about, licking his dangly bits."

"Honestly, that pet name kind of suits me. But if you don't like it then by all means suggest another."

"We could try John Thomas, but that seems a bit obvious. Let's call you J-Ho and see if you can live up to that sobriquet."

"I like the sound of it. Now, let's head back into town and give me a proper christening."

"Wait a damn minute," Danny barked, prying lose Christie's talons from his arm. "It's my party, so I'm the one who decides whether you stay or go."

"Actually you don't," Max said, tossing his empty cup in the trash. "I shouldn't have come out here tonight. We're leaving, whether you like it or not."

J-Ho was waiting to fill Max's empty hand with a beer. Max wasn't sure if the Scotch had loosened his tongue or opened his eyes. Either way, it was suddenly clear he was trying to fit in where he didn't belong. Mixing people together at these kinds of events was a lot like Christie's pink punch. The resulting concoction was potent, but it made you sick.

"You sure?"

"Definitely."

Secretly, Max hoped Danny would try harder to get him to stay, but he wasn't going to find out. It was time to cut his losses and call it a day. With the setting sun, all the fantasies he'd had about his last summer with Danny had gone dark.

The hard trek back across the dune made Max even more determined to ignore all the foolish distractions and just focus on his music. The past was like the footsteps he'd left in the sand. Each one marked where he'd been, but the wind quickly erased any traces of his passing. It was time to stop looking backward and start moving in a new direction. Maybe it really was true that for one door to open, another had to close.

By HIS suggestive tone, Max wasn't sure whether J-Ho was offering a ride in his Range Rover or suggesting a threesome when he asked if the guys wanted to load their bikes into his trunk. Either way, Max decided to let Liam be the one to find out.

"You two go ahead and drive back without me. I'll take my bike and meet you at the Boatslip."

A hard ride and some fresh air was just what Max needed shrug off his mood. It would also give him a chance to burn off the empty calories that made the Scotch taste so good.

Rather than retrace a course back along the over-used bike trail, Max went all out, sailing down Race Point Road and across Route 6.

It might have been superstition or just exhaustion, but he stopped pedaling and let the bike glide when he passed by the cemetery.

James Cavanaugh. Forrest Woodside. Miguel Balais.

The names and dates etched into the weathered stones marked the passing of people who had spent too much of their short lives in one place. These good men, gone too soon, had never had the chance to leave their mark. Max wasn't going to just live a simple life in Provincetown and join them in a silent, unforgiving grave. Whatever time he had was going to count for something. Music wouldn't make him immortal, but it was the next best thing.

It usually took twenty minutes to bike from the beach back into town, but Max made it back in less than ten. Instead of turning right to go home, he made a hard left and headed up Commercial Street. Hopefully, the thumping bass from the music at the Boatslip would be loud enough to drown out the talk track of the things Max had wanted to say to Danny. Now, he probably never would.

Leaning his bike against the empty rack, Max raked a hand through his disheveled hair and walked down the steep driveway to the Boatslip's entrance. Layers of dark blackout curtains blocked the view from the street, but you could almost feel the wave of human current surging on the other side. This was where he belonged. Without thinking, Max hardened his face into a grimace and took a deep breath to inflate his muscles. It was a cheap trick, but it worked. This time the bouncer waved him right in.

Even with traffic, it would've taken twice as long to get back into town by bike than by car. Liam and J-Ho were probably already two drinks in at the side bar. Rather than rejoin them right off, Max decided to do a quick lap and check out the scene. It was a warm night and the back deck was thick with handsome men. High on cocktails and the promise of fun, everyone was generous with glances and smiles. Even though the sun had set, a warm afterglow reflected off the harbor. Max would have been happy to just hang out and enjoy the view, but he was nursing a bad emotional hangover from the party on the beach. The only thing that would ease his suffering was some hair of the dog that bit him.

On his second pass around the venue, Max spotted Liam leaning halfway over the bar trying his best to engage the busy bartender in conversation. No one could blame him for flirting. The guy was a real looker. Max would have made a play for him too, but hitting on a guy you'd known since kindergarten felt too much like inbreeding.

"Hey, Ryan! I never expected to see you at the Boatslip. What are you doing here?"

"Well, I'm definitely not here to pick up chicks. I'm tending bar."

"Seriously?" Max understood how hard it was to find a good summer job, but working at the Boatslip was a strange career choice for a guy with a fiancée and a toddler at home. "Your girl doesn't mind all these dudes ogling you every night?"

"No way. The wages are shit, but I've already emptied my tip jar twice."

"Nice work if you can get it," Max said, noticing all the fives and tens overflowing from a tin pail next to the register. The only thing more conspicuous than the money Ryan was pulling in was the white waistband of his Calvin Klein underwear peeking out from beneath his tight camo shorts.

"Don't worry," Max said above the roar of conversation and dance anthem. "I won't tell anyone you're straight."

"Tell anyone you want, bro. Most guys find that a total turn-on. I guess there's something sexy about wanting someone you can never have."

"Can't have or can't afford," Liam interjected, stepping forward to join in the conversation. "I'm not usually a kerb crawler, but I've never met a rentboy I couldn't do business with for the right price."

To make his point, Liam pulled a couple of twenties from his wallet and stuffed the cash down the front of the bartender's shorts.

"Does your friend speak English?" Ryan asked Max as he transferred the money into his front pocket. Turning back to Liam, he flashed a threatening grimace, but also poured his patron another drink. "This one's on me."

As amusing as it was to watch Liam try to negotiate a gay-for-pay transaction, Max was more interested in the tall, bearded guy standing a few feet away.

"Captain Avellar. What are you doing here?"

"Max, please. Call me by my first name when we aren't at work," Jasper said in a tone that made his request sound more like an order.

"Right now I'm looking for my better half. Byron went off to help one of his girlfriends fix her face and he never came back."

As usual, Max smiled and tried his best to keep up with the conversation. He didn't know whether his boss was talking about a real woman or just another drag queen, but it didn't matter either way. Luckily, Byron appeared from out of nowhere with two towering beauties in tow.

"There you are *meu amor*. I've been looking for you everywhere," Byron said, with hands on his hips and elbows turned outward. "I should have known I'd find you out on the deck, gazing off at the sea. And who may I ask is this blond Adonis?"

"You know Max Balais. He's a member of my crew."

"Of course! Well, hello there, young man," Byron said with the kind of smile that would've made even the gruffest leather-bear feel like a ten-year old. "My goodness! You've certainly filled out since the last time I last saw you."

Max didn't mind being objectified, but not by his captain's boyfriend. The last thing he needed was for Jasper to get jealous and take it out on him at work. To make matters worse, Max had the sinking feeling Liam had given up on Ryan and moved on to his next conquest. Balancing a dirty martini in each hand, he was gliding like a torpedo across the deck.

"Why don't you go join your friend," Jasper said to Max. Casually, he slipped an arm around Byron and began rubbing his shoulder. "I'm done with my beer. We should head off to bed and let the young ones play."

"Aye, aye, Captain!" Byron said snapping to attention and proffering an exaggerated salute. "I need to get this gorgeous man out of this meat market before someone steals him away!"

"You're sweet to say such things, but no matter where I get my appetite, I always come home for dinner," Jasper said, kissing Byron on the head and handing his full bottle of beer to the nearest barhop. "Come, let's go home."

Suddenly alone in a sea of men, Max started swimming. By the time he reached the nearest island of open space, Liam and a new friend were busy getting acquainted. The guy was significantly older with salt-and-pepper hair and dark eyes. You could say a lot about Liam's insatiable libido, but at least he had impeccable taste.

"And here's my chum now."

The obvious look of confusion on the older man's face confirmed what Max already knew. Liam had never bothered to mention he was out with friends. Max and the handsome stranger eyed each other coolly as each tried to figure out which was the third wheel. Considering the size of the town and the chances of bumping into one another again, it made sense to play it cool and make the best of an awkward situation.

"Hi, I'm Max. It's nice to meet you."

"Likewise," the older man said, extending his hand. "My name's Bill Woodside. But everyone around town just calls me Billy."

"So, William," Liam said, eager to re-establish his position as the suitor du jour. "Where's this 'Dick Dock' I've been hearing so much about?"

"You're standing on it. Actually, all of the real action takes place down below on the sand."

"Sounds manky," Liam said, finishing his martini and handing the empty glass to Max. "I'd love to check it out. Anyone interested in joining me downstairs for a knee trembler?"

"I'm always up for a friendly tussle," Max said, trying his best not to blush and spoil what he hoped was coming off as youthful bravado. "But ten-on-one doesn't sound like much of a fair fight."

"Think of it more as a square dance," Bill said, slipping a little too easily into the role of the experienced, silver daddy. "You spend a little time with one partner, then someone calls out, and everyone switches."

"Sounds like just the ticket. Shall we?" asked Liam.

"Are you kidding?" Max asked what he hoped was a rhetorical question. Liam's harmless fantasy had fiendishly morphed into a reckless plan. "Those kinds of cruising spots are for old men and sexual deviants."

"Let's go." Liam and Bill said together.

"You're just going to leave me high and dry?" Max asked Liam, trying to sound surprised, not desperate. "I thought we were going to pick up where we left off last night?"

"Don't be cross. We had fun. Now, it's time to move on to the next adventure. We're bound to bump into each other again. After all, this is Provincetown, not Paris, right?"

A GROUP of guys waiting in line at the entrance playfully called for him to come back and stay, but Max was done for the night. In four long strides he was at the top of the steep asphalt driveway and pulling on the handlebars of his bike. After a couple failed attempts to free it from the rack, Max realized his predicament. Apparently he'd arrived at the Boatslip *before*, not after, his friends. Rather than leave his bike in the Range Rover, Liam had walked it to the club and locked their frames together. Ironically, Max was stuck with the guy that had just cut him loose. Channeling his anger, Max grabbed a length of the cable in each hand and pulled with all his might.

"Are you seriously trying to break an iron chain with your bare hands? You might look like Russell Crowe, but this isn't *Gladiator*. Nobody can pull off a stunt like that in real life."

Danny showing up at just the right moment was either serendipity or dumb luck. Either way, the sheer coincidence of running into each other again was enough to defuse the smoldering powder keg that had been lit out on the beach.

"You wouldn't happen to have a pair of bolt cutters on you?"

"Afraid not."

"What are you doing here," Max asked as he abandoned his shackled bike and led Danny across the street to avoid the steady stream of patrons walking up and down the driveway. He probably had a better chance picking the padlock than getting Danny to give him a straight answer, but it was worth a shot. "Did Christie puke and pass out from too much pink punch?"

"Not quite. She decided to move the party back to her house. I thought I'd take a walk and check out some of the architectural properties my dad has been researching. Apparently, the town council is meeting at the end of the month to vote on some big, new development plan."

"Well, you've come to the right place," Max said, leaning over the white picket fence bordering the sidewalk. "This house is my favorite."

"Then tell me all about it."

It had been a couple of years since Max had sat through his high school history class, listening to his teacher lecture on about various historic structures around town. Luckily, he'd checked out a couple of architecture books so he'd have something to talk about with Danny's dad. Some of the more obscure properties went unnoticed, but locals knew the story of the heroic white house at 160 Commercial Street. Wearing an ornate cupola like a fascinator, the stately manor had a history as colorful as a drag queen's dress.

"Captain Joseph Atkins built the place back in 1830, but everyone refers to it as Grozier House, since the Grozier family lived here for more than half of the 20th century. In 1963, Reggie Cabral, the son of a Portuguese fisherman, purchased Grozier House and Grozier Park across the street. A year after moving into the house, the Cabrals offered the town a chance to acquire the park for $75,000. When the town declined, Reggie built the Boatslip Motor Inn, a 200-foot-long structure that obscured almost every bay view from the houses between Atlantic Avenue and Central Street. Reggie moved out of Grozier House in 1994 and died two years later. Since then, his daughters have been fighting a protracted legal battle over its ownership. I really don't care who wins the custody fight, as long as someone restores the place to its former glory."

"Nice job. My dad would be impressed."

Max wasn't sure whether Danny had actually meant it as a compliment, but at least they were talking again. After what happened out at the beach, it was probably better to stick to a safe topic like architecture. That was easier said than done. Max had only had a couple fingers of Scotch, but all he could think about was how much he wanted to talk about how their friendship had unexpectedly caught fire.

"I'm sorry about earlier. The night was a total bust."

"I don't know," Danny said, shoving his hands into his pockets and taking a step closer. "Technically, the evening isn't over yet."

Without thinking, Max leaned forward until their foreheads touched. Although less passionate than the kiss at the club, the gesture was more intimate and reckless. Like a game of chicken, they were driving toward each other on a collision course. The only question was whether one of them would swerve.

"I can't do this in front of the Boatslip on Commercial Street," Danny whispered in a voice that was dry and hoarse. "I'm going to head back out to the beach. Wanna come?"

"That's a terrible idea."

"Probably the worst."

"We should just go our separate ways."

"And pretend this never happened."

Summer days felt longer than twenty-four hours, but this one was a marathon. Tomorrow was Monday, which meant Max worked a double shift at the docks. He needed sleep, not drama. Being alone with Danny under a sky full of stars was a dangerous proposition. Given their history and pent-up feelings, chances were pretty good they'd end up fighting or fooling around. Either way, someone was going to get hurt. Given the odds and the wager at stake, there was only one safe bet.

MAX AND Danny had snuck off to the beach together too many times to count, but something about the crashing surf and the full moon made it feel like a brand new adventure. Alone at last, Danny grabbed a blanket from the trunk of his car and led Max down to the waterline. At first, everything seemed almost normal, but then Danny decided alcohol would make it easier for them to talk. Luckily, there was still a case of beer left over from the party. Two bottles led to three and, after the first six-pack, they both lost count.

Danny had started to drift off listening to Max tell a story about two gay penguins trying to hatch a rock as if it were an egg. On any other night, Max would've stumbled home to his own bed, but then Danny did something that changed everything. Half-drunk and mostly asleep, he'd mumbled to himself and pulled Max into a bear hug.

"Cuddle. Sleep."

Falling into Danny's arms was like swimming in the Atlantic Ocean. The water was too cold to dive right in, but the summer sun was so warm you just couldn't resist. At first, nothing happened, but eventually Max broke free of Danny's platonic spooning and rolled over to face him. Face-to-face with bodies pressed together, the rest seemed to happen of its own volition. Lips touched and hands wandered. By morning, Max's skin looked angry and red. The friction of Danny's stubble had scraped his face raw. Angelo mercilessly teased him about his unexpected "sunburn," but Max didn't mind the pain.

Nothing had ever hurt so good.

CHAPTER 8

"**S**IS, WAKE up...."

"No, not the couch again," Josie mumbled into her pillow as she pulled up the blankets to hide her face. "This is the second time this week."

Max wanted to tell her it was actually the third, but he'd come down with an incurable case of the giggles. The image of a grown man sneaking a guy into the tiny bedroom he shared with his sister would've been funny if it wasn't so tragic. Max had tried crashing at Danny's place a couple of times, but without a proper lock on the cupola door, what had started out as a romantic sleepover quickly turned into a slumber party when Sam showed up with comic books and a sleeping bag. Max was tired of the clandestine rendezvous, but a few stolen hours together were better than nothing. After a couple more failed attempts to speak between bouts of stifled laughter, his boyfriend stepped forward to make their case.

"Come on, Nosy Josie. I'm about to rip your brother's clothes off. Be a good sport and give us the room?"

"O.K., but you owe me, Cavanaugh. And don't think I'm not going to collect on it."

Max helped his sister get settled on the couch and then turned off the living room lights. Luckily, his mom was working the graveyard shift at the diner. By the time Lara got home, she'd be too tired to question why Josie wasn't in her own bed. Max would just say his snoring had driven his sister away. In the morning, Danny would be gone and everyone would be back where he or she belonged. Max didn't like the idea of lying to his mom, but what Lara didn't know wouldn't hurt her.

Max had barely gotten the bedroom door locked before Danny was all over him. Lips touched and hands tugged to pull down underwear that had suddenly become too tight. The absence of light in the room seemed to heighten the other senses. Taste and touch replaced sight. Fingers and tongues were like eyes, tracing out the lines and contours of a body each man knew as well as his own.

"Do you have any stuff?" Danny asked, breathless between kisses. "You know...slippery stuff?"

"We can't. I mean I want to. I *definitely* want to. But not here, in the apartment, with my sister in the next room."

"Damn. Cockblocked again by my own wingman. If I didn't know better, Balais, I'd think you were playing hard to get."

"Oh, I'm playing hard alright," Max grunted as he guided Danny's hand under the sheets to prove his point.

Having sex in a single bed took skill and courage. Naked and sweaty, two entwined bodies essentially occupied the same space, but there was no way to retreat to the other side of the bed after the deed was done. Even though Max had been hooking up with Danny for almost a month, he was still getting used to the concept of cool down time and afterplay.

Straight guys were like Jekyll and Hyde. In the heat of the moment, a lover would whisper "please" when he begged you not to stop. But sex was like a secret serum. Once a trick had drunk his fill, it was hard to predict how quickly the monster's nature would turn dark. In high school, "safe sex" was about more than condoms and bodily fluids. To reduce his risk of getting hurt, Max had kept things simple and played by the other guy's rules. The actors and settings of those random encounters varied as much as any good porn movie, but the plot was always the same. Finish fast and make a clean getaway.

The best part about having a real sex life was the unpredictability of what would happen next. Just when Max thought he'd figured out the choreography, Danny would switch things up and try something new. That's what made being together so exciting. It was also scary as hell.

Only three weeks had passed since that fateful night when Danny had conveniently bumped into Max outside the Boatslip and convinced him to go back out to beach. The first time with anyone new was usually a little clunky, but Danny literally blew Max away with moves that were more than just beginner's luck. After a couple false starts and mumbled explanations, Danny finally confessed that he'd spent most of his last semester at school hooking up with guys. Always a little fluid, his sexual orientation unexpectedly took a hard turn after the kiss with Max on New Year's Eve.

Now, with the curtains drawn, dawn was creeping in through the bedroom window. Outside, the sun was rising over the bay. Max needed to get up and dressed before his mom woke up. Unfortunately, his boyfriend had something else in mind.

"Stay just like that. Don't move a muscle."

Max took a deep breath and exhaled. He was trying to relax and enjoy himself, but the muscles in his back were already getting stiff. With each passing minute it was getting harder and harder to keep still and not reciprocate the attention. Pressed up against the bedroom wall, Danny was doing all the work while Max just laid back and smiled.

Max was physically uncomfortable, but he loved the way Danny looked at him when he sketched. Eyes measured the size and proportions of muscle and bone as fingers traced the outline of his body onto the notebook page. Grainy and gray, the graphite from the flat edge of the pencil shaded out the shape while the tip gave the drawing definition and detail. Danny squinted and took a deep breath in through his nose. Leaning forward, he kissed Max tenderly on the mouth and whispered into his ear.

"I smell coffee."

All Max could smell was the stink off the harbor. People thought living on the water was romantic, but when the tide went out anything left on the sand shriveled up and died in the sun. The stench of rotting seaweed and clams was enough to make even a fisherman sick. Max got used to it after a while, but extended exposure had left him smell blind.

"Josie must have the early shift at the diner. We'll go out in a minute. Let me see how it turned out."

Max broke his pose and crawled across the narrow bed to pull the sketchbook from Danny's hands. The drawing was primitive and rushed, but it captured the essential nature of his form.

"This is *really* good."

"It better be after all the time I've spent studying the subject matter," Danny said playfully as he tweaked Max's nipple. "I've also taken a couple art classes. My teacher thinks I have a good eye."

Max was dying to make a cheesy "one-eyed" joke about Danny being his teacher's only pupil, but it was time to get serious and listen. After almost a month together, his boyfriend was finally starting to open up and share something serious about his other life. Somewhere close, the engine of a delivery truck bleated like an old alarm clock. Max would have killed for another hour of pillow talk, but the old adage was true: the time and tides wait for no man.

"Shit! It's almost six. I've got to get to work. Come on, I'll treat you to coffee at Tips."

With Danny in tow, Max closed the bedroom door and tiptoed across the living room. The creaks and groans of the pine floorboards were part of the rustic charm of living in an old building. Normally, the sound of her kids moving around wouldn't have roused Lara. After eight hours on her feet at the diner, she could pretty much sleep through anything. That's why it was such a surprise to find her sipping coffee in the kitchen.

"Good morning."

Fully dressed, but still half-asleep, Max and Danny looked like they'd just rolled out of the same bed. It wasn't as if his mom had walked in and caught them in the act. Danny had stayed over lots of times before. Still, something about the look on her weary face made it clear she'd finally connected the dots.

"Hey, Mrs. Balais," Danny said, sheepishly glancing over at Max for a signal about how to handle the situation. "I drank a little too much last night, so Josie took the couch and let me crash in her bed."

"Honey, we both know that's not true, so let's cut the bullshit. Why don't you grab some coffee and head on home? I need to speak to my son, alone."

Out in the living room, a shadowy figure rose up from the sofa. Mouth open and eyes closed, Josie staggered across the living room toward her bed like a zombie from *Dawn of the Dead*. The slamming of the door behind her sounded ominous, but it was nothing compared to the horror show that was about to start in the kitchen.

Max filled a ceramic mug with Maxwell House and handed it to Danny. Although their eye contact was brief, it spoke volumes. The only thing worse than having the sex talk with your mom was having it with your boyfriend in the room. The last thing Lara needed was a visual of what she was already imagining in her head.

"I really need to get to work," Max said, launching a pre-emptive strike as soon as Danny was out the door. "Any chance we could save this for another time?"

"Please sit down. I'll make you something to eat."

Max melted into his usual chair and watched as his mom lit the stove and cracked eggs into an iron skillet. All the really heavy stuff in the Balais family always seemed to go down at the kitchen table. Max could still remember the strange feeling of excitement and detachment when his parents sat him down to explain his dad's cancer. Medical terms he couldn't pronounce quickly became the common tongue of a language he was expected to learn. Coming out to his mom hardly qualified as a life or death scenario, but it marked another critical rite of passage Max wanted to postpone until he was away at college. Once the cat was out of the proverbial closet, everyone in the apartment would have to start thinking and acting like adults.

"So," he began, grabbing a piece of toast from the small stack and slathering it with butter. "When did you figure it out?"

"That you're gay or that you're having sex with Danny?"

"Either? Both?"

"Ironically, I think I knew before you did. Any fool could see you've been crazy for that boy since the first time he followed you home."

"How come you waited so long to let me in on the secret?"

"I was going to bring it up when you came to the diner for breakfast last month, but then you knocked the wind out of me with the news that you'd spent the night with a boy you'd just met. Please tell me you were safe with Liam?"

"Totally," Max said as he reached for the glass in front of him and slurped down a mouthful of water. "But you're just going to have to trust me on that because I'm not giving you a blow-by-blow of what happened."

It was an interesting choice of words, but Max had made his point. As usual, he was making Lara work a double shift. Being a single parent meant she had to be both mother and father to her kids. Although Josie had her fair share of boy troubles, the real challenge was keeping up with Max. At every turn, her firstborn seemed determined to challenge his mom's parenting skills with growing pains that were beyond her limited experience. Luckily, Lara's gay friends were more than willing to answer the intimate questions she'd been too embarrassed to ask their family doctor. Lara had never considered herself a prude, but it wasn't easy to raise a teenager whose sex drive was almost as voracious as his appetite.

"Three eggs, sunny side up."

"Thanks."

"Sooo," Lara said, stretching out the word as a verbal cue she was about to ask the big question that had been keeping her awake all night. "Are you boys just 'friends with benefits' or have things gotten serious?"

This was Max's chance to pass off what was going on with Danny as something meaningless, or at least casual, but he owed his mom the truth.

"It's still too early to call," Max said, inhaling his rest of his food and putting the empty plate in the sink. "But when I figure everything out, I'll let you know. Good enough?"

"*Perfeito.* Thanks, son."

"No problem, *mamãe*, but I've got to bolt or I'm going to miss the boat," Max said as he grabbed his jacket and headed out the door. "Later."

Lara closed her eyes and chuckled. "To be continued" was the tagline of her life.

THE EMPTY streets of Provincetown were practically begging to be run on. Sprinting at full speed, Max made it to the MacMillan Pier with five whole minutes to spare. It was an unusually cold morning and most of the crewmembers were bundled up in heavy sweatshirts and thick canvas pants. Standing alone in short-shorts and a bright pink hoodie, Angelo was trying to stay warm by dancing in place to the soundtrack playing in his head.

Max wasn't the only one who'd noticed the recent changes in his friend's appearance. A few of the saltier crewmembers had complained about sharing the head with a "trannie." Captain Avellar had already cautioned Angelo about going AWOL and sending Angelique to work in his place, but he'd also told his men to hold their tongues. In the end, it was Max who'd brokered an agreement between the two factions.

"Yo, Angel."

"Buenos días, Max Factor!"

It wasn't easy to live down a nickname that was synonymous with women's makeup, but it was a step up from being called "Maxi Pad." Max was still doing penance for convincing Angelique to make peace with the rest of the crew by trading her stage pseudonym for a less flamboyant name that was used by girls and boys.

The embarrassing pet names started shortly after, but it sort of made sense since Angel had become Max's work spouse. As the only two gay guys on the *La Benedita*, it was an obvious match. Still, they'd spent a few too many late nights consummating their common law marriage with drinking binges and shirtless dancing at the A-House. And Danny didn't seem to mind being able to have a gorgeous beard on his arm whenever he was out in public. Flawlessly adorned, Angel could pass as his girlfriend if he inadvertently bumped into a family friend.

"Oh good," she said, twirling to a stop and leading Max by both hands to the nearest bench. "We have time for the latest installment of my favorite telenovela soap opera, '*Paneleiro de Nossas Vidas*.'"

"Which means?"

"Gays of our Lives."

"Very funny."

"Yes, I'm a fucking hoot. Now, let's stop beating around the bush (so to speak) and talk about your red-hot love life. What happened last night? Did Danny finally make it impossible for you to wear white at your wedding?"

"Angel, stop." Max said, lowering his voice and looking around to make sure no one was listening. "We're still having fun doing all the *other* stuff. We both agreed to wait for the right time and place before we go all the way."

"All I know is you better get that kitty punched before you head off to Berklee. Those city boys can smell a virgin a mile away."

The howl of a foghorn saved him from having to tell Angel how he suddenly wasn't so eager to head off to school and leave his boyfriend behind. Ironically, his dad had abandoned New Haven to come to Provincetown and paint. For as long as he could remember, Max had fantasized about running off to make a life in Boston. Now, the same small streets that had always made him claustrophobic seemed charming and quaint. Music was his way out, the chance to escape from a world that was smaller than his ambitions. But what did you do when real life was better than your dreams?

"All aboard."

Moving en masse, the crew discarded Styrofoam cups and extinguished cigarettes before heading down the metal gangplank that connected the jetty to the pier. Captain Avellar was already standing in his usual spot at the helm. As the engines sputtered to life and the boat lurched forward, each member of the crew took his appointed place on deck.

Standing at the bow, Max watched the seascape expand as the boat left the harbor and sailed out into open water. Maybe his problem was really just a matter of perspective. The closer he got to Danny, the bigger his world seemed to be. Leaving now, without giving their relationship a chance, might be something he'd live to regret.

Like his father before him, Max tried to imagine a future in Provincetown. If he worked hard and kept his nose clean, Captain Avellar would eventually promote him to first mate. Fishing wasn't as glamorous as performing at Carnegie Hall, but it was honest work and a steady paycheck.

Hovering overhead, a pair of gulls glided on invisible drafts of wind. Cawing to each other and playing in the sun, the birds had figured out the secret of happiness. Maybe it was time for Max to stop fighting so hard to figure out which way to go and just let the summer winds carry him forward.

CHAPTER 9

I N Provincetown, July 4th felt more like a bachelor party than a national holiday. The eager bands of shirtless men roaming the streets were more interested in hedonism than patriotism. Already high on summer, the boys were happy for any excuse to come out and play. Since Independence Day marked the official start of the season, most of the locals made the extra effort to charm and woo the scourge of tourists who kept their small economy afloat. It was unquestionably a marriage of convenience, not love.

Over the years, Max had grown accustomed to the particular rhythm of the day. All the B&Bs spoiled their guests with picnics of grilled hotdogs, potato salad, and the obligatory apple pie. Down at the Boatslip, imported DJs from Madrid and Barcelona spun exotic dance mixes. Despite the raging bass and unbroken tempo, none of the Yankee Doodle dandies would have any trouble keeping it up. Although they'd never be handy with the girls, these born dancers could mind the music and the step.

By the time Max made his way to Commercial Street, the men and boys were as thick as hasty pudding on the already-crowded sidewalk. Everyone wanted a prime spot to watch the parade of politicians, rotary club members, and colorful characters riding through town in vintage convertibles. Baking in the sun, the summer dignitaries smiled and waved as the high school band played the same tired John Philip Sousa march on an endless loop. A court of drag queens floated up and down the sidelines, doling out royal waves and air kisses to their adoring subjects. Rain or shine, tourists and natives would spend the day squeezing in as much merriment as the law would allow.

Max wasn't into all the pomp and circumstance, but he was jazzed that his mom and sister had made plans to go out for dinner and watch the pyrotechnics display over the harbor. Alone with Danny in the apartment, he was going to make sure there were enough sparks to set off his own fireworks.

With his audition at Berklee less than a month away, Max would have preferred to spend his day off practicing his trumpet, but he'd promised to make an appearance at the Cavanaughs' party at the marina. Moored at the end of the pier, the family's wooden schooner wasn't the biggest boat in the harbor, but it was the most majestic. Like the rest of the town, it was tarted up with tri-colored bunting and American flags.

Even from a distance, Max could see the gala was unusually well attended. Guests ebbed and flowed from the deck of the ship out onto the adjoining jetty. Strategically sequestered in the wings, a brass band regaled the crowd with up-tempo bluegrass and jazz. Max didn't recognize any of the numbers, but the sound of a slide trombone and a dueling banjo made him wish he'd brought along his horn. Music played on as the crème-de-la-crème of Provincetown and Boston milled about with empty plates and full glasses. As usual, the Cavanaughs had gone all out to make sure their friends enjoyed the best that money could buy. Although the hospitality was genuine, Michael Cavanaugh considered the expense an investment, not a gift. Eager to make an exit before he ran up a tab, Max hurried over to where Danny and his father were knee-deep in conversation with a distinguished, older gentleman.

"So, Patrick," Michael said with a look that acknowledged Max, but also made it clear that he should be seen, not heard. "I'm sure if you spoke up, the town council would quash Bill Woodside's development proposal. If he gets his way, the Foundation will lose six of our most important properties. Do you really want to see all that rich history replaced with cheap townhouses?"

"At a million dollars a pop, I'd hardly call those places cheap! I admire your passion, but Forest Woodside was one of my biggest supporters. I can't risk alienating half of Beacon Hill by blackballing his only child, especially during an election year."

"I'm also a major donor. If I can't count on you for support when

I need it, then I'll have to start putting a few of my golden eggs in your opponent's basket."

"Don't make ugly threats, Mickey. This is Provincetown, not Dorchester. Let's not let a silly real estate deal ruin a perfectly good holiday. Danny Boy, help me out and say something clever to distract your father."

"Small talk really isn't my forte, Senator Donovan. It's nice to see you again, sir."

"Well, it's good to be seen young man. How are things at Holy Cross?"

"Actually, I just graduated from Dartmouth."

"I stand corrected," Donovan said, raising his eyebrows to make it clear he was impressed with Danny's intellectual prowess. "If you were a few years older, we'd have matched you with my daughter Melody. Now *that* would have been an interesting union."

"You can say that again."

Max stepped forward and pressed a cold beer into Danny's sweaty palm. The gesture was a little too intimate, especially since they were the only two guys at the party without dates. Most of the town thought of Danny as a playboy, but that was a calculated move on his part. Perpetually dating gave him the perfect excuse to sidestep introductions to the eligible daughters of his parents' friends. Danny would extend a casual acquaintanceship for as long as he could, but as soon as things started to heat up or fizzle out, he'd quickly move onto someone else. Showing up stag to the party was like hanging out a "vacancy" sign at the Red Inn. It wouldn't take very long for prospective suitors to start checking in.

Having Max at his side was only making things worse. Hanging out together at the apartment was one thing, but lately, anytime they got within three feet of each other, there was a static charge that raised hairs. By the end of the night, his parents' friends would be whispering about the noticeable chemistry between the two young men. Now, it was too late to do anything about such idle gossip except explain that Danny wanted to spend what was left of the summer having fun with his childhood friend. The best lie, he quietly reminded himself, was always grounded in the truth.

"Senator Donovan, this is Max Balais, my best buddy."

"Balais. That's Portuguese. Do I know your father?

"Not likely, sir."

"Really? Well, any friend of a Cavanaugh is a friend of mine. Where are you at school?"

"I'll be starting at the Berklee College of Music in the fall."

Now it was Michael Cavanaugh's turn to raise an eyebrow in surprise. Danny rarely volunteered information about his personal life, but not mentioning Max's plans to move to Boston felt like more than just a simple oversight. Cavorting over the summer break was one thing, but Michael and his son had an unspoken agreement: what happens in Provincetown stays in Provincetown. In September, Danny was going to have to get serious about his future and focus on work. The last thing he needed was another distraction.

Now more than ever, the Cavanaugh Foundation needed everyone in the family's undivided attention. Bill Woodside had done his homework and already secured the backing of two key members of the select board. If the hearing next month went the wrong way, the 100-year land leases would expire, and possession would revert back to the town. Woodside was determined to buy the land and replace the structures with something expensive, but culturally unremarkable. Michael wasn't going to sit back and let that happen. Watching the demolition of the historic sites he'd spent his life trying to save would be like losing a child.

The sudden arrival of two new guests was enough to derail the Senator from his linear train of thought. Michael Cavanaugh used the unexpected break in the conversation to pour more Hendrick's gin in his old friend's drink. A less scrupulous lobbyist would've resorted to something boorish, like bribery or blackmail, to weaken the venerated statesman's resolve. Alcohol, however, was more effective and cheaper.

"Danny! Max! Over here."

Using wit and wiles, Liam had managed to finagle an invitation to the party from Danny. He was wearing a perfectly pressed linen shirt and the long mane of red hair that usually blazed from the top of his head had been slicked back into a classic coif. It was probably a mistake to let the red fox into the henhouse, but at least he'd arrived with a suitable escort. Perfectly appointed in a blue-striped seersucker suit and scarlet pocket square, Trey Taft looked every bit the head of state that his surname implied.

"Excuse me," Danny said as Senator Donovan discreetly downed most of his refreshed drink. "My other friends have arrived and I should go greet them. I hope you enjoy the rest of the holiday. Please give my best to Melody?"

"Of course, my boy. I'm sure you and your pals would rather spend the day chasing after pretty girls than hobnobbing with stuffy, old men."

It was a sin of omission not to correct such an obvious falsehood. Still, the Senator had given Danny the perfect excuse to duck out of his parents' party. The best way to throw his family off the scent was to mask the smell of pheromones with testosterone. Two guys were a couple, but four were a gang. As usual, Max was already a step ahead, charting an intercept course to rendezvous with the rest of their squad.

"We just dropped by to make a quick appearance," Trey said as he grabbed two fresh drinks from the bartender. "I'm taking Liam to a house party in Truro. You boys are welcome to come along."

"Why would we haul ass all the way down there when there's plenty of free food and drink right here?"

"Because, my dear Max," Liam said in a voice just above a whisper, "Our party will be teeming with handsome men. There's a strict 'no girls allowed' policy, if you catch my drift?"

"What do you say, Danny?" Max asked, suddenly excited by the prospect of being seen on the arm of Provincetown's most eligible bachelor. "Want to go as my date?"

Danny took a long swallow of beer and thought about the question. It was one thing to grab a drink together at the Boatslip and another to show up as a couple to an all-gay event. Silently, he played a quick game of Six Degrees of Separation and mentally calculated how long it would take for a careless rumor to make its way from Truro to Telegraph Hill. Going public with their romance was a risky proposition, but that's exactly what made it so tempting.

"It sounds epic. Let's go."

"Well, well, well..." Trey said as he finished the rest of his own drink and reached for the spare he'd intended for Liam. "Mr. Cavanaugh, you're full of surprises."

Without missing a beat, Danny took the full glass of alcohol from his friend's hand and lifted it in a mock toast.

"J-Ho, my good man. You have no idea."

EXCEPT FOR the full moon and perfect weather, "it was a dark and stormy night" was the perfect way to describe the sense of impending doom that loomed as the Rainbow Cab hurtled up the coast on Route 6. It wasn't unusual for the popular kids to show up at a party uninvited. Still, Max had a sinking suspicion Trey was leading them on a fool's errand, since no one seemed to actually know the address of where they were going. Luckily, Danny had divined the street on which their mysterious host lived and told the driver where to drop them.

"The Marilyn Monroe Garage."

The murals on the wooden doors of the car barn had been painted in homage to Andy Warhol, but the twin portraits looked more like a bad drag queen than a Hollywood icon. Even so, it was the closest thing Truro had to a local landmark. Psychedelic paint colors and a dense canopy of trees made the unpaved lane look even more enchanted. Considering the number of charming princes frolicking up at the ball, the fairy tale setting was ironically apropos. Max was just about to suggest he and Danny sneak back to the apartment to act out their own version of happily-ever-after when Bill Woodside materialized like a dark knight in a silver sports car.

"You boys look lost. Can I help you find your way?"

"We seem to have gotten turned around," Liam said, leaning suggestively against the passenger side door. "We're looking for the party at John Derek's house. Is it #6?"

"Actually, it's #13 at the end of block. I'm on my way there. Can I give you a lift?"

That felt like a trick question since there were four of them and only one vacant seat in the roadster. Max didn't know much about cars, but he was pretty sure Billy's Porsche Carrera cost more than four years of tuition at Berklee. And the swishy "S" after the cursive-style emblem on the back came at a price that would've covered the cost of his room and board. Billy was looking for an expensive piece of arm candy to accessorize his Armani polo and Banana Republic chinos. Although their destination was less than a block away, Max suspected that even with a seatbelt, it was sure to be a bumpy ride.

"Thanks, but no." Liam said, abruptly answering for the group. "We'll meet you there?"

"I'm looking forward to it."

Getting the host's address was more dumb luck than kismet. Even Christie McLean could've figured out which house was hosting a gay birthday party for Uncle Sam. The thumping bass from an endless track of dance music was more obvious than a rainbow flag.

By the time they reached the house, the valet had already parked Billy's sports car and tethered the shiny key to a pegboard near the mailbox. Max was trying to act confident and cool, but anyone could see he looked more like the hired help than a distinguished guest. Since they'd arrived on foot, the attendant looked the other way as the four friends ambled up the crushed-clamshell walkway. Without a flashy automobile and a wad of cash for a tip, the pedestrians were invisible.

The bouncers at the gate, however, were another story.

"Password?"

Star-Spangled Boner. Yankee-Doodle Dildo. Boston-Tea-Bag Party.

There were a thousand clever guesses to make, but the odds were not in their favor. More for show than security, the two sentinels guarding the entrance were dressed in black with designer sunglasses that distorted the guests' reflections like a funhouse mirror. It was going to take more than good looks or a parlor trick to get them into the exclusive venue. Luckily, Liam understood it wasn't what but *who* you knew that opened doors.

"We're with Billy."

The first guard stepped forward and extended his hand as a signal for them to stop while the other touched his earpiece and mumbled something unintelligible. Getting turned away at the door of a local bar was no big deal. The bouncers would send you off with a wink and a playful admonition to come back when you were legal or could spring for a fake ID. Max suspected there'd be more significant consequences from trying to crash this party.

"Go right in, sir."

The back patio was nearly as big as the deck at the Boatslip with a view that was even more impressive. Across the harbor, the twinkling lights of Provincetown stretched up the length of the isthmus before turning back on themselves in a hook. The dramatic panorama reminded Max that he'd grown up at the end of the world, on a sliver of land surrounded by water. It was strange, then, how the lingering quality of Provincetown was neither the sea nor the sand. For him, home would always be about the light, reflected.

The shimmer from distant stars dulled in comparison to the sparkling personalities that had assembled for John Derek's soirée. The fact that the event was being hosted in Truro only seemed to enhance the exotic appeal. Guests milled about eating canapés and drinking from heavy crystal glasses. Except for the hunky waiters in red, white, and blue Speedos, the affair felt a lot like the one they'd just left.

The first rule of party crashing was to keep a low profile and try to blend in. Unfortunately, Max was learning the hard way why being "fashionably late" was actually a thing. Deliberately arriving after an event had started didn't seem to him like a very effective way to improve your social status, but he realized he was suddenly the center of attention. A dozen hungry stares made him feel like the main course at an all-you-can-eat buffet. There were plenty of hot dishes to go around, but these Provincetown regulars were tired of settling for the same old summer fare. After a dull afternoon drinking and gossiping with each other, John Derek's guests were eager to sample the fresh amuse-bouches that had just been served. Suddenly self-conscious, Max fastened two buttons on his partially open shirt and tried not to blush. If people were going to shamelessly objectify him, then he'd at least make an effort to serve them a covered dish.

"Why is it that the men who never seek attention are usually the ones you should be giving it to?"

Some guys seemed to have a knack for making even the most innocent question sound dirty. Max felt his pulse quicken as Bill Woodside placed a hand on his broad shoulder and squeezed. A month ago, he would've gotten off thinking about a hot "Bruce Wayne" like Bill giving it to him all night long. But that was before Danny. Now, all he could think about was whether what they felt for each other would last. If boyfriends were like handcuffs, Max was ready to lock up his heart and throw away the key.

"I've never really been a big fan of Truro," Bill whispered under his breath to keep their host from overhearing. "But there aren't many vacant lots left in P-Town. New men with new money are content buying the same old houses. Not everyone has the courage or imagination to let go of the past and build something new. It might cost more and take twice the time, but in the end, you get exactly what you want. Don't you agree?"

"I live in an apartment that's probably the size of your closet, so I wouldn't know."

Bill took another sip of his drink and winced. His attempt at pleasant conversation had unexpectedly backfired. Rather than dance around the subject, he decided to set a trap for his young friend and then rescue him from the snare.

"So, how do you know our host?"

"Honestly, I don't," Max confessed, looking around as though someone were about to step forward to show him the door. "Liam and J-Ho...I mean Trey...invited us to tag along."

"The guest list for J.D.'s parties is usually chiseled in stone, but I'm not surprised he made an exception and let you in. You're quite an impressive piece of real estate, Mr. Balais. I'm looking forward to getting to know you better."

"I'm flattered, but I think my boyfriend is getting ready to sign a long-term lease," Max said, looking down into his empty glass to avoid eye contact. "He's lurking around here somewhere."

"Or maybe he's just enjoying a summer rental? Either way, he's a lucky guy," Bill said, flashing a peace sign to the nearest waiter who quickly darted off to fetch them fresh drinks. "I look forward to meeting him soon."

"Meeting whom? Me, I hope?"

The tone and accent were always a dead giveaway. Without waiting for a reply, Liam stepped forward and wedged his body into the tight space between Max and Billy. Although the memory of their first and only sexual encounter had cooled, the contact of arms touching arms was a better electrical conductor than water. Max stepped to the right and shifted his stance to break the current. Bill smiled at the tactical move. It was a refreshing change of pace for Bill to watch the interplay between himself and his young acquaintances. Liam had made it painfully clear he was ripe for the taking, but Bill had another conquest in mind. For once, he was in the enviable position of being both the pursuer and the pursued.

The old saying about "safety in numbers" usually meant you're safer in a group than alone. That interpretation, however, could get you into a lot of trouble when the duo next to you both wanted to tear off your clothes. Max could usually hold his own against unwelcomed advances, but tonight it was two against one. Luckily, his wingman stepped in, ready to even the odds.

"Hey, handsome," Danny said, sliding his arm around Max and pulling him close. "I've been looking for you everywhere. I should have known you'd be out here enjoying the view. Why don't you come inside with me and join the party?"

"Or you could just stay here and help us bring the fun outdoors," Liam said, boldly reaching out to finger the collar of Danny's shirt. "If we could just get you chaps to loosen up, I'm sure we could make a nice foursome."

"You should stop letting your fingers do the walking before someone breaks one of them off."

"Now, boys, play nice." Bill said, modulating his voice to assume the role of the wise, older uncle. "You'll have to forgive Liam. As a Brit, he thinks it's his duty to the Queen to spend Independence Day subjugating every red-blooded American boy he meets." Turning to Danny, he said, "I don't think we've met. I'm Bill Woodside, but people just call me Billy."

"I know who you are, Mr. Woodside. Michael Cavanaugh is my father."

"So, you must be Sam?

"He's my younger brother. I'm Danny."

"Well, it's good to meet you," Bill said, extending his hand as a polite gesture. "And please, let's not stand on formality. Just call me Bill."

The last thing Danny wanted to do was exchange pleasantries with his father's nemesis. He would have preferred to avoid physical contact and just "knock gloves" like prizefighters, but decorum demanded an even higher civility between enemies than friends. Billy seemed like the kind of guy who used subtle charm, not brute force, to get his way. Tonight, however, he was determined to make different kind of first impression. Offering his right hand, he used his left to grab onto Danny's wrist and held on tight. The intimacy of the gesture made it seem like they were close friends, but nothing could have been further from the truth.

"My grandparents got married in the chapel you're planning to tear to the ground," Danny said, as he took a step forward and looked his opponent squarely in the eye. He was careful not to raise his voice and spoke clearly so his next words wouldn't be misunderstood. "You and I both like men, but when it comes to Provincetown, we're looking for very different things."

"We may not see eye to eye when it comes to land development," Bill said, as he casually glanced at Max to make his next point. "But as far as I can tell, we're after the same prize. Unfortunately, only one of us is going to end up on top."

"You talk like you've got game," Danny said with a chuckle, "But you come off like a spoiled little boy. Why don't you scurry on back to your mama's little guesthouse and tell her all about your big plans?"

Words hit like fists as Danny delivered a crippling body blow. Max didn't wait for the sound of the bell to jump in and pull his fighter back. Right on cue, Liam took Bill by the arm and led him back into the safety of the party.

Don't hate the player. Hate the game.

Danny seemed unnerved by the whole encounter, but it was nothing time and gin couldn't fix. Luckily, Max had picked up a few new tricks from Bill and discreetly flashed the bartender their order. In less time than it would've taken to get a beer at the A-House, the server appeared with another round of freshly mixed drinks.

"Bill Woodside is going to be trouble," Danny said, lifting a new glass from the waiter's silver tray. "I should've never let him push my buttons. I've got a bad feeling we haven't seen the last of him."

"Probably not, but he's just one guy. How much harm could he do?"

LIKE TRURO and Provincetown, the future and the present were two distinct places. Max spent the short shuttle ride back thinking about the life he'd been dreaming about in Boston and the one that was waiting for him in town. Danny had made it clear at the bus stop that he needed time alone to think. Sitting in his own seat across the aisle, he stared out the open window as wind, warm and salty, blew his hair back into an exaggerated pompadour.

Max knew Danny was probably replaying the scene at the party in his mind, rewriting the dialogue to avoid the ugly confrontation with Bill. Although Max had made the mistake of telling Bill he had a boyfriend, it was Danny who'd stepped forward and proved it was true. In giving up his secret identity, he'd recklessly given his father's enemy a valuable piece of information. All Bill had to do was casually mention that he'd seen Danny with Max at the party. Michael Cavanaugh was a bright guy who wouldn't need any help connecting the dots.

When the bus finally pulled into the parking lot off Ryder Street, Max was the first one off. There were other stops that would have put him closer to home, but he wasn't ready to call it a night. Besides, the long walk up a crowded Commercial Street would remind him why he wanted to get away from Provincetown. Max was almost to the corner when he heard the heavy footfall of someone running up behind him.

"Screw Woodside," Danny exclaimed, grabbing Max in a playful bear hug. "I'm not going to let some asshole with an attitude ruin our night. Let's head back to Telegraph Hill. We can grab a couple beers and watch the fireworks from the roof."

Before Max could answer, a drunken tourist plowed into him and dumped most of her Sea Breeze onto his chest.

"Oh my god! I am so sorry," she said, giggling to her friend in a way that almost made it sound like the scene had been staged as part of some sadistic comedy routine. "My bad."

"No worries."

Max should have been frustrated with the flippant apology, but the anger and frustration that had been building up all evening suddenly melted away. Sometimes, when a bad situation gets even worse, it puts everything in perspective, and the mood comes full circle. Max pulled off his shirt and wrung it out over the sidewalk. It was an unusually warm night for July, but the sight of his bulging muscles raised the temperature.

"Damn! You are hawt! Wanna make out?"

Max smiled and blushed at the offer. Even though he wasn't into girls, it felt good to be admired.

"Sorry, ladies" Danny said, taking Max by the hand and leading him down a quieter street. "This boy's taken."

"Why are the good ones *always* gay?"

Considering it was Provincetown, the girl's question was definitely rhetorical. Rather than justify it with a response, Max slowly backed away as he shrugged his shoulders and raised his hands with both palms turned toward the sky.

Once the reset button on the night had been pushed, Danny and Max were ready to play. Neither of them was particularly keen on spending any more time with a bunch of gay guys who were more interested in drama than a good time. There was only one place in town where they were guaranteed to find some quality entertainment. Luckily, the Crown & Anchor was only a few blocks away.

Divas and understudies fanned out across Commercial Street handing out glossy flyers for the show. Angel waved wildly and jumped up and down as soon as Max and Danny came into view. She had dressed for the day, wearing a royal blue crop top with a red anchor conspicuously placed on her chest. White short-shorts and kitten heels accentuated her toned legs, and her shoulder-length bob was topped off with a sailor's hat set askew. As usual, her makeup was flawless. Even Max had to admit Angel looked like a star.

"*Guapos*, I am sooooo glad to see you," she said, fanning herself with a thick stack of handbills. "I've been working the street for three hours and my dogs are BARKING! I need to take a break and get off my feet."

Danny and Max were just about to offer Angel a double round of cocktails and hugs when one of the onlookers stepped forward and grabbed her by the hand.

"You can hop on my lap, pretty little lady."

"I think I'd rather stand."

"Or maybe you'd rather sit on my face?"

"That's enough," Max said, startled by the thundering bass of his own voice. "She isn't interested."

The stranger had already planned his next move. Angel was a professional when it came to walking on high heels, but the man knew how to use her weight against her. Tugging hard to throw her off balance, he pulled her helplessly into his waiting arms. It looked like Angel was going to just get up and laugh it off, but Max knew she had other plans by the way her arm was cocked. Like a spring that had been wound too tight, it recoiled and her open hand slapped the stranger hard across his face. Determined to prove Newton's third law that every action has an equal and opposite reaction, the man responded with a hard backhand that connected squarely with Angel's rouged cheek and sent her tumbling to the ground. The scene played out in the blink of an eye, but what happened next was in slow motion.

Acting on instinct, Danny scooped Angel off the ground as Max went into action. Without stopping to think, he clenched his hand into a solid fist and threw his weight into the punch. Months of training had turned him into a weapon that could be used to stop others from hurting the people he loved. The fight was over in two hits, Max hitting the bully and the bully hitting the ground. He had defended his friend and protected her honor, but the pain in his wrist burned like white lighting. The numbness that followed was even worse.

"It's definitely starting to swell up." Max said, using his good hand to cradle the other limp and lifeless appendage. "I need to get it iced."

"We need to get you to a hospital," Danny said, even though he knew the nearest one was an hour away. "You probably need an x-ray."

"That sounds expensive, and you know I don't have medical insurance."

Danny wasn't about to make a bad situation worse by offering to pay. He laid a gentle hand on Max's shoulder and guided him farther down Commercial Street toward the East End. Danny only knew one doctor in town. She might not be the most logical choice to provide medical care, but she was close by and Danny knew from experience she was someone he could trust.

"HERE'S THE technical explanation of your condition: When your moving hand hits a hard surface, the force of the impact bends it back toward your forearm. This can stretch the ligaments that connect the wrist and hand bones a little too far. The result is tiny tears or even worse, a complete break to the ligament."

"In other words, I busted my hand on that loser's fat face."

"Exactly."

Max probably shouldn't have put so much faith in the diagnosis since Dr. Lynn Morris was a psychologist, not a medical doctor. But she had kind eyes and a gentle touch. And if Danny trusted her judgment, that was good enough for Max.

"So, it's not broken." Danny said as a statement of fact, even though the ugly purple bruising on Max's wrist suggested otherwise. "He just needs to take Tylenol and get rest?"

"Ibuprofen is better. You need to keep your wrist immobilized and use ice to reduce the pain and swelling. Do it for 20-30 minutes every three to four hours for two to three days. Once the pain is gone, you'll need to wrap it with a bandage and keep it immobile for at least three weeks."

"Thanks, Dr. Morris. I really appreciate the free care."

"Call me Lynn, please. And since all my medical knowledge comes from WebMD and watching episodes of ER, you might want to get a second opinion."

"I'll make sure to stop over to the Provincetown Health Center in the morning and have them check it out. Although I'm not sure how much faith I have in a medical facility that prominently advertises that its urgent-care services include 'fish hook removal.'"

The abatement of pain was less about the extent of his injuries and had more to do with the pink tablets of Percocet Angel had managed to scrounge from one of the other Ladies of the Crown who'd pulled her hamstring back in May. Max could feel his eyelids getting heavier by the minute and it was getting harder to keep up with the conversation.

"Thanks, Doc. I'll get him home safe. Can we keep this little incident just between us?"

"A bully getting punched in the nose will probably be front-page news in the Provincetown Gazette, but your secrets are always safe with me, Danny."

It was only eleven, but the streets had already thinned out. After the fireworks, the tourists and families were ready to get some rest. Danny and Max walked back through town without saying a word. It wasn't the kind of ending either of them had expected, but Danny was proud as hell of Max for standing up to a jerk and defending Angel. The muscle Max had packed on during the winter was giving him the confidence and courage he'd need to make it in Boston. Danny had to admit that his Max was turning into someone he hardly recognized.

The alleyway that led to the steps to the apartment was pitch dark. After so many nights sneaking around, neither guy needed any light to find the way. Once he was sure they were alone, Danny led Max into the space beneath the stairs and kissed him hard on the mouth. In spite of the narcotics coursing through his blood, Max responded with equal measure.

"I kind of like having a boyfriend who's a total badass."

"Is that what I am now?"

"A badass?"

"A boyfriend?"

Danny answered the question with his mouth, but not his words. Careful to avoid the injured limb, he tugged at Max's leather belt and undid the button at the top of his shorts. Sliding them down just enough, he dropped to his knees and swallowed Max all the way up to the hilt.

"Damn. When did you learn that move?"

"I've been eating a lot of popsicles."

Max used his good hand to guide Danny's head up and down while he thrust rhythmically in and out of his boyfriend's warm, wet mouth. Pain and adrenaline mixed with desire to heighten his arousal. As usual, it didn't take very long for Danny to take him right to the edge.

"I'm close." Max said in a breathless whisper. That was Danny's cue to pull away, but instead, he wrapped his hands around Max's torso and pulled him in deeper. "Babe, stop. You're going to make me cum."

By the time Max got the words out, it was too late. For a couple of seconds, the pain in his wrist was eclipsed by a wave of ecstasy. Danny waited to make sure he was finished and then wiped Max from his lips. The statement made by what he'd just done was even more satisfying than getting off. Medicated and spent, Max could only smile and try to catch his breath as Danny stood and kissed him tenderly on the forehead.

"You didn't have to do that."

"A hero's reward."

"But it wasn't safe."

"It was safe enough. You aren't the only one who's allowed to take risks."

Max was much too tired to argue. Besides, he understood that Danny had just unofficially taken their relationship to the next level. If it weren't for his injury, Max would have taken Danny upstairs and offered him something of commensurate value in return. Thinking about where and when they'd find enough privacy to do what they'd been talking about all summer, he handed Danny the apartment keys and focused what was left of his dwindling strength to climb the flight of stairs to the door. Injured, but satisfied, he wanted nothing more than rest. Tonight, they could definitely sleep with the bedroom door unlocked.

CHAPTER 10

I T WAS going to take more than the mechanical grind of a few garbage trucks to wake the dead. Outside, Provincetown was nursing a whopper of a hangover from a daylong binge of Independence Day festivities. Inside, Danny was slowly coming back to life after a fitful night watching Max lie motionless in a narcotic-induced sleep. Elevated on a couple lumpy couch cushions, his boyfriend's black-and-blue wrist looked even more painful in the half-light of morning.

Danny pulled back the covers and leaned across the narrow space between the twin beds. More ice would help with the swelling, but it was going to take a couple weeks for the strained tendons to heal. Moving like a cat burglar, he opened the bedroom door and tiptoed through the living room and into the kitchen. The sun wasn't up yet, but after weeks of sneaking in and out of the apartment, it was easy enough to find his way around without the lights.

Working quickly and quietly, Danny grabbed a white plastic grocery bag from a stash under the sink and filled it with ice. He'd only been gone a couple of minutes, but by the time he got back Max was sitting on the edge of his bed with both feet planted on the floor.

"No way, mister. You're staying put."

"I gotta get to work."

Max winced as he tried to wipe the sleep from his eyes with his bad hand. The combination of drugs and ibuprofen had dulled the pain, but he was overdue for a booster. Danny pulled a couple pink pills from his pocket and palmed them off with a glass of water. Too tired and hurt to argue, Max swallowed the cocktail of meds and fell back onto his pillow.

"I'm going to run down to the pier and talk to Jasper," Danny said, pulling on his wrinkled polo and K-Swiss tennis shoes. "I'm sure he'll understand why you need some sick leave when I explain what's happened."

By the time he was finished double-tying the laces, his patient was fast asleep.

Danny repositioned Max's arm on the pillows and carefully placed the icepack on his wrist. His injury meant he'd be out of commission for the rest of the month. Even after the tendons healed, there was no way he'd be able to lift any real weight. Lara Balais needed her son's paycheck to make rent and Max needed to save money for school. That meant Danny had to find his boyfriend some other kind of gainful employment and convince Jasper to hold his spot on the crew.

Kissing Max tenderly on the lips, Danny grabbed the baseball cap hanging from the headboard and shoved it onto his head. After almost three months without his usual cut, his closely cropped hair had grown out into long, curly locks. Michael Cavanaugh wasn't happy with his son's new look, but there wasn't much he could do about it now that Danny was 21. Still, he'd be willing to barter to get what he wanted. That was a good thing since Danny was about to ask for a huge favor. It probably wouldn't take much convincing to get his dad to agree to the arrangement, but he was going to need all the leverage he could get.

By THE time Max finally woke up, the bag of ice on his wrist was full of lukewarm water and the sun was shining through the open window. Despite having gotten ten hours of sleep, his eyes were still heavy and his back was stiff. Using only his abdominal muscles, he sat up in bed and looked around the empty room. Although Max had no real sense of how much time had passed, it felt like Danny had been gone too long. An angry growl from his empty stomach reminded him how much he needed food. There was no point calling out to his mom or sister for help since they were already at work. Besides, he wasn't ready to explain how he'd gotten hurt or what actually happened last night. Right now, Max had more questions than answers.

If Danny had slugged Bill Woodside, why was Max the one with the busted wrist? When did Liam get a shiny silver sports car? Why was Senator Donovan with Marilyn Monroe at a party in Truro?

The sequence of events from the night before was a total blur. People, places, and things traded verbs and adjectives to form a looking-glass narrative that was more twisted than a Lewis Carroll novel. Max needed to get some food into his system to counteract the drugs that were keeping him in a pain-free fog. Moving like a wounded bird, he pressed his bruised wrist into his hip and hobbled into the kitchen.

It took twice as long to make a bologna sandwich with one hand, but Max managed to load up a plate with leftovers from the diner and carry it back to the couch. Turning on the TV, he realized he had no clue what was on in the middle of the day. With only three working channels, it didn't take long to find out. Max wasn't particularly interested in talk shows or soap operas, but at least the latter had hot, shirtless guys. Instinctively, he started to slip a hand down his pants, but stopped short and winced at the pain. There wasn't much a righty could do with his left hand, so Max finished his meal and pulled a heavy afghan over his body. With the TV droning on in the background, he quickly fell back to sleep.

WAKE UP *little man. You are going to sleep your life away.*

It was still daytime, but the room was strangely shadowed and lit with small pools of light like the set on a stage. Wearing a pink, polka-dotted nightie and sitting cross-legged, a miniature version of Josie was planted at the foot of a familiar green, plaid couch. Staring at the TV, she watched a teenage girl named Blossom dream about what life would be like in a family that wasn't run by men. At her side, a much younger Lara Balais provided the show's laugh track as she brushed out her daughter's dark hair and twisted it into a long braid that fell down her back.

I have something to show you, mijo. Come see what I've made.

Max rose from the couch and followed the disembodied voice into the small alcove off the living room that doubled as a studio. The padded footies sewn into his pajamas muffled the patter of his small feet as he scampered across the hardwood floor. Looking tired but satisfied, the artist sat on the edge of a three-legged stool, studying the painting in front of him. Max walked toward the figure with outstretched arms.

You can look, but don't touch. The paint is still wet.

The blazing colors swirling inside on the canvas seemed to harden and crystallize until the smooth surface became a mirror, reflecting the image of Max, with his mother and sister in the distant background.

What will you make with your life, my son?

Tiny, trembling hands tried to hold on, but his father was already slipping away. A sudden, urgent pain pulled Max back through a dark, narrow corridor, out of his subconscious, and into the bright light of day. Still lingering in the space between sleep and wakefulness, he closed his eyes and tried to call back the dream. But the images were like water. No matter how tightly he laced his fingers together, the memories were already slipping through the cracks.

The same drugs that kept the pain at bay were making him feel too much. Since Max suddenly had a lot of free time on his hands (or *hand* as the case may be), he decided to take a long walk to clear the muddled thoughts from his head. Pulling an old canvas belt from the cardboard box beneath his bed, Max looped it around his neck and slid his right arm through the opening. The makeshift sling wasn't legit enough to earn him a First Aid merit badge, but at least it would keep his wrist elevated and immobile. Danny would probably give him hell for disregarding his prescription for bed rest, but Max needed some fresh air and a change of scenery.

THE GALLERIES of the East End were the closest thing Provincetown had to a museum. Brightly lit, the window displays were meant to highlight the work of local artists and attract buyers. More often than not, they just gave tourists something pretty to look at on their way to somewhere else. Like the architectural design of the town, the style of the various salons ranged from traditional cottages to chic lofts. There were dozens of options to choose from, but Max was searching for one place in particular. He didn't remember the name of the gallery, but his father had been on good terms with the owner and Max had been there enough that he knew he would recognize it when he saw it. Luckily, it was conveniently located right on the main drag. With its doors and windows open, art overflowed from the front showroom walls and onto the street.

"Good afternoon."

A painter on the sidewalk tossed out a friendly greeting, even as his eyes stayed focused on his canvas. Like most artists, he seemed to be able to sense when someone was admiring his work. The same was true with music. Max could always tell when someone was really listening to him play or just pretending to be polite.

"Is the owner around? I was hoping he'd let me have a quick look inside."

"That would be me. Please, be my guest."

Max pretended not to notice the starving artist leering at him like he was a piece of meat. Despite his sunken cheeks and deep smile lines, there was something about his eyes that suggested he'd once been quite handsome. Still, time and circumstances had apparently made him neglectful of his general appearance. Shirtless and barefooted, his denim overalls were tattered and splattered with paint.

"My name's Doug. You look familiar. Do you work out at Muscle Beach?"

"I've been a regular there since January. I think I may have seen you there a couple times."

Doug smiled to acknowledge what they both knew to be the truth. Anyone could see by his lithe frame that he wasn't going to the gym to build muscle. In fact, he'd been hanging out in the locker room, shamelessly cruising Max for months.

"I'm just going to pop my head inside for a peek."

"Pop away."

This was one of those times when Max wished he could hide under a brimmed hat and dark sunglasses. It felt great to get attention from someone you liked, but when it was unsolicited, it just felt dirty and gross. Max wanted to tell Doug to go take a cold shower, but by the smell of it, he probably hadn't bathed in a week.

"See anything you like?"

The duplicity of the question was annoying, not sexy. Max decided right away to make it clear he wasn't just another pretty face.

"Not yet. I'm more into the postmodern stuff – Jackson Pollock and Miró."

"Is that so? Well, I have a couple of smaller pieces in the storeroom you might want to see. Follow me."

It seemed like more than just a coincidence that Grace Jones was singing "I Need A Man" as Doug led Max through the warren-like rooms of the gallery and into the back. At what appeared to be a dead-end hallway, he opened a hidden door and switched on the light. True to its name, the storage space was packed with rows of canvases, ordered alphabetically by the artist's last name.

"So Pollock, huh?" Doug asked, intentionally brushing up against Max from behind as he squeezed by him and pulled a few canvases from the pile. "Here's one from the school."

The first piece was colorful and complex, but derivative. Even though the artist had replicated the technique, he'd missed the point. Anyone with an eye could see it was nothing more than a random splattering of paint.

"No? Well, maybe something a bit more in the style of Miró?"

Max sucked in a breath of stale air when Doug presented the next canvas for inspection. The yellow triangles, red circle, and purple cubes reminded him of the toy blocks he'd played with as a kid. A tight knot of anticipation in his stomach felt like Christmas morning and his birthday all rolled into one. It would have been easy enough to look in the lower right corner and see the name of the artist scribbled in black ink but there was no need. Max would've known his father's work anywhere.

"Miguel Balais."

"Actually, yes. He was a talented, local artist." Doug didn't bother hiding how impressed he was with Max's prowess. "Wow, you really know your stuff."

"I want it," Max blurted out as he reached for his empty wallet. "How much?"

"It's marked $750, but for you, I could probably do $500."

"That's still too much," Max said, feeling the first droplets of sweat slide down his back as he thought about someone else buying what should have been his by right. "I only have $250 in my savings account. Can we work something out?"

"I already gave you the 'friends and family' price," Doug said, shaking his head from side to side as he bit down seductively on his lower lip. "Sounds like you're looking for the 'friends with benefits' discount."

Max closed his eyes and swallowed. A month ago, he would have gladly gone down on this creep if it meant getting a piece of his dad back. Now, everything was different.

Not saying "no" wasn't the same as a "yes," but it was good enough for Doug. Stepping closer, he unsnapped the buckles of overalls and let them fall to the floor. Fully clothed, Max suddenly felt naked and vulnerable. He closed his eyes and told himself that it would all be over in a few minutes. What Danny didn't know, wouldn't hurt him.

"Hello? Is anybody here?"

The muffled bass of a man's voice reverberated through the walls. Even though they were well hidden, the unexpected interruption seemed to break Doug's concentration. Worried that he'd change his mind and call off the deal, Max leaned forward and kissed him tentatively on the lips.

"Come out, come out, wherever you are."

The voice was suddenly louder. Whoever it was, was getting closer.

"Damn," Doug cursed under his breath. By the look of it, he'd had plenty of practice getting dressed in a hurry, but it was going to take more than a thin swath of denim to cover up the raging boner that was poking out from between his legs. He'd only managed to push it down and snap one of the buckles of his overalls into place before the customer appeared in the doorway.

Even though Bill Woodside seemed like the kind of guy who would have been in favor of transactional sex, the look on his face betrayed his anger. For whatever reason, catching Doug with Max had clearly set him off.

"I'd hoped we'd meet again," Bill said to Max. "But this wasn't what I had in mind. Please excuse us. I need to speak with my old friend alone."

"Now, Billy. You of all people wouldn't deny me a little fun. Max has a great body and I suspect he knows how to use it to get what he wants. Go wait for us out front. This won't take very long."

"Douglas!" Bill shouted out his friend's name as a warning that his patience was quickly wearing thin. "You won't be doing *anything* with this young man. Not today, not ever. Do we understand each other?"

Taut with anger and sharpened with the trace of a Scottish brogue, Bill's admonition was like an arrow that had hit its target. Doug looked him squarely in the eye and nodded once to show his agreement. Max wasn't sure what was going on, but he knew from experience that it would be a mistake to get in the middle of a fight between friends.

Outside on the sidewalk, a cacophony of street noise kept Max from hearing the heated conversation that was undoubtedly taking place in the backroom. When Bill finally emerged, he was carrying a small package under his arm. Wrapped in brown paper and tied with twine, the purchase was apparently a consolation prize for Doug's bruised libido.

"Come on," Bill said, putting on a pair of expensive sunglasses and walking decisively up the street. "I think we could both use a stiff drink. I'm buying."

Max had been prepared for a long trek back to the Boatslip, but Bill steered them straight for the nearest bar. Given the time of day, the place was dead. Selecting the most private spot in a room full of empty tables, Max took a seat while Bill gestured for service.

"Two shots of Patrón," he ordered without even bothering to confer with Max. "And bring the bottle." Less than a minute later, the waitress was back with the drinks and a plate of fresh limes.

"I don't like tequila," Max said pushing his glass away and helping himself to one of the wedges of fruit.

"Neither do I, but we aren't drinking it for the taste." Bill tossed back the first shot and quickly poured another.

"You need to promise me you won't go back to that gallery again. Douglas can be charming in his own way, but he isn't someone you can trust."

"And *you* are? Give me a break. I appreciate your concern, but I'll decide what I do and who I do it with."

"It's 'whom,' but that's entirely beside the point," Bill said, falling back into the role of teacher once again. "You need to understand something. Douglas is sick..."

"He might be a little sexually compulsive, but I'd hardly call him 'sick.'"

"Listen to me," Bill said, lowering his voice and leaning forward across the table. "He has AIDS."

Without thinking, Max lifted the shot of tequila with his good hand and drank it down in one hard swallow. Wincing from the taste, he tried not to think about how close he'd come to making a terrible mistake. Bill reached across the table and refilled his glass.

"Thank you."

Max wasn't just talking about the drink and they both knew it. He should have said more, but the gravity of the situation left him at a loss for words. Luckily, Bill stood up to leave before the silence became too awkward, tossing a wad of cash on the table.

"Hey, wait. You're forgetting your package."

As soon as he lifted it, Max realized what Bill had done. Even wrapped in brown paper, he could tell by the size and weight what was inside.

"I didn't buy it for me. That belongs to you."

For the second time this afternoon, Max had misjudged another man's intentions. Maybe, just maybe, it was time to stop thinking of Bill as the enemy and start giving him the benefit of the doubt.

ALCOHOL AND opioids made for a dangerous cocktail. Max didn't remember very much about the long walk home, but somehow he managed to make it back to the apartment in one piece. Once inside, Max cut through the twine and tore apart the brown paper wrapping. For a second he froze, worried that this was all some elaborate practical joke or another psychedelic dream. Taking a deep breath, he carefully propped the canvas up against the back of one of the kitchen chairs. Max squatted down on his haunches and studied it up close. Now that it was his to keep, the colors seemed even brighter.

When he was sure that the pattern was burned into his memory, Max picked up the painting and hung it on a hook protruding from the otherwise empty wall. Staggering back to the couch, he reapplied a fresh bag of ice to his throbbing wrist and leaned back into the cushions. The pills had just about worn off, but he didn't mind the pain anymore. The image of circles and squares floating in space stayed with him, even after he closed his eyes and drifted back to sleep. For the first time in as long as he could remember, it felt like his family was whole again.

WHEN MAX opened his eyes, Danny was sitting on the edge of the couch, looking exhausted and stinking of fish.

"What time is it? Where have you been?"

"I just got back from a meeting with my father, but I spent most of the day about a mile offshore in the Atlantic."

"I don't understand. You went boating with your dad??"

"No more drugs for you," Danny said lifting Max's legs high enough so he could slide underneath and take a seat. "Captain Avellar agreed to let me sub for you until your hand is better."

"Wait. You were out on *La Benedita* today?"

"Don't sound so surprised. I've been sailing since I was two. We may not have hoists and nets on our boat, but my dad taught me everything I needed to know about taking care of myself out at sea."

Danny proceeded to recount his experiences as the newest member of Jasper's crew, but the mixture of narcotics, alcohol, and too much sleep made the story sound a lot like a lost episode of *Gilligan's Island*. Max closed his eyes and tried to imagine his boyfriend shoveling cod into the hold and hosing down the deck. It was hard to imagine a Cavanaugh doing hard, manual labor. It was also pretty hot.

"I also stopped by the pharmacy and picked up a proper sling for your arm. I figured you'd want a black one so you could pretend you were a pirate when we go out later."

"You're thinking of an eye patch. Besides, I don't really feel like doing any swashbuckling tonight. I'd just rather hang around here with you and watch TV."

"Come on, Maxie. It's a beautiful summer evening and the fresh air will do you good."

MAX ASSUMED "going out" meant grabbing a slice of pizza at Spiritus, not taking in the show at the Crown & Anchor. The last thing he wanted to do was sit around a bar watching Danny drink all night, but it probably wasn't a bad idea to drop by to check up on Angel. Max was used to being dazzled by her show. Even so, he wasn't prepared for the reception waiting for him just inside the door.

Right on cue, the house lights dimmed and the soundtrack began to play. Max had seen *Footloose* at the local movie house enough times to recognize Bonnie Tyler's "Holding Out For a Hero" from the first pulses of the heavy-handed synths. As the piano-led choral riffs rang out, Angelique parted the heavy velvet curtains and stepped into the waiting spotlight. Looking even better than Lynda Carter, she took center stage wearing knee-high red leather boots and a matching cape that furled out behind her when she twirled.

Dressed as Wonder Woman, Angelique used the lyrics and the choreography to process the violence that had been done to her the night before. This time, however, the "pretty little lady" was fighting back. Angelique lip-synced perfectly to the music as she threw punches into the air and deflected invisible bullets off her Bracelets of Submission. From the safety of their seats, the audience went wild. Always the consummate entertainer, she finished the number by playfully tying up one of the boys near the stage with her Lasso of Truth. When Angelique willingly fell into his waiting lap, the song ended and the spot went dark.

The crowd was still clapping when Angel scurried over to Max and Danny's table and took the only empty seat. Standing ready for her cue, the waitress brought over a chilled bottle of champagne and three empty glasses. Angel threw back her head and let out a wicked laugh. Tonight, the bubbly was on the house.

"Wow, that bruise looks ugly." Max said, leaning closer to inspect the purple discoloration on Angel's cheek while Danny popped the cork. "Maybe you can try to cover it up with some concealer?"

"Lady Angelique does not wear makeup to look better. She wears it to look *even* better."

The shock and indignation was feigned, but the feeling behind the sentiment was all too real. Max suspected it wasn't the first time Angel had been the victim of violence and it probably wouldn't be the last. Hiding behind false bravado was the only way to protect her heart from a world that wasn't ready to accept the fluidity of her identity and appearance.

"The show was great, but we're going to have to call it a night."

Danny got up from the table and downed his champagne as a subtle signal to Max that it was time to leave.

"Why so soon? You simply *must* stay for my second show."

"We'd love to, but Max has a busy day tomorrow. He's starting a new job."

"What?" Max jumped in to ask before Angel had time to react. "I thought you worked it all out with Jasper?"

"I did. As long as I keep showing up each morning, your spot on the crew is secure and you'll keep getting paid. It's not like I need the cash, and given how many nights I've been staying over, I want to kick in for rent. I also found another job that you can do one-handed while you're healing."

"And what, pray tell, is this fabulous new vocation?"

"You're going to be working at the Foundation."

Max felt his stomach rise and fall. Two paychecks meant he could save for school and help his mom with the bills. But beyond a passing interest in historic preservation, Max had zero professional experience to bring to the job. Working at the Foundation office also meant spending a lot of time alone with Michael Cavanaugh. It was one thing to blend into the background at a family party and another to work side-by-side with your boyfriend's dad.

Head swimming and drowning in problems, Max needed some time to think things through and get used to the idea of doing something more with his life than just fish. It was undeniably a great opportunity, one that he never expected and really didn't deserve. The night, like Danny Cavanaugh, was full of surprises.

CHAPTER 11

I N AUGUST, time seemed to pass more quickly as the days got hotter and shorter. After only a month on the job, Max had gone from cataloguing old photographs and collating files, to researching properties and preparing grant applications. Michael Cavanaugh had always been kind, but now, after working so closely together, he was starting to treat his son's friend like a trusted member of the family.

"That wasn't the amount we discussed. It's not even close." Michael said into the telephone receiver as he entered the room and headed straight to his desk without a greeting or even a perfunctory nod to Max. "I've got the written estimate right here...."

Michael rifled through a tall stack of papers with a look of panic on his face. Although his tone was even and measured, he was clearly becoming more agitated by the minute. Max still hadn't improved his verbal skills, but he had developed a sixth sense about his employer's mercurial moods. Using his good hand, he deftly pulled a file from the cabinet and slid the right page into his boss's field of vision. Michael quickly scanned the document and then resumed his call.

"The exact amount of the quote was $950,463.28. And there's a note that confirms we sent a written acceptance of the contract two days ago. What do you mean you never received it?"

Max had already anticipated the crooked contractor's next move. Stepping forward, he flipped the file over and pointed at the delivery slip conveniently stapled to a photocopy of the quote.

"The FedEx envelope was delivered to you at 3:11 p.m. on Monday. If you'd like, I can fax you a copy of the receipt with your signature on it?"

Max held his breath and waited for his boss to speak. For a moment, he thought the contractor had hung up, but then Michael smiled and gave him a thumbs-up.

"That's great, Ronnie. I'll have my associate give you a call in the morning to schedule a site inspection. His name is Max Balais. We'll talk again soon."

Michael Cavanaugh pushed a button on the cordless phone and cradled it back on the charger. His footfall on the hardwood floors sounded loud and imposing as he crossed the room to where his newest employee was pretending to study the contents of a book on local zoning ordinances. Max felt his heart skip a beat when Danny's dad put a heavy hand on his shoulder and began to speak.

"You went ahead and finalized a million dollar deal without waiting for me to tell you to send back the paperwork."

Swallowing hard, Max closed the book and turned around in his chair. Although Michael had signed off on the quote and told him to include the expense in the next quarterly budget, his boss was right. It was one thing to organize files and quite another to legally commit the Foundation's money to a project.

"And by doing so, you just saved us over two hundred thousand dollars."

If his arm hadn't been in a sling, Max would've crushed Michael in a bear hug. Instead, he settled for a left-handed shake and a smile.

"Keep up the good work, Mr. Balais. You're doing a great job."

"Sorry, Dad. Am I interrupting something important?"

The voice may have sounded familiar, but the guy standing in the entryway was a changed man. Wearing a faded gray t-shirt and three days worth of stubble, Danny looked every bit the salty seaman he'd unexpectedly become.

"Not at all, son," Michael said, handing Max the file and heading toward the door. "I have a meeting with the mayor in less than an hour. Apparently, this guy Bill Woodside has put together a formal proposal to purchase and develop the four parcels of land we've been trying to preserve."

"How can he do that? I thought your grandfather held all the titles."

"He did, but the properties were conveyed to him as a lease for a term of ninety-nine years in 1901. That means the land and everything on it reverts back to the town at the end of this year. We've been in negotiations to extend the lease, but the council could decide it would be easier and more lucrative to just sell off the properties to the highest bidder. There's a town hall meeting scheduled for Thursday night. Max, I'll want you to be there with me."

"Of course."

"You can't do that," Danny said, stepping forward and taking the file from Max's hand. "I know you want to help, but you have your audition at Berklee on Friday afternoon."

"I can do the meeting and catch the first ferry to Boston in the morning. That'll leave me more than enough time to hoof it over to Park Street and catch the Green Line across town."

"You need to spend Thursday rehearsing the piece, not pushing paper. There's no way I'm going to let you risk your future for me."

Danny seemed to be forgetting that his dad was still in the room.

"I'm going to give you boys some privacy so you can talk this out," Michael said as he stealthily moved toward the nearest exit. "But for once, my son and I are in complete agreement. It would've been good optics to have a native son standing by my side to make our case to the council, but I can handle the presentation. Go do what you need to do in Boston."

Michael closed the pocket doors behind him and hurried off for his next meeting. Danny watched from the window as his dad made his way down the back steps and along the long, winding trail that connected Telegraph Hill to the West End.

"Alone at last," Max gasped, finally able to find his voice after what felt like two of the longest minutes of his life. "Now get over here, Mr. Cavanaugh, and show me some appreciation for saving your family a buttload of cash."

Danny put out his hand as a sign for his boyfriend to wait and then touched his index finger to his lips. Seconds ticked by as he listened for the telltale creaks of the old house that signaled someone else was at home. Even though Danny had watched his mom drive away with his little brother securely belted into the back seat, Sam was like a private detective. It would've been just like him to double back on foot and do some undercover reconnaissance on his older sibling. Just to be on the safe side, Danny locked the library doors and tested them to make sure they wouldn't open. It was one thing for his family to suspect what was going on and another for them to walk in and catch him in the act.

"Fun fact," Max said as he pretended to turn his attention back to one of the thickest books on his small desk. "A 'buttload' is actually 126 gallons of wine. The word 'butt' comes from 'botte,' the French word for boot. Seafaring merchants shipped wine in large wooden casks. I can just imagine a twelfth-century Captain Avellar telling some hunky winemaker to put a load in his butt."

"Enough showing off," Danny whispered as he swiveled Max around in the chair and grazed his lips across the sweet spot on the back of his boyfriend's neck. "You're a walking encyclopedia of historic trivia, but I'm right about skipping the town hall. You need to focus on your music and forget about this preservation nonsense."

"It isn't nonsense and you know it."

"All I *know* is that you need to ace that audition. And I'm going to make sure you get there on time if I have to drive you to Boston myself."

"Is that a threat or a promise?"

"Both. But right now, I've got a serious question to ask you. Feel like getting wet?"

MAX HAD been so caught up in his work on land that he'd forgotten what it felt like to be at sea. It was a warm August day, but the temperature was at least ten degrees cooler out on the Atlantic. Initially, he'd bristled at the suggestion to postpone their "afternoon delight" so Danny could pick up an extra shift on *La Benedita*. But in the buff or fully clothed, Max didn't mind giving up his free afternoon, as long as he got to spend it with his boyfriend. What really bugged him was how quickly Danny had ingratiated himself to Captain Avellar.

Newbies usually spent their first month on the job making deliveries and working the pier. Few, if any, got the chance to crew a full shift and get out on the open water. Even then, chances were good they'd spend most of the long trip relocating several thousand pounds of ice to one side, packing the fish, and then shoveling the ice all back over the daily catch. That's why Max was so surprised to see Danny working up in the bow with the senior deckhands, checking the lines and preparing the nets.

High above, a squadron of seagulls was spoiling for a dogfight. Like kamikaze pilots, they took turns dive-bombing toward the fishing trawler only to pull up at the very last moment and bank away on an invisible draft of wind. The spray of water off the surface made good on Danny's promise. They were only an hour into the shift and Max was already soaked.

Thirty-one. Twenty-nine. Thirty.

For some reason, Max couldn't remember how many days were left until the start of the fall semester. It was unlike him to lose track of the calendar, but over the past week, he'd been so busy doing research and cataloging properties that he'd hardly even thought about Berklee. Fate definitely had a wicked sense of humor. After spending the better part of the last decade dreaming about escaping to Boston, he was squandering what was left of his last summer learning everything he could about the place he was about to leave behind.

Towering over the two-story buildings nestled around its base, the Pilgrim Monument was easily the most recognized structure in Provincetown. Most people could have guessed by its name that the stately monolith was built to commemorate the first landfall of the Pilgrims in 1620. Some of the old-timers might even recall how a contest had been held to choose its design or that President Teddy Roosevelt actually laid the cornerstone in 1907. But only a true history buff knew the winning entry by Willard T. Sears was based upon the *Torre del Mangia* in Siena or that, at 252 feet, the campanile is the tallest all-granite structure in the United States.

There were dozens of architectural treasures hidden in the shadows of the modern monstrosities that had sprung up like mushrooms. For the first time, Max could see there was more to the little fishing village than just trendy gay bars and trashy t-shirt shops.

Staying or going?

The nagging existential question echoed in his mind. A few months ago, the answer was crystal clear. There was a time, not so long ago, when all Max wanted was a fresh start in a world full of possibilities. Now, he had a bona fide boyfriend and a promising future to consider. Going to Berklee and composing music was all he'd ever cared about, but after just a month on the job, Max was starting to wonder whether it was better to spend his life creating something new or preserving something worth saving. It would take him years of hard work to earn his degree. Even then, he probably wouldn't get a job nearly as interesting as the one he had right now at the Cavanaugh Foundation. After all that had happened over the summer, Max couldn't help but wonder whether he was leaning toward the future or just running from his past.

Jasper seemed to be reading Max's mind as he abruptly brought the ship around and cut the engines. Down at the stern, a mechanical drum winch unspooled heavy nets off the back of the boat and into the churning water. Waiting in the wings, Danny jumped in and completed the deployment by extending the long metal booms out over the port and starboard sides like outstretched arms. It was a routine maneuver that anyone with experience could manage. Unfortunately, his training had mostly been "learn as you go." That's why he didn't see the gravity of his mistake until it was too late.

Even from the upper deck, Max could see that Danny was in trouble. The line that secured the fishing nets to the boat was caught in the wheel of the boom pulley. In a few seconds, the nets would fill up with fish, but there'd be no way haul the catch into the hold. Wrapping the full length of the loose coil around his left arm, Danny grabbed the rope with both gloved hands and pulled with all his might. It only took one good tug to set the wheel back in place, but he was so focused on fixing the rig that he forgot to secure the end of line to the deck mooring.

Deep beneath the surface of the water, a school of trapped fish was frantically swimming to escape. The only thing keeping them tied to *La Benedita* was the length of nylon cord securely wound around Danny's forearm. Max saw the thick, white rope go taunt and called out for Danny to untangle himself from the line, but it was already too late. Danny grabbed onto the railing and held tight. For a brief moment, it seemed like he'd managed to right himself. Then, a split second later, the tension of the line yanked him off his feet and over the side of the boat.

Jasper sprang into action, sliding down the rails from the boathouse to the main deck like a fireman on a pole. No one knew where to look or what to do next. Without thinking, Angel grabbed an unsheathed fishing knife and dove straight into the sea.

Time slowed to a crawl as the crew stared into the spray where both young men had disappeared.

Twelve. Sixteen. Twenty.

Max counted to himself and held his breath as the collective life he'd shared with Danny Cavanaugh flashed before his eyes. The last two months together had been amazing, but their romance was just the latest chapter of a friendship that had carried them through the darkest of days. It was Danny who had sat with Max for hours at his father's funeral, whispering words of comfort and consolation as scores of strangers stopped by to pay their respects.

In the cold winter months that followed, it was Danny who had shown up at Max's front door every Saturday morning with a box of glazed doughnuts and a half-gallon of chocolate milk. Side by side, they'd sat on the wooden staircase outside the apartment and binged in silence until the sugar kicked in. Then, the two friends spent the rest of the short day roaming the empty streets until the cold drove them back indoors. Danny's smile had been the only glimpse of sunlight in that long, bleak winter.

Now, it was Max's turn to call his friend back into the world of the living. Closing his eyes, he silently offered a prayer to pay whatever ransom came due to guarantee Danny's safe return.

A moment later, Angel and Danny broke the surface, coughing and sputtering as water-soaked lungs sucked in air. There was a collective cheer from the crew as three of them jumped into the ocean and helped their men overboard swim back to the ship.

White-knuckled, Jasper held onto the railing of the deck with both hands and cried. In twenty years, he'd never lost a member of his crew. Today, he had almost lost two. The shredded remnants of the fishing net drifted on the open water. Empty, it was a chilling reminder of what had almost been lost.

Danny spent the ride back to shore below deck, wrapped in warm blankets with a tall glass of whiskey in his trembling hands. Growing up near the sea, he'd seen its destructive force before, but this was the first time he'd ever been on the receiving end.

A lingering sense of disappointment, not dread, had his nerves on edge. It wasn't like he wanted to drown. Rather, it was the feeling that he wouldn't have minded so much if Angel hadn't managed to cut him free. There was certain poetry to the idea of being pulled under the waves. For years, he'd felt trapped, unable to escape from his parents' expectations about the role he was supposed to play. Occasionally, he managed to break the surface and catch a breath, but mostly he was just treading water.

A brush with death had triggered a powerful fight or flight response. Danny's first impulse was to pack a duffle bag and catch the first plane back to Lisbon. His parents would never finance another trip abroad, but there was enough graduation money left in his savings to buy a round-trip ticket and Eurail pass. He could already imagine long, hot days sketching with charcoal pencils and cool nights drinking sweet, red wine with other artists. Admittedly, working odd jobs and couch surfing with friends wasn't the most glamorous way to see the world. The rudimentary plan swirling in his head created more problems than it solved, but at least Danny would finally be living life on his own terms.

Without thinking, he drained the glass of whiskey in one long gulp. Danny could leave tonight, fly away and disappear without a trace, but there was someone he would miss. Max was the only thing about his crazy summer that actually made sense. Truth be told, Danny had been happier spending time with his boyfriend and working on *La Benedita* than he'd ever been trotting around the globe. That, among other things, would change in September.

Max poked his head into the cabin. Somehow, he looked even worse than Danny felt.

"Can I come in?"

"When did you ever need an invitation?"

"So, what was the deal with that lame stunt walking the plank? I thought we agreed I was the one who got to play pirate? I've got the black sling, remember?"

"I think it's supposed to be an eye patch..."

Before Danny could even finish the sentence Max grabbed both sides of his face and pulled him in for a long, deep kiss. The hot breath passing between them was a poignant reminder that Danny was still alive. Max didn't particularly enjoy the backwash of cheap whiskey, but given the circumstances, he wasn't in a position to complain.

"I'm done with Berklee. This summer with you and Angel made me realize I don't need to move to the big city or get some fancy degree to be happy. Everything I've ever needed has been right in front of me the whole time. I've always had the courage, the brains, and the heart to make a life for myself right here in Provincetown. I want to keep working at the Foundation and be with you. This is my home and it's where I'm meant to be.

The laughter that came out of Danny quickly dissolved into a mean sounding cough. Given all the saltwater he'd swallowed, it was probably going to take few days for him to fully recover.

"You realize that your eloquent soliloquy was straight out of *The Wizard of Oz*?"

"What? No! Crap."

"You're adorable, but there's no way I'm letting you give up on your dream of living in Boston. Oz is only a ferryboat ride away, so click those ruby slippers three times and repeat after me....

There's no place like home.

CHAPTER 12

"**C**'MON, COACH!" Max pleaded from the small stoop just outside the apartment. "I've been training all week. Don't I get some kind of reward for all my hard work?"

Danny stood cross-armed at the bottom of the wooden steps wearing a dour look that already answered his boyfriend's question. The "no-sex-before-sports rule" was rooted in a fear that ejaculation saps men of their testosterone and energy, thereby harming their athletic performance. Although there was zero science behind the half-cocked theory, Danny wasn't about to risk Max's future for the sake of a little nookie.

"After the audition, I'm all yours. Until then, the only thing you're going to be blowing is your horn."

Max pantomimed a shot to the heart as he fell against the doorpost in feigned agony. The only thing hotter than sex with Danny was the anticipation of having it. Luckily, he was the king of delayed gratification. Tomorrow was the day Max had been waiting for – his one chance to dazzle the Admissions Committee at Berklee. But first he had to get through the evening, knowing that his boss was making their case to the town council without his trusted associate by his side.

Max had spent most of the morning printing and binding the final handout materials. It was doubtful there'd be very many people in attendance at the hearing, but he'd produced a dozen extra copies, just in case. Strangely, Michael Cavanaugh had disappeared from the office right after lunch. The cryptic note he'd left behind wished Max good luck with his audition and told him to take the rest of the day off. That just meant Max had even more time to sit around worrying about the outcome of the meeting. The council wouldn't issue its formal decision until sometime next week, but they'd probably know which way the wind was blowing based on the questions and tone. Too bad Max would have to hear about it second-hand from Danny during the ferry ride to Boston in the morning.

"How about I treat you to a pizza with 'the works'?"

"Sex is off the table, but anchovies are suddenly fair game?"

Max skipped every other step on his way down to the parking lot, but by the time he reached the bottom, Danny was already a safe distance away. Even though their romance was one of the worst kept secrets in town, Max had begrudgingly promised to help Danny hide the truth from his parent's until the end of summer. That's why it was such a surprise when he took Max's hand and held it tight as they walked up Commercial Street.

"Is this O.K.?"

"Well, it is my *only* good hand."

"And you might need to catch a fly ball."

"Or hail a taxi cab."

The unexpected kiss that followed conveyed everything that had gone unsaid between Max and Danny since the incident on *La Benedita*. PDA had always been completely off the table, so the impromptu gesture was both intimate and erotic. Although neither of them had worked up the nerve to say the actual words "I love you," it was unquestionably the pink elephant in the room.

Outside Spiritus, the line snaking down the sidewalk was a sobering reminder that, in August, the town belonged to the tourists. Max cracked his knuckles and hummed along to the score of trumpet music playing in his head while Danny fiddled with his new cellular phone. His Nokia 3310 was smaller than a TV remote, but it was even more effective when it came to keeping him connected to the world beyond Provincetown.

"Fuck. Fuck. Fuck."

"I knew you'd crack on this no-sex rule, Cavanaugh. Let's head back to the apartment..."

"I just got a Mobile Chat from my dad. Apparently, he drove to Hyannis this afternoon to try, one last time, to convince Senator Donovan to join him at the town hall tonight. The two of them are en route, but there was a four-car pile-up on Route 6. He doesn't think they'll make it back in time. Wait, there's a voicemail message."

Danny felt his stomach drop before he switched to speaker and hit "play." Even before he heard the recording, Danny knew what his father was going to say.

"Hello, son. We just heard traffic is gridlocked from Wellfleet to Orleans and even the Senator's credentials won't get us past the state troopers. I need you to take my place at the town hall. Max has already prepared the handout materials and my notes are on the cue cards in the top drawer of my desk. This has always been my fight, not yours, but you're a Cavanaugh. The family is counting on you. I know you won't let us down."

Danny listened to the message again, then pushed the "delete" button. Stepping forward in the queue, he closed his eyes and tried to wrap his head around the heavy mantle that had been placed on his shoulders. Over the past month, he'd purposely zoned out any time his dad or Max had brought up the subject of preservation. To make matters worse, he'd never even taken the time to visit the sites or learn anything about their historical significance. Danny was about as unprepared for the hearing as he'd been for navigating his new relationship with Max. Although he'd had plenty of time and experience to draw from when it came to figuring out his love life, the whole "fake it til you make it" strategy wasn't going to work against such a formidable opponent.

Bill Woodside was a savvy entrepreneur who knew how to sell a business plan. The word on the street was he already had four of the seven council members locked to vote his way. That meant Danny would have to convince at least two of them to change their minds or the negotiations to extend the land leases would fail.

"Before you say anything," Danny said, taking Max by the hand and looking straight into his smoldering blue eyes. "You should know I've already changed my mind about this evening. I need you so frickin' bad."

"For sex or the town hall?"

"What do you think?"

Max stepped forward to the takeout window and ordered a large cheese pizza with the works.

"Staying or going?"

This time, he didn't hesitate with his answer to Gus. Tonight, everything was on the line.

"We're going."

THE TOWN hall looked more like a grade school spelling bee than a formal, administrative hearing. All of the council members had opted for "summer casual," wearing short-sleeve shirts and Dockers pants. Only the mayor had bothered to get dressed up. Donning a dark gabardine suite and paisley silk tie, he looked every bit the town patriarch as he prepared to preside over the meeting with his dick and gavel in hand.

Danny thumbed through a stack of index cards and tried to invoke his father's forceful rebuttal to the proposed development plans. Local business owners and life-long busybodies would inevitably step up to voice their opinions about what the council should or shouldn't do, but everybody knew this was the Cavanaugh's fight. Win, lose, or draw, it was up to Danny to take up the family's cause. Even though Max was practically an expert on each of the historic sites in question, he had been relegated to a supporting role. Rather than just sit back in the gallery and do nothing, he decided to do a little reconnaissance over at the enemy camp.

Bill Woodside looked even wiser and more handsome in his Italian linen jacket and crisp white shirt. Although he was flying solo, he had an army of easels standing at attention around him. Each one displayed an artist's rendering of the various stages of his proposed development projects. Unlike the gaudy structures that had been cropping up around town like weeds, these architectural designs were elegant and understated. The clapboard-covered cottages and cedar-roofed townhomes blended in seamlessly with the classic Provincetown neighborhoods. Bill had even commissioned a firm to create model dioramas of a few of the developments to give the council a three-dimensional view of the future.

"Hey there, Billy," Max said, trying to sound friendly, but not too familiar. The last thing he needed was to give anyone the false impression he was sleeping with the enemy. "How's it going?"

"Sorry, young man. I know we've met before, but I can't seem to recall you."

Max looked more hurt than annoyed as he pursed his lips and tried not to frown. Growing up in a small town, he'd grown accustomed to neighbors knowing one another, but the shelf life of his first impression had seemingly expired after just a month. As a businessman, Bill only bothered to remember the kind of influential people who could advance his cause. Unable to offer him any real value, Max had quickly become forgettable. Still, after the incidents at the Boatslip, the party in Truro, and the art gallery, he had expected Bill to at least remember his face, if not his name.

"We have a mutual friend – Liam?"

A look of recognition passed over Bill Woodside's face as he fumbled with the papers on the table in front of him. It was clear from his reaction that his dalliance with a much younger man was not one of the subjects he was prepared to discuss at the public hearing. Given his own experiences with Liam, Max could appreciate the sentiment.

"Come to order. Come to order. Everyone please settle down." The mayor's directions and gavel strikes were merely ceremonial since the audience was already sitting quietly in their seats. "This meeting of the Provincetown Council is now in session. The Honorable Mayor John Jacob Masterson is in attendance and hereby presiding."

Referring to oneself in the third person was never a good sign of humility, but in a small seafaring town with a year-round population of only 3,400, beggars couldn't be choosers. Following the brief discussion of a litany of agenda items that ranged from raccoons in the dumpsters to sex in the dunes, the council finally got around to the main event. Under normal circumstances, the zoning discussion would have started with a review of the proposed development plan, but the mayor was determined to give the Cavanaughs the home field advantage.

Although Danny did a capable job of delivering his father's scripted narrative, he stumbled when it came to answering the tough questions. He tried his best to project the Cavanaugh confidence and swagger, but like a little kid trying to walk a big dog, the issues were simply too much for him to handle alone. In the end, the council thanked him for his presentation and then turned the floor over to Bill Woodside.

"Good evening, Mr. Mayor and esteemed members of the Provincetown Council..."

Max knew as soon as the words left Billy's mouth, they were in serious trouble. Every talking point that followed was poised and polished. For almost an hour, the experienced businessman systematically explained the ways his proposal would benefit local businesses and the community at large. Danny Cavanaugh was unquestionably a prince of Provincetown, but Billy made the case that cash is king. The longer he spoke, the more evident it became that the Cavanaughs were fighting a losing battle.

"Mr. Woodside," the mayor said, stopping Bill just when he seemed to be hitting his stride. "This council appreciates the time and money you've invested in this project. Your proposal has a great deal of merit, but as an outsider, you may not fully appreciate Mr. Cavanaugh's interest in protecting the rich, historic integrity of our little fishing village."

"With all due respect, Mr. Mayor," Bill said, trying his best to hide the fact that he secretly thought none was owed to the pompous bureaucrat. "My mother has lived in her house on Bayard Street for over forty years, and I've recently taken up residence in her guesthouse on the property. I may not have deep roots yet, but I'm determined to make Provincetown my permanent home."

"Thank you for volunteering that information. The council will take your comments and presentation under advisement before we make our final decision. Is there anyone else in the audience that would like to come forward at this time and make a statement on this matter? Speak now or forever hold your peace."

The half-full gallery of spectators looked at each other in silence. True to form, the stoic locals seemed determined to prove John Updike's observation that the New England spirit never seeks solutions in a crowd. After a long, pregnant pause, one young man stood and walked up to the podium stationed in the front of the room. Unfolding a piece of notebook paper, he adjusted the microphone and cleared his throat.

"Good evening, Mr. Mayor and members of the council. My name is Max Balais. I've lived in Provincetown my whole life. I've never been the kind of guy to get on my soapbox and preach, but tonight, I've got something to say."

The statement that followed was less practiced and refined than his opponent's presentation. Still, Max had clearly done his homework and was speaking from his heart. He'd only been allotted ten minutes to make his case, but sometimes when you talk less, you say more. Weaving together colorful strands of folklore, historical facts, and hard legal precedent, Max managed to make a compelling argument against approving the proposed development plan.

"Thank you, Mr. Balais. The council will certainly weigh your testimony before we render our final decision," the mayor said, shuffling the stack of papers in front of him to signal his intent to move on to other matters. "I'd like to add that it is refreshing to see such passion and enthusiasm from such a young man. You've given us a lot to think about tonight."

LIKE PRACTICED altar boys, Danny and Max walked in lockstep up the center aisle and out the polished wooden doors of the meeting room. There was no point in sticking around to hear old Mrs. Dewire complain about the noise from the Boatslip or Mr. Harrigan ask again when the council intended to repaint the park benches. It was the same recycled grievances they'd all heard before. For all intents and purposes, the town hall was over.

Luckily, Angel and Josie were waiting for them down on the red brick sidewalk holding a Big Gulp cup.

"Please tell me this is spiked with something stronger than sugar and caffeine," Danny asked as he took the drink and raised it in a mock toast to his inglorious defeat.

"It's as virgin as *moi*," Angel sarcastically quipped as she grabbed her own cocktail from the bench and clinked it against Danny's giant plastic cup. "Cheers, queers!"

"How did it go?"

"I choked." Danny said, ironically coughing up a swallow of a drink that was light on soda and heavy on rum. "Your big brother was the rock star tonight. He had the council and audience eating out of the palm of his hand. Any chance we might still have is because of him, not me."

"Oh, P-L-E-A-S-E!" Josie wailed, taking back the drink from Danny and playfully slapping Max's hand when he reached for a sip. "Don't keep flattering him or his big, swollen head will get even bigger. If I have to hear one more time about that original composition or his rising music career, I swear I'll be sick."

"Sister-to-sister, I know your pain is real," Angel groaned as she joined in to commiserate with Josie. "My mama thinks the sun rises and sets in her only son's big, brown eyes. She acts like he's God's gift to the world or something. Ever since we were kids, all I'd hear, day and night, was '*Hija*, why can't you be more like *su hermano*?'"

"I never knew you had an older brother. What's his name?"

"That's the most delicious part. His name is JESUS!"

"Shut up! Are you serious?"

"No, it's Gino, but it makes for a much better story, *n'est-ce pas*?"

The group was still laughing at Angel's punch line when Max spotted the flashing lights of a police motorcade as it cleared a path up Commercial Street. Trolling a respectable distance behind, a dark sedan with D.C. license plates heralded the arrival of Senator Patrick Donovan.

"That's our cue to skedaddle. See you back at the apartment."

Angel and Josie took what was left of the beverages and scurried up the sidewalk just as the Senator's town car pulled up to the curb. Donovan stepped out of the passenger side and focused his attention on Danny, but Michael Cavanaugh unexpectedly paused as he crossed in front of the car. Anyone else would've written off Angel without a second look, but his honed parental instincts warned him to stop and take notice. Somehow, he knew the young woman was a part of his son's inner circle.

The sight of his father sent Danny's heart into overdrive. If the universe had set up the hearing as some kind of twisted test of his skill and passion for preservation work, then he'd clearly failed. Danny Cavanaugh had many positive attributes, but tonight he'd proved that, when it came to the Foundation, he was not his father's son. Tomorrow morning, his dad would be waiting for him at the breakfast table with an update from the mayor and a look of utter disappointment. The conversation that was sure to follow would dash any lingering doubts either of them had about Danny's future in the family business. As his father traversed the short distance between the car and the sidewalk, there was only one word to describe the feeling that was making Danny's head spin.

Relief.

Twice in one week, his life flashed before his eyes. This time, it was a glimpse of the future, not the past. A big win at the hearing would have sealed Danny's fate. Luckily, that realization came to him early enough to do something about it. Since each of his dad's talking points had been neatly organized on five-by-seven note cards, any fatal mistakes during the formal presentation would have been too obvious. The Q&A was the perfect opportunity for Danny to take advantage of his lack of preparation. With an Ivy League degree, it was hard to come up with dumb answers to easy questions, but he'd managed to pull it off. The entire family would be disappointed by the final outcome, but there were other projects to pursue and better historic properties to save. Danny only had one life to live and he wasn't about to waste it chained to his father's desk.

"Is the hearing over already?" Donovan asked as he consulted his expensive timepiece to confirm what he already knew. They'd arrived too late.

"I'm afraid so, sir."

"How did it go?"

The repetition of the question didn't make it any easier for Danny to look into his father's eyes when he gave the answer. "As well as could be expected, given the circumstances."

"Actually, I think it went great," Max said as he stepped forward to join in on the conversation. "Danny hit all the major points in his presentation and somehow managed to draw out old Mrs. Mooney during the Q&A. I'm pretty sure she's one of the holdout votes we need."

"That's good news, son," Michael said, exhaling in relief at Max's reassurance that there was still some hope for success. "We put you in a difficult spot, but I knew you'd rise to the occasion. You're a Cavanaugh and a born fighter. Let's head home and you can fill me in on all the details."

"Actually, I was planning to crash over at Max's place so we can get an early start in the morning. The first ferry leaves at 8:00 a.m."

"What do you mean? I had no idea you were going to tag along with Max to his audition. I need you here." Michael didn't bother to hide his displeasure at his son's unexpected plans. "I wish you'd bothered to tell me this before now."

"And I didn't know you were going to run off to Hyannis and leave me holding the bag tonight. I guess we're both just full of surprises."

"Danny, I...."

Michael Cavanaugh never got a chance to finish his sentence. Bill Woodside sauntered toward them with his fine linen blazer casually slung over his shoulder. The tension of the situation was made worse by the obvious look of satisfaction on his face. Despite Max's assertions to the contrary, Michael knew his unplanned absence from the town hall had put them at a serious disadvantage.

"It's nice to see you finally made it, Michael." Having a captive audience only seemed to embolden Bill to rub salt in his opponents' open wounds. He may have had many positive attributes, but being a good sport wasn't one of them. "It's a shame you couldn't have gotten here sooner. I'm sure the council would have been impressed with a statement from Senator Donovan."

"Good evening, Bill. I heard you did a fine job making your case. Well done."

Michael Cavanaugh was determined to treat his adversary with decorum and respect, no matter the cost. Danny may have bungled the meeting, but the Cavanaughs still had their family name and reputation. Bill may have had a good night in front of the council, but just being a Woodside wasn't going to get him very far. He'd learn soon enough that in a close-knit community of old families and trusted friends, he could win the battle, but lose the war.

"Can we convince you to join us for a whiskey over at The Mews?"

"I'm afraid I have other plans, but thank you for the invitation, Senator. Good effort tonight, Danny. Better luck next time."

Max felt his face burn red with anger as he watched Bill disappear into the swollen stream of pedestrian traffic on Commercial Street. Michael and Danny seemed to be taking the loss in stride, but Max was far from ready to give up the fight. It was time to stop playing by the rules and steal a page from the varsity playbook. There was one sure thing he'd learned from his nefarious encounters with Liam and Douglas.

Every man has his price.

CHAPTER 13

MAX WOKE to the sound of running water. Instinctively, he pushed his bare bottom toward the wall and tried to make his body as small as possible to squeeze into his single bed. After a month bunking next to Danny, they'd both gotten used to conserving space. He was just drifting back to sleep when a familiar voice called out.

"Rise and shine, Sleeping Beauty."

Max extended a muscled arm to reach for his boyfriend. To his surprise, there were yards of bed, but no body lying next to him. Sighing in relief, he rolled over, and burrowed his face into a mound of down-filled pillows. The freshly pressed linen smelled like lavender and a hot summer night. A noticeable upgrade from his lumpy mattress and musty bedding was the first clue that something was off, but the absence of traffic sounds and the stink of the harbor was a dead giveaway. Begrudgingly, Max opened his eyes to find himself alone in a strange room.

"I'll be out in a minute," Danny's voice echoed from the en suite bathroom, as steam poured out from a partially open door. "It's still early, but we should grab some breakfast and get going."

Shielding his eyes from the sunlight shining in from the windows, Max threw back the blankets and jumped out of the king-sized bed. Despite the August heat, an unnatural chill from the central air conditioning made him shiver. Using his big toe, he poked through the piles of clothes littered across the floor until he found his discarded t-shirt and shorts. The expensive furniture and elegant silk wallpaper on the walls told Max what he already knew: Dorothy wasn't in Kansas anymore.

A cyclone of events from the night before whirled around in his head. By the time he and Danny had finally gotten back to the apartment, they were both too tired to sleep. Adrenaline from the town hall and apprehension about his impending audition had been more potent than caffeine. Sometime after midnight, Danny had come up with a plan to borrow his mom's car and drive them to Boston. The only thing crazier than a late-night road trip was the prospect of spending six long hours tossing and turning in a twin-sized bed. Wide-awake and crawling out of his skin, Max had grabbed his trumpet case and backpack without even bothering to turn on the light.

The open road and a cool breeze were the perfect cure for a bad case of the nerves. Max spent most of the drive staring up through the open sunroof at a sky full of stars while Danny hummed along to a medley of James Taylor's songs on the radio. After a few failed attempts at stilted conversation, they'd fallen into a comfortable silence. Inevitably, they'd have to talk about what would happen come September, but for now, there was too much to say about a future that was still uncertain.

Less than two hours later, Danny inched his mom's Range Rover up a narrow cobblestone street and made a sharp left turn into a gated driveway. The Cavanaugh's Beacon Hill residence seemed even more majestic by the light of gas lanterns and a pale, full moon. Exhausted from the journey, Max followed his boyfriend through the darkened house and right into his bed.

Luckily, what their sleep lacked in quantity, it made up for in quality. Now, instead of waking up early to catch the ferry, they could just relax and enjoy the morning.

Danny emerged from the hot shower, dripping wet, with a towel wrapped loosely around his waist.

"Can you grab me a clean pair of shorts? They're in my closet."

Max wandered into the cavernous walk-in and began rummaging through a built-in dresser. The top shelf revealed a fine leather case with a dozen expensive watches synchronously ticking off the seconds. Locked beneath a layer of glass, each of the Swiss-made timepieces cost more than a fisherman made all summer. The rest of the drawer was devoted to cufflinks and other tuxedo attire. Without thinking, Max grabbed one of the black satin ties and draped it loosely around his neck. It was easy to imagine being a stylish accessory on the arm of Mr. Daniel Cavanaugh as he sauntered into an exclusive party or some swanky event.

After a few false starts, Max finally discovered Danny's unmentionables. Not surprisingly, the rows of perfectly folded briefs looked like a department store display. After spending too much time fingering the soft cotton, he selected a pair of classic white boxers from the bottom of the stack. Max wasn't sure how you could stitch two pieces of cloth together without any visible seams, but apparently "Barneys New York" knew how to do it. Just for fun, he strutted out of the closet wearing nothing but the black satin ribbon hanging loosely around his neck.

"Do you even know how to tie one of those things?" Danny asked as he dropped his damp towel and slipped into the shorts. "Come here and I'll show you."

Danny took Max by the shoulders and spun him a quarter-turn to face the mirror. In less time than it would have taken most guys to tie their shoes, he'd reached around and twisted the loose ends of the fabric into a perfect bow. Satisfied with his handiwork, Danny rested his chin in the crook of Max's neck and let out a breathy whisper.

"Damn, you look hot."

"If this thing with Berklee doesn't pan out, I can always audition for Chippendales."

"You'd be the star of the show. I'd better start saving up my ones for tips."

"Ones? You'll have to make it rain twenties if you want a lap dance from me."

To prove he had the moves to back up his boast, Max did a couple of deep, sexy grinds and arched his back. Right on cue, Danny hooked his thumbs around Max's hip bones and pulled him closer until he felt the hardness of his crotch pressing into the cleft of his boyfriend's ass. The moan that followed told him he was hitting the right spot.

Danny had never dared to have sex under his parent's roof, but the need to have Max was making him reckless. It was impossible to explain the feeling with words, but his body was making the point, loud and clear. Even though the boxer shorts he was wearing didn't have seams, it looked like he was about to bust right out of them.

"I thought you'd be exhausted from last night."

"We did get in pretty late."

"And you did all the driving. Maybe it's my turn to give you a ride?"

"Stop," Danny growled, kissing Max hard to shut him up. "I love the sexual banter, but let's not start something we don't have time to finish."

"What do you mean? My audition isn't until one o'clock. We've got the rest of the morning to play and we have the whole house all to ourselves. Let's take advantage of the privacy and christen every room."

"I guess you forgot about the maid and the butler who live upstairs?"

"I thought you told me the staff kept mostly to themselves when your parents were away?"

"They do, but I'm not sure Martha would appreciate having to wipe your sweaty ass prints off the kitchen counter. Besides, we've got the rest of the weekend to fool around. Today, we're going to put your mouth where the money is. Grab your horn and let's go."

"Like this?"

"I meant your trumpet. Seriously, Max. Put on some pants on and let's roll."

EVEN IN the peak of summer, Harvard Square was abuzz with visitors. Berklee was waiting on the other side of the Charles River, but Danny wanted to give Max a taste of what it would be like to live as a student in Boston.

"So why is the Harvard bookstore called 'The COOP?' Please tell me it's not because they sell chickens."

"Actually, livestock's one of the only things they don't sell in there. It's not what you'd call a traditional bookstore," Danny said, leading Max out the front door and back into the open square. "It's a co-operative organization that students can join for just a buck a year. The COOP shares a portion of its sales profits to its members in the form of a 10% discount. I'm not exactly sure how it works, but apparently they keep the profit margin on textbooks low for the benefit of students and offer higher margin merchandise to the general public."

"That's a pretty modern business arrangement for such an old school."

"Actually, The COOP opened for business back in 1882. There are a couple other locations, but I wanted you to see this one. I also think Harvard Square is a great spot for you to warm up for your big audition."

"Here? Now?"

"No time like the present. Let's see what you've got."

Max cracked his knuckles and gently deposited his trumpet case on the sidewalk at his feet. Beneath the lid, his shiny brass instrument was resting on a soft bed of purple velvet. Applause from an audience was just what he needed to boost his confidence. The blare of car horns and the grating sound of a truck shifting gears would be the perfect accompaniment for his original composition about life in the big city.

As he'd done hundreds of times before, Max wiped down his horn with a clean cloth and opened the smaller compartment inside so he could assemble his instrument.

"No! This isn't possible."

"What's wrong?"

"My mouthpiece. It's not here."

Max checked the pockets of his shorts, but they were empty. As panic took hold, he turned the trumpet case upside down and shook it hard. Hidden inside the lining, a few nickels and dimes fell out and clinked against the sidewalk. Even though there was no place else to look, Max repeated the process again, hoping for a different result. Each time he came up empty handed.

"When was the last time you practiced?"

"Yesterday," Max said, mentally retracing his steps back to the apartment. He remembered going through each of his audition pieces twice. It had taken almost an hour for him to clean the instrument and oil the valves. Max used to joke that he could put his horn back together with his eyes closed. Although he couldn't remember doing it, he must have left the mouthpiece in the dish drainer next to the kitchen sink.

"There's no way I can play this afternoon."

"You'll just have to call Berklee and explain what happened. I'm sure they'll let you reschedule."

"No way. I got the last spot. The secretary told me the Admissions Committee meets Monday morning to make their final decision about how to fill the last few vacancies. School starts in less than a month."

Instead of screaming out loud and cursing his fate, Max gently interred his trumpet in its casket and shut the lid. There was no one to blame but himself for such a bonehead move. Like a bad Greek tragedy, the mighty hero had ended up being his own worst enemy. Now, the story was over. It was time to just go home and accept his fate.

"There's no way we're giving up without a fight," Danny said, slapping Max on the back and scanning the names of the storefronts. "Stay here. I'll be right back."

Without waiting for a response, Danny darted into The COOP while Max slumped down onto one of the benches. It was a beautiful summer day and the square was packed. On a nearby corner, a handsome, young musician was gently strumming an acoustic guitar. He was too far away to make out the song, but Max could tell by size of the crowd that the guy was really good.

Hot, wet tears rolled down his face as Max thought about the music he'd never make. Secretly, a small part of him was relieved to know he'd be staying in Provincetown. Assuming the town council decided in their favor, he could probably convince Michael to keep him on full-time at the Foundation. It would be hard to work alongside Danny every day and keep their relationship hidden, but eventually the Cavanaughs would figure out the truth about their son and his friend. Max was starting to see how he could parlay his mistake into a real future. Still, it would have been nice to have actually chosen that option rather than ending up there by default.

In less time than it took for him to start feeling sorry for himself, Danny was back, wearing a grin that instantly filled Max with both dread and hope.

"We're in business."

"Are you kidding me? The COOP sells musical instruments?"

"Even *you* aren't that lucky," Danny said, picking up Max's trumpet case and leading him across the sidewalk toward one of Harvard's entrance gates. "I noticed one of the stock boys checking you out. He was dressed all in black and seemed like the artsy type. His name is Winston, and it turns out he's got a friend who plays in a jazz band. He'll make a call and meet us over by the dorms in twenty minutes."

Harvard Yard was like the eye of a hurricane. Outside campus, traffic zoomed up and down Mass Ave as tourists frequented the eclectic restaurants and shops. But inside the ivy-covered walls, the mood could only be described as serene. Max had focused so much on his audition that he'd forgotten his plans to attend Berklee also included taking classes and making new friends. Even with a good job and a great boyfriend, he'd never have the opportunity to experience much beyond the insulated community where he'd lived his whole life if he stayed in Provincetown. Suddenly aware that he might be losing more than the chance to make music, Max slumped down on the concrete steps outside one of the old, venerated halls and watched as the rest of the world passed him by.

The next ten minutes were the longest of his life. Just when he was ready to give up, a slovenly dressed sophomore came barreling across the yard on a ten-speed bike.

"Hey, I'm Jamie," the young man called out, introducing himself as he braked hard and skidded to a stop. "Which one of you guys is the musician?"

Visibly blushing, Max raised his right hand and stepped forward. Holding his breath, he waited to find out whether there was still a chance for him to get his shot.

"I got you two mouthpieces. They're used, but the guy who gave them to me went to Exeter, so you'll probably be O.K. putting your mouth on them. Put one in your case and give the other to your friend for safekeeping."

Max took the metal pieces and a tattered scrap of paper from Jamie. He stuffed the note and one of the mouthpieces inside his trumpet case and handed Danny the spare. Without waiting to be thanked, Jamie lifted his bike off the ground and pointed it back in the opposite direction.

"Wait! Can I pay you for these?"

"Nah, we're good. I gave you my contact information. Look me up when you get back to town and we can grab coffee – your treat."

"Deal!"

Max was more than happy to agree to the arrangement, especially since he only had seven bucks left in his wallet. Walking in a daze, he followed Danny back to the square and pulled his trumpet from the case. The borrowed mouthpieces may have been used, but they looked practically new. Max fitted one into the neck of his instrument and raised it to his lips. Unlike reeds and strings, you didn't need to break in a horn. By all rights, he should've been able to just pick up his instrument and play, but something was holding him back.

Max stared at a fixed point on the ground and tried to block out the distractions. The sidewalk in front of Town Hall had its fair share of colorful characters, but there was a big difference between playing over the din of a crying kid and blocking out the discord of a major city. Pulling in a breath, he held it in his diaphragm and listened for the first note inside his head. Once it was firmly in place, Max depressed the first and third valves of his trumpet and blasted out a run.

It wasn't long before a small crowd gathered around. Unlike the other beatniks performing around the Square, the blond-haired, blue-eyed musician looked as good as he played. Max tried to keep his attention focused on the melody and rhythm of the song, but too many eyes felt like ants crawling over his skin. He barely managed to make it through the set before his breath faltered and the music slipped away.

Like minnows in a tidal pond, the audience scattered. Although a few people lingered around the periphery to see if the musician would do an encore, the look on his face made it clear the show was over. At first, Danny assumed Max was just concerned about how long it would take to get over to Berklee, but something about the tightness of his movements suggested he was worried about more than the time.

"Why did you stop? That was perfect."

"No, it wasn't. I messed up a couple different times in the second movement."

"You could've fooled me."

"That wouldn't be very hard to do," Max said, slamming his trumpet case closed and spinning around to face Danny. "You've always had a tin ear. You wouldn't know an F sharp if it bit you on the ass."

"Stop trying to pick a fight and tell me what's really going on."

"You heard me play. I'm just an average street performer, nothing more. I was kidding myself to think I could actually get into a REAL music school. Maybe forgetting my mouthpiece was just my subconscious saving me from making an ass of myself at this audition."

"O.K., stop. I know this is a lot to take in and coming to Harvard Square was probably a mistake. Let's go somewhere quiet and chill."

"I need to head over to my audition. I'm going to be late…"

"It's not even eleven yet, so we still have a couple hours to kill," Danny said, holding up his hand to signal for a cab. "Come with me. There's a someplace I want you to see."

"THIS IS *not* what I thought you had in mind when you said you were taking me to 'Pleasure Bay,'" Max quipped as he walked beside Danny along the scenic Boston Harbor Walk. "You know we've got pretty nice views of the ocean back in Provincetown, right?"

Despite the sarcasm, Max seemed noticeably more relaxed as his eyes charted the vast archipelago of islands scattered across the bay. The wind off the open water was noticeably cooler and the air smelled like home.

"Right now, we're on Castle Island. Over there is Pleasure Bay Beach. Back in high school, my dad used to bring me here when I needed a break from the city. I wanted you to see this place and experience Fort Independence. I'm sure a history buff like you already knows all about it."

"Actually, no."

"The first known garrison at this site dates back to 1630, which makes this one of the oldest fortified English military sites in North America. During the Revolutionary War, the British occupied it as Fort William and Mary until George Washington scared them away with an arsenal of cannons. The Redcoats burned the citadel to the ground and retreated all the way back to Halifax, Nova Scotia. It was eventually rebuilt in granite and renamed Fort Independence. Edgar Allan Poe was stationed here for five months in 1827 and was inspired to write the short story *The Cask of Amontillado* based on an old Castle Island legend."

"If this is your idea of nerdy foreplay," Max said, leaning closer to whisper discreetly into Danny's ear. "You should know, it's working. Keep talking."

"My family wasn't always rich. The Cavanaughs originally hail from a neighborhood that's not far from here called Dorchester Heights. Until recently, it was just a working class, Irish-American neighborhood of South Boston."

"Yeah, until Matt Damon and Ben Affleck put 'Southie' on the map in *Good Will Hunting*," Max said, feeling more anxious than aroused as the minutes ticked on. "Now, it's one of the city's hottest real estate markets. Your great-great-grandfather may have had humble beginnings, but at least he was living in a city and not stuck in the middle of nowhere."

"That's where you're wrong. Originally, Boston was a water-locked peninsula that was only connected to the mainland by a narrow isthmus called the Roxbury Neck. Eventually, the surrounding area was filled in and the land became part of the South End. Even though it's no longer considered separate from Boston, there was a time not so long ago when Dorchester Heights probably felt a lot like Provincetown. Hell, there's even a neighborhood called Telegraph Hill."

"And your point is...?"

"You're bigger than the place you came from," Danny said as he pulled his boyfriend into his arms and held him tight. The very public display of affection was attracting more attention than Max's recent performance, but he didn't mind.

"I'm not sure if I even want to go to Berklee anymore," Max whispered into Danny's shoulder as he looked out across the vast expanse of ocean toward home. "I love my job at the Foundation and, if I wait another year, I'll have even more money saved for school. That would also give us more time to figure out how we can make this relationship work. It's a win-win for everyone."

"Sorry, Champ. Life isn't a non-contact sport where you get a trophy for showing up. If you want a win, you've got to earn it. Now, let's get you over to Berklee. There's an Admissions Committee that's waiting to hear you play."

DANNY PACED up and down the sidewalk outside the Performance Center. Unlike Harvard or Dartmouth, Berklee was an urban school made of concrete and chrome, not brick and mortar. In stark contrast to the stuffy institutions choking on ivy and tradition, the contemporary look and feel of the campus reflected the vibrant creative energy of its students and curriculum.

Danny had just got done holding the door open for a trio of musicians burdened with instrument cases when he spotted Max in the lobby, talking to a stern-faced woman who was barely half his size. Dressed in vintage Chanel with her auburn hair in a tight bun, she was either a world-famous performer or a member of the faculty. Danny couldn't shake the sense that he'd seen her before, so chances are she was both. Trying not to be obvious, he stood just inside the entrance closer and waited.

After what seemed like forever, Max shook the woman's well-manicured hand and made a beeline for the nearest exit. Luckily, his boyfriend was waiting for him at the door.

"How did it go?"

"I bombed."

"Seriously?"

"Nope. I totally nailed it."

Without thinking, Danny pulled Max into his arms and kissed him. Even though his lips were still numb from playing, Max could still feel the pressure.

"I knew you'd blow them away. I'm so proud of you."

Max felt like his heart was going to explode inside his chest. All his life, he'd been fighting to prove himself to the world. Now, Danny's opinion was the only one that mattered.

"So, I wanted to give you something."

"If it's some more PDA, I'll take it," Max said as he tried to pull his boyfriend in for another kiss.

"No, I mean I actually got you a present."

Danny handed Max a plastic bag and led him over to a nearby bench to sit down. Max reached inside and pulled out a heavy hooded sweatshirt with the word "BERKLEE" embroidered in block letters across the front.

"Isn't this bad luck? I haven't gotten in yet."

"That's just a technicality. You'll need this come winter."

"I'd rather have your arms to keep me warm."

"I think you've earned that and more. Let's go home."

Max would have preferred to take the "T" back to Beacon Hill, but a taxi was faster than the subway. As instructed, the driver dropped them at the bottom of the cobblestone street rather than taking them up to the house. Walking a respectable distance apart in case someone was watching on the closed-circuit security cameras, Max followed as Danny led him across the courtyard and through the back door.

A CHILLED bottle of Dom Perignon and two crystal flutes were waiting on the bedside table in Danny's softly lit room.

"Champagne?" Max asked as he felt his heart skip a beat. "I thought we were trying to be discreet?"

"We are. I asked Jeffrey to set this up and then gave him my credit card to take Martha out for a night on the town. We've got the whole place to ourselves."

Danny Cavanaugh had been Max's best friend for as long as he could remember, but the man standing in front of him felt like a stranger. The romantic gestures only punctuated the significance of the occasion. Exhaustion or lack of opportunity had always been a convenient excuse to put off going "all the way." In truth, fooling around had turned out to be anything but. Max was no virgin, but he was about to do something with Danny he'd never done before. Sex was just sex, until it wasn't. What was about to happen would confirm what he was already feeling, something that was undeniably love. Once he admitted the truth to himself and Danny, there'd be no going back.

"Hey, breathe."

Danny kicked off his worn-in docksiders and slinked out of his polo. Like a game of strip poker without the playing cards, Max matched his boyfriend's wager, hand for hand, until they were both all in.

Shirt. Pants. Boxers.

Each piece of clothing that fell to the floor was like another barrier between them gone. It would have been easy enough to just fall back into their usual routine, but they'd built it up too much to chicken out now.

"So, how do we figure out who is going to do who?"

"Actually, it's 'do whom,' but I get what you mean."

"Let's just say if we flipped a coin, I'd call tails."

"Got it."

Since Max and Danny's first time together, the choreography of sex had always been linear. Kissing led to touching and tugging until one of them went down on the other. They might switch off a couple of times and take turns, but it was never very long before one of them got too excited and shot his load. The finish for whoever came last was almost always a little bit awkward. Even when the sex was hot, and it usually was, there was a sense of disappointment about a solo ending.

Danny hovered over Max. The lust smoldering behind his eyes had been replaced with a look of sheer determination. Unlike so many uncertainties in his life, this was exactly what he wanted. Wrapping his arms around Max, he pulled him into a tight embrace and rolled them both over. As Max pulled away and sat up, Danny grabbed his hamstrings and lifted his knees toward his chest.

With an unsteady hand, Max snatched the small bottle of lube from his backpack and squirted a generous portion into his palm. Careful not to spill any on the expensive Oriental carpet, he slathered a thick glob on himself and rubbed the rest into the gully of Danny's ass.

"Fuck! How is that jelly so ice-cold?"

"Shhhhh! You'll ruin the mood."

Max scooted forward into position and used his thumbs and fingers to bend his hard-on to the right angle. Following his boyfriend's lead, Danny pulled his knees back even further into his chest and lifted his ass. As the head of his cock pressed into the warm, soft spot, Max felt Danny's body tense up in anticipation.

"Hey, breathe."

Annoyed at hearing his own words repeated back to him, Danny emptied his lungs in three short puffs and filled them up again with one long inhale. It was hard not to wonder how many of his ex-girlfriends had silently endured a similar discomfort because of his haste and inexperience. Tonight, he was finding out the hard way that karma was a bitch. What was happening felt more clinical than carnal, but it was too late to turn back now.

"I'm ready, but go slow."

Max inched the tip of his shaft forward and applied steady pressure. The opening was as tight as a fist, but with persistence and a little probing, the muscle relaxed and he slid inside Danny like a key into a lock. Certain that the worst was behind them, Max stopped and waited for Danny to get used to the sensation. As the seconds passed, he felt his strained triceps began to tremble under the weight of his upper body. A few minor adjustments would have eased his discomfort, but it was a small price to pay for the privilege of being Danny's first. It was such a cruel paradox. How could something that brought one guy so much pleasure cause his lover so much pain? Max had just wondered whether he should pull out and take a break when Danny cupped his buttocks and pulled him in.

With his fingertips firmly rooted on Max's hips, Danny controlled the speed and depth of each penetration. Every nerve in his body told him to push harder and go faster, but Max willed himself to stay in the moment and be cool. After a dozen slow, shallow thrusts, he leaned forward to wipe his boyfriend's sweaty brow.

"It feels amazing," Danny gasped. "Give me more."

Max felt a part of him let go as he grabbed onto Danny's ankles and lifted them onto his shoulders. The passionate kisses and soft moans confirmed that it was time to take things to the next level. Even though Max loved the sensation of being inside another body, watching his boyfriend get off was even hotter than the sex. Slower, longer, deeper strokes or short, rapid thrusts – for every action there was an equal and opposite reaction. Danny may have been on the bottom, but he was giving his top the ride of his life.

In less time than he'd expected, Max sensed the shift in his body that signaled he was heading toward an epic climax. Without thinking, he clutched Danny's erection and began rhythmically stroking it to match the pace of his strokes.

"Stop," Danny pleaded as he grabbed the back of Max's head and pulled him close. "You're going to make me come."

"Don't worry, I'm close too. Just relax and let go."

The end, when it finally came, was epic. Just as Danny began to shoot, Max felt the tight muscles around his cock contract in a spasm that took him right over the edge. Gasping for air, he managed to lock eyes with Danny at just the right moment. The look on his face was the answer to every question Max had ever had about the future.

Thirty minutes later, Max emerged from a hot, steamy shower to find Danny waiting for him in a freshly made bed. Clean and satisfied, he stumbled across the room on legs that had turned to rubber and climbed under the comforter.

"Please tell me that Martha didn't sneak in and switch out the dirty sheets while we were in the shower."

"You may not believe this, but I know how to find the linen closet. All the forensic evidence is down in the washing machine. I'll get up early and put everything away before we head back to Provincetown."

"Tomorrow? I was hoping we could spend the weekend exploring Boston."

"I wish we could." Danny said, forcing back a yawn. "But I have a shift on *La Benedita* tomorrow afternoon and a thing with my parents on Sunday. Still...."

"We've got tonight."

"Who needs tomorrow?"

"Let's make it last."

"Let's find a way."

CHAPTER 14

THE ATLANTIC Ocean stretched out to the horizon as the ferry inched its way toward Provincetown. Hugging close to the coast, the boat bounced over white caps, rocking to and fro in a rhythmic motion that made Max feel sleepy and most of the other passengers sick. Fortunately, the crew was ready with ginger-flavored lollipops for nausea and barf bags for the handful of landlubbers who were too far gone. With the end of summer just a few weeks away and traffic backed up to Plymouth, Danny had decided to leave his car in Boston. Given the unique geography of Provincetown, drivers had no choice but to take the same road out and back. Yearning for fresh air and a change of scenery, he and Max had grabbed two large coffees from Dunkin' Donuts and caught the high-speed ferry home.

Like *Top Gun* fighter pilots, a squadron of black-hooded laughing gulls drifted on thermals in the skies above the boat. Using the position of their wings to deflect the currents of warm air downward, the birds created an updraft that kept them aloft. Gliding motionless, the keen hunters studied the surface of the water and executed a stooping dive, straight down, to catch their prey. As a fisherman, Max had a fractured peace with the birds, but he'd always been impressed by their devotion. Like penguins and eagles, seagulls were monogamous creatures that mated for life.

After only ninety minutes, the boat rounded the horn of Cape Cod at the very tip, where a thin neck of sea grass and sand connected Long Point to the mainland. Tall and slender, the Pilgrim Monument loomed in the distance, welcoming tourists to Provincetown as its short, squatty cousin kept vigil over the harbor. Described in the U.S. Coast Guard list as a "white square tower," the simple lighthouse was constructed in 1827 to warn ships of the sandbar that extended a quarter mile from the shore out to sea. Although the light was no longer needed for navigation, automation and solar power kept the flashing green signal shining for historic and aesthetic purposes.

The motors of the ferry ground down to a mechanical hum as the boat adjusted its speed and direction. To the untrained eye, it looked as though it was on a collision course with the end of MacMillan Pier, but at the last moment, the captain reversed the engines and the boat lurched backward.

Like a foul witches' brew, the water around the hull churned and bubbled as the acrid stench of diesel fuel polluted the air. Max watched the deckhands spring to life, securing the mooring lines, and dragging the metal gangplank into place. Reflexively, he rubbed his wrist and fought the urge to step in and help. Even though the tendons in his hand had healed, Danny had offered to finish out the season on *La Benedita*. If everything went according to plan with Berklee, Max would have to give his coveted spot on the crew to someone else.

Although they'd only been gone for a day, Max sensed a subtle change as soon as he stepped off the ferry. The weather was still hot and balmy, but the light was different in a way that signaled the coming of fall. Tossing his backpack over his shoulder, he led the way as they walked toward Commercial Street.

At the end of the pier, where the weathered wooded planks transitioned to concrete, Michael Cavanaugh was waiting. Just off to the side, his luxury car was parked inside the painted white stripes with its hazard lights flashing. Even without such an obvious signal, it was clear that Danny's dad was about to deliver bad news.

"Good morning," Michael said, trying to sound cheerful as he forced out a weak smile. "I hope you boys had an easy trip back."

"There was a fair amount of chop, but nothing we couldn't handle," Danny said as he walked right past the waiting car. Unfortunately, his dad wasn't about to let him slip away again.

"Let me drive you home," Michael said. He didn't seem angry or put out, but it was clear from his tone that he was giving an order, not making a request.

"Actually, a ride sounds better than walking all the way back through town," Max said, trying his best to mend the sudden rift that had opened between father and son. Rather than make Danny nostalgic for his family, their night at the house on Beacon Hill had only confirmed the adage Max had been struggling with all summer— you can't go home again.

"Sorry, but I need to speak with my son, alone. We have something important to discuss."

"Anything you have to say to me, you can say in front of him. Max is my best friend."

"Let's stop with the pretense," Michael said, putting up both his hands as a signal for Danny to step back from the proverbial cliff where he was standing. "We both know he's more than that. Max is an important part of the work we are doing at the Foundation, but this is a family matter."

"Max is my family, dad. Until you accept that, we've got nothing to discuss."

"Fair enough," Michael said, leaning back against his car and crossing his arms. "I'll save you the trouble of having to tell him the news yourself later. Yesterday, Bill Woodside stopped by the house to tell me he's received a verbal approval from the mayor to move forward with his development plan. Given that he already had most of the votes he needed, it wasn't a total surprise. I spent half the night sitting out on the deck, crying in my beer, but this morning I got up and started making phone calls. One of my contacts in Lisbon, João-Filipe Pires, owns a ruined Franciscan abbey near the Santuario da Peninha in Sintra, and he's looking for an angel funder to oversee the restoration. It's a five-year initiative that will involve architects and historians from Universidade de Lisboa. Given that you're fluent in Portuguese and have experience with construction, we think you should be the one to head up the project."

Too late, Danny realized how he'd forced his father's hand by sabotaging his presentation at the town hall. If Bill Woodside's plans were approved, there'd be no local properties to preserve and no Foundation job in Provincetown. The only thing Michael Cavanaugh cared about more than his work was his family. Determined to keep his son on the straight and narrow path, he'd come up with an elaborate plan that would take Danny far from home.

Max pretended to study the horizon as he fought back tears. In the clear, bright morning light, the hulls of the boats bobbing on the harbor seemed Technicolor. Two small children were flying a kite down on the ribbon of beach that separated Commercial Street from the sea. Like a pair of gulls, their playful shrieks and cries rang out each time another gust of wind pulled the toy higher and further into the air.

Last night, Danny had been on cloud nine, but his father's offer had just brought him crashing back down to earth. Suddenly, his pipe dream of going back to Portugal and building a new life was a viable option. Even with a full-time job, he'd still have evenings and weekends free to sketch and hang out with his friends. As much as Danny hated the idea of leaving Max behind, this was his one chance to do something creative in a place he loved.

"I need to go somewhere quiet to work all this through."

"Let's head back to the house, son. We can open a bottle of Jameson Reserve and talk about your future." Michael's tone was noticeably kinder now that his trap had been sprung. "I promised João we'd get him a commitment letter by the end of the week."

"You shouldn't make promises you can't keep," Danny growled at his father through clenched teeth. "I just told you I needed time and space to think. I'm taking the sailboat out, but I'll be back before dark."

Instinctively, Max started to follow him back down the pier toward the Cavanaugh slip, but he only got a few feet before Danny spun around and gave him a look that warned him to keep his distance.

"I really want to be alone. I'll come find you later."

Without waiting for a reply, Danny took off and disappeared into the steady stream of tourists still disembarking from the morning ferry. Eager to start a weeklong summer vacation, their laughter and chatter was louder than the engines. Unlike other hubs that were a layover on the way to someplace else, Provincetown was everyone's final destination. Waiting in a long line that snaked down the edge of the pier, their doppelgangers wore a look of sadness and despair as they waited to take the ferry back to Boston. Max knew exactly how they were feeling. The party was over.

A HALF a mile offshore, in the middle of harbor, Max sat on a huge granite boulder and stared out at the panoramic view of Provincetown. During the day, adventurists loved to hike across the uneven stones that extended from Stevens Point across House Point Island Flats to the sandy spit at Wood End. Although tourists affectionately referred to the man-made structure as the Breakwater, it was actually the Long Point Dike, built to prevent the kind of erosive flooding that would've isolated the narrow peninsula from the mainland and filled the western half of the harbor with sand. Most locals just called it the jetty. Although well intentioned, the construction of the massive embankment may have caused more harm than good by impeding the ebb and flow of water into the salt marsh.

Secretly, Max wondered if he was also risking irreparable damage by tampering with the fragile ecosystem he'd created with Danny, trying to hold back the tides that were pulling them away. Scheming and dreaming, Max had done everything he could to escape a life that was too small for his ambitions. How could he deny Danny the same chance for happiness? Staring down into the jade-green tidal pool for an answer, Max tossed a small piece of driftwood into the water and watched as the current carried it back toward shore. Provincetown seemed to have a way of reclaiming its own.

Despite his promise to bring the boat back before dark, Danny radioed his dad before sundown to let him know he'd decided to extend his trip. He ended up staying out at sea for three long days. Like a good sailor, he'd routinely checked in to let his parents know he was okay, but his prolonged absence felt like an ominous S.O.S.

Max was almost back to shore when he noticed a figure making his way toward him across the jetty. It was almost dark and the tide was coming in fast, but Danny was moving like a man on a mission. Skipping across the broken surface of the rocks, he'd made the trip enough times to know all the hidden pitfalls along the way.

"I got back about an hour ago, but I stopped by the house to talk to my dad and grab something from my room."

"So, it sounds like you're seriously considering his offer."

"If things had worked out differently at the town hall, I'd stay. But as things stand, I don't really have any choice."

"You could come with me to Boston," Max said, knowing even as the words left his mouth that Danny wasn't about to follow him to Berklee and live in his shadow. Besides, he'd been talking about his adventures at ULisboa since his junior year abroad.

"I think you need to go make music and I need to do my own thing in Portugal."

"So, where does that leave *us*? You're going to just fly away and forget all about me?"

"You are many things, Max Balais, but forgettable is not one of them. I know Lisbon is far away, but we've been friends forever. If anyone can manage a long-distance relationship, it's us. I promise to keep in touch, and we'll spend time together over the summer holidays."

"You shouldn't make promises you can't keep."

"Please don't use my own words against me," Danny said, as he pulled something from his pocket and placed it in Max's open hand. "Maybe what you need is an old-school, romantic gesture to show you how I feel."

Careful not to drop it, Max extended a length of gold chain and let the ring attached to it dangle in front of him. The failing sunlight danced across the gilded surface as he touched it with his fingertips and brought it closer for inspection. Max didn't speak Latin, but the etched insignia on the face of the signet and the word "Dartmouth" were a dead giveaway.

"Are you seriously asking me to 'go steady'?"

"Not quite, but I do want you to wear it. That way, even when I'm away, a part of me will still be with you."

"You know most guys wear a ring on their finger. What's the deal with the chain?"

"I'm not ready for the whole world to know about *us* just yet. Besides, this way you can keep it close to your heart."

"Given how often I'm shirtless, I should probably tuck it away until I get to Boston."

"You've got a point, but just don't lose it."

Max slipped the chain into his front pocket and fingered the outline of the ring through the fabric of his shorts to make sure it was safe and sound. Due east, far across the Atlantic, Lisbon was waiting. Max knew Danny meant every word he was saying, but the road to hell was paved with good intentions. Time and distance might make their relationship stronger, but it was also possible that it would tear it apart. Max needed to get at least one of the local properties back into play so there'd be work to keep Danny in Provincetown. Since the town council had already signaled their intent to approve the development proposal, there was only one person who could make that happen. Bill Woodside was a shrewd businessman, but Liam had said it best that first night at the Boatslip.

Everyone has a price. You just have to find out what it is.

Savvy men bartered with money or power, but Max didn't have either of those things at his disposal. Luckily, he had something else of value to offer. Max was going to make Billy an offer he couldn't refuse.

THE LATCH to the front gate creaked out a warning as Max slipped inside Florence Woodside's yard. The street was dark, but the full moon illuminated a path of flagstones that snaked past the main house and into the back. A single light twinkled in one of the upstairs bedrooms as lace curtains billowed out of the open window. For a second, Max though he saw a face, white like a ghost, staring down at him. But when he looked again, there was no one there.

Bill Woodside's guest cottage was a miniature version of his mother's house. Nestled between two young maple trees, the one-bedroom bungalow had a gabled roof and a fire engine-red door flanked by four-paned windows. Sitting in a rocking chair on the front porch, Bill looked as if he'd been waiting for Max to arrive.

"Grrrrrr. Whoof."

The scruffy little dog's growl sounded less like a warning and more like a motor that needed to be tuned. By the look of it, the animal couldn't have weighed more than ten pounds. Even so, it was clear from his demeanor that the Jack Russell terrier had developed an incurable case of Small Dog Syndrome: standing tall on its hind legs, the little pup seemed convinced he was the leader of his pack. Max dropped down to his haunches and stretched out a hand. Sniffing the air, the temperamental cur took a few tentative steps backward and quickly scurried away.

"Don't take it personally," a disembodied voice said from the shadows of the porch. "Chance is a male, but he can be a real bitch. I'm his master and he acts like he doesn't even trust me."

"Well, you know what they say," Max asked, rising up to his full height and thrusting out his chest. "You can't fool kids or dogs."

"Ouch! That hurts."

Bill Woodside chuckled at the subtle dig and struck a match. The momentary burst of light illuminated his face as he lit a citronella candle and then sank back into his chair.

"So, to what do I owe the pleasure of this visit? Don't tell me you've come to congratulate me on my impending victory over the noble Cavanaughs?"

"It looks like you're doing a pretty good job celebrating on your own," Max said, glancing down at the nearly empty bottle of Grey Goose sitting on the first step of the porch. Given Bill's glossy eyes and red glow, Max suspected it had probably been full when the evening began.

"I've been toasting my success, but I hate to drink alone. Will you join me?"

"Sure."

Bill poured some vodka into a glass and passed it to his guest. As Max took it, their fingers touched and a spark of electricity passed between them. It was then that he knew for sure his plan could work. With his fortune already made, Bill Woodside wanted what his money couldn't buy. Max knew he'd jump at the chance to feel young and desired, but the illusion required the younger man to be the aggressor and make the first move.

"Let's cut to the chase," Max said, lifting the glass to his lips and pretending to drink. "We both know there are a couple properties in the mix that don't really fit into your plan. I was hoping you might just let the Foundation have them as a consolation prize."

"Come on, Max. There's a big difference between gifting you an oil painting and giving away a valuable parcel of land."

"Even if I was willing to make you the same offer I made your friend Douglas at the gallery?"

"Ah, well." Bill said, taking a long swallow of his drink before he stood up and answered the question. "Now, *that's* a different kind of proposition."

"Do we have a deal?" Max asked in a low, deep voice as he stepped forward and undid the top button of his shirt. "Let's shake on it."

Without waiting for an affirmative reply, Max cupped the front of Bill's pants and squeezed. Dozing beneath a thin layer of fabric, Bill's flaccid cock stirred awake and stiffened. Breathing hard, Bill leaned in for a kiss, but Max abruptly turned his head away.

"No. Anything but that."

"But *that's* the best part. Look, if you're not really feeling this, then maybe we should call the whole thing off. You're either all in or you're not."

Max closed his eyes and pictured Danny standing at the Breakwater, promising not to forget him. Giving himself to Bill was the only way to make sure that didn't happen. One night meant nothing in the grand scheme of things if it bought Max a future of tomorrows with Danny.

Max lifted his chin and looked Bill squarely in the eyes. Slowly, he wrapped both hands around the back of Bill's head and pulled him in for a passionate kiss. His lips were soft, but his breath tasted sour, like premium vodka and cheap lies. Like a good performer, Max knew how to put on a show, even when he wasn't down with the vibe. Knowing what would turn him on, Max slid his tongue in and out of Bill's open mouth and bit down gently on his bottom lip.

"Maybe we should take this inside."

Max followed Bill up the steps of his porch but stopped short outside the front door. Having sex was one thing, but he wasn't about to let another guy take him to his bed. Without stopping to consider the consequences, Max pulled off his shirt and slipped out of his cargo shorts.

"Right here?" Bill asked in a voice that was heady with liquor and lust. "How do you want this to happen?"

"Do me."

Max turned around and grabbed on tight to the wooden railing in front of him. With his knees slightly bent, he lifted his ass into the air and pushed it back suggestively into Bill's crotch. Hot breath on the small of Max's back sent a shiver up his spine as Bill grabbed his hips and pulled him closer. Suddenly, the same tongue that had just been in Max's mouth began poking and prodding as a preview of what was to come.

Moving at a slow, deliberate pace, Bill savored his young lover's ass like an ice cream cone, licking rapidly around the rim and circling in long, fervent swirls. Just when Max thought he'd explode from the sensation, he felt one finger, then two, slip deep inside him. Instead of roughly plunging in and out, Bill bent his digits back in a "come here" motion that put just the right amount of pressure on the perfect spot.

Max tried to stay detached from what was happening, but what the sex lacked in romance, it made up for in heat.

"That feels amazing."

"It's about to get even better."

"Wait!" Max gasped, grabbing his shorts from the ground and rummaging through the pockets.

"Hate the game, not the player," Bill whispered under his breath as he watched Max pull out a condom and a small plastic vial of lube. Eager to suit up before his partner changed his mind, Bill unrolled a sheath onto his hard-on and slathered himself with the slippery gel.

Max expected discomfort, the all-too-familiar burning sensation that seemed an intrinsic part of the experience when a man forced himself into his inner core. What he never anticipated was how good it would feel to be with someone who knew how to separate pleasure from the pain. With each tug and thrust, Max felt himself surrendering to the intensity of the moment. Somewhere along the way, he stopped thinking about Danny and focused his full attention on the man rutting inside him. Instead of feeling disgusted and repulsed, Max was secretly reveling in a sense of power and control he'd never known before.

After what felt like forever, Bill wrapped his hands around Max's broad shoulders and rammed the full weight of his body forward. Engaging his core to stabilize his frame, Max took a deep breath and closed his eyes. Bill repeated the move in four quick successions before he gasped and collapsed. One last time, he leaned forward and tenderly kissed Max on the lips. Although brief, the intimacy of the gesture made it clear he was feeling something more than lust. Sex was just sex, until it wasn't.

Wearing a look that warned he was satisfied but not finished, Bill carefully pulled out and dropped down to his knees.

"Wait!" Max said as he grabbed Bill by the shoulders to hold him back. "You don't need to do that."

"You just gave me the fuck of my life. There's no way I'm sending you home without getting you off."

Reluctantly, Max leaned back against the railing and pulled his hands away. Over the years, he'd had his fair share of hurried blowjobs, but Bill was teaching a master class in the art of oral sex. With unexpected proficiency, he used his tongue and hands to finish Max off in a climax that left him breathless. The only thing stronger than the feeling of satisfaction was the sickening pang of regret.

The tenet that the means justifies the ends echoed in Max's head as he considered the gravity of what he'd done. It really didn't matter if he was prostituting himself for multimillion-dollar real estate or pocket change. Now that he'd given Bill his body, they were merely haggling over the price.

With the deal consummated, Max quickly dressed and ran a hand through his tousled hair. He was ready to put what had just happened behind him, but Bill seemed interested in a little post-coital pillow talk.

"I hope Cavanaugh appreciates your loyalty. There aren't many guys who'd put themselves out like that for a job."

"I didn't do it for the Foundation or for Michael. I did it so Danny would have a reason to stay in Provincetown. I did it to keep from losing him."

Bill had done more deals than he could count, but suddenly the weight of what Max had sacrificed for love softened his jaded heart.

"Here," Bill said as he took a swig from his half-empty glass and handed the rest to Max. "You need this more than I do."

Max didn't bother arguing with him. He tilted back the glass and drank every last drop.

"So, this really was just a business transaction?"

"It would be a lot easier if it was, but I'd be lying if I said I didn't enjoy it."

"Well, that's always nice to hear. Now, go find your guy. Do *not* tell him about what happened tonight. What he doesn't know won't hurt him."

It was hard to hold back the tears that were sure to come, so Max said a quick good-bye and retraced his route out the gate and back into town. Danny had a social obligation with his parents, so they'd agreed to meet up in the morning for breakfast. Given the circumstances, Max was relieved to know he'd have a quiet night alone to work through his feelings.

Commercial Street was still jumping as Max crossed over and hurried down the alley that led back to the apartment. Taking the steps two at a time, he climbed the wooden staircase and slid his key into the lock. It was still too early for his mom or Josie to be home from work, so Max had the place all to himself. Moving in slow motion, he pulled the lube and condoms out of his pocket and tucked them away in his bedside table. His body was exhausted, but his head told him to hit the shower and rinse away any evidence of Bill.

For the second time in under an hour, Max stripped out of his clothes and headed for the bathroom. Just as he turned on the water, the kitchen phone began to ring.

"Hello?"

"Hi."

"Hey."

At the sound of Danny's voice, the gravity of what Max had done came crashing down like a wave. Naked and ashamed, he snatched a dishtowel and used it to cover up his private parts. The illuminated clock on the kitchen stove marked each pregnant moment of silence. Max had learned the hard way that keeping a secret from Danny was like holding his breath; ultimately, it would be a question of when, not if, he'd have to exhale. The longer he waited, the worse it would be. Max opened his mouth to speak, to confess the truth before the lie had a chance to take root, but Danny interrupted him before he had the chance.

"I love you."

All Max had ever wanted was to hear those three words. Now, Danny's profession of devotion made it painfully clear that Max had just put everything at risk to protect what he already had.

"Did you hear me, Maxie?" Danny said, trying to cover up his disappointment with a chuckle. "I said 'I love you.'"

"Thanks."

The polite acknowledgement of Danny's feelings was almost as shitty as saying nothing at all, but it the best Max could manage. Tomorrow, he'd find a way to make things right, but tonight, it was all he could do to hold it together.

"You sound strange. Are you okay?"

"Just on pins and needles about Berklee. I should hear something soon. I'll be fine after some sleep." Max needed to end the conversation now, before he said something they'd regret. Bill Woodside was right—what Danny didn't know couldn't hurt him. "Still, want to meet for breakfast?"

"Or I could sneak over now..."

"I was just about to turn out the light and crash. I think we both need some rest. I'll see you first thing in the morning."

"Sleep tight."

Max put the phone back in its cradle and stumbled into bed. Burying his face into his pillow, he pulled the blanket around him and heaved the first, heavy sob. Suddenly, he was ten years old again, grieving for his dad and knowing his world would never be the same. In all the years since, the walls around Max's heart had protected him from getting hurt, even if it kept him from feeling anything at all. Now, that same sense of loss had returned, sharper and more heartbreaking with the knowledge that he'd brought this all on himself.

As much as Max hated duplicity, the truth seemed less noble than a lie. The odds were against him, but he wasn't going to give up without a fight. Alone in the dark, Max stared up at the ceiling and practiced the lines he'd tell Danny in the morning. Only time would tell whether Bill Woodside would rat him out or renege on their deal, but there was one thing that was certain.

It was going to be a long night.

CHAPTER 15

A T 5:59 A.M., Max slipped out of bed and tiptoed to the bathroom. After working the graveyard shift, Josie and his mom would be asleep for at least a couple more hours. That meant he could take his time in the shower without having to worry about using up the hot water.

The failing boiler that serviced the apartment building had been on life support all summer, so Max didn't even bother turning on the cold faucet. Within minutes, the bathroom was filled with a dense bank of steam that was almost as thick as the fog in his head. Max washed once, then again, using the orange bar of soap like a pumice rock to slough off the remnants of Bill from his body. By the time he stepped out of the tub, his skin was pink from the friction and heat.

Back in the bedroom, the clock warned it was already 6:15. That only left him fifteen minutes to make it all the way to the diner for breakfast. Grabbing a fresh pair of cargo shorts from the box beneath his bed, he sniffed-checked an already worn t-shirt hanging on the back of the door and snatched his keys from the top of the dresser. Max was almost to the front door when he realized his outfit was incomplete without one critical accessory.

Careful not to wake his sleeping sister, Max snuck back into the bedroom and grabbed the shorts he'd worn the night before from the plastic laundry hamper. One empty pocket wasn't cause for alarm. With six in total, the odds were pretty low that he'd guess it right the first time. But a sinking feeling of dread shook him awake when he searched through the rest of the compartments and came up empty-handed. Suddenly, Max was back in Harvard Square without a mouthpiece. But this time, no one was going to come riding in to save the day. Although he knew it was unlikely, Max checked the back pockets again and violently shook the shorts as if Danny's ring was mischievously hiding inside. No longer concerned about waking his sister, he dumped the contents of the laundry basket onto the floor and carefully inspected each article of clothing.

Under the bed. Inside the nightstand. On the white porcelain sink.

Each promising lead turned out to be another dead end. The realization of what must have happened hit him like a punch to the gut. The ring and chain must have fallen out of his pocket at Bill's, when Max had rifled through his shorts for the condoms and lube. His first instinct was to bolt back over to find it, but that would mean ditching Danny for breakfast. There was no way Bill would be awake yet anyway, especially considering how hard he partied last night. Max could grab a bite and do a quick drive-by to grab the ring on his way to work.

IF DANNY sensed anything was amiss, he certainly didn't show it. The conversation, like the food, was lukewarm and bland. Worried about his already strained finances, Max ordered the blue-plate special and spent the next five minutes explaining to Danny how his lower cost meal got its name from plates sold during The Depression, which had separate compartments for different foods, and were only available in the color blue. In truth, Max was drawn to it because the adjective matched his melancholy mood.

"Anything else I can get you boys?" the waitress asked as she cleared away the dirty dishes. Max was just about to reach for the check when Danny snatched a laminated menu off the table.

"Can I get a 'Noah's Boy' and put some shoes on it?"

"Wow," Max said, smiling at Danny's humorous attempt at diner lingo. "I guess you couldn't have just asked for the ham and eggs to go? How can you still be hungry after eating a tall stack of pancakes?"

"The order is for my dad. I told him I'd stop by the office this morning to review the plans for the abbey and discuss logistics."

Max only had a split second to think of a reason not to walk to the Foundation together so he could circle back to Bill's and search for the ring. Luckily, lying was like playing the trumpet—the more you practiced, the better you sounded.

"I'm going to go over to the library to see if I can find any books on the Franciscan order. Understanding how the monks lived and worked will give you a better appreciation of the functional design of the community."

"Good thinking, Maxie. I'll see you at the office."

"Later."

EXCEPT FOR a few delivery trucks and dog walkers, Commercial Street was still empty. While Danny waited for his takeout order, Max sprinted off toward Bill's cottage in the West End. If all went as planned, he'd find the ring and make it back from the library before anyone even noticed. Although he made record time getting across town, he stopped short at the gate.

Standing between Max and Bill's front porch, Florence Woodside was already busy tending to her roses. Luckily, the wide-brimmed hat that shaded her milky complexion from the morning sun also obstructed her view of the road. Given Bill's sexual proclivities, she was probably well accustomed to the parade of scantily clad tricks making their walk of shame from his love shack. But Max wasn't in the mood to stand around while a nosy old lady gave him the third-degree. Cursing under his breath, he turned back toward town and tried to not to think about what would happen if Danny got handsy and discovered the ring was missing from his boyfriend's pocket. It would be nearly impossible for Max to sneak away from the office during the day, but he could try again on his way home from work. By sundown, he'd have the ring back and no one would be the wiser.

Back on Commercial Street, an overly attentive librarian helped Max find the books he needed and, in less than an hour, he was on his way back to the office. Max felt like a character in a story, waiting around for the writer to decide his fate. It was doubtful that Bill Woodside would hold up his end of the bargain. Given the circumstances, Max would be happy if he just kept his mouth shut about what happened between them. Even if he didn't, Max felt better knowing that without any witnesses, it would be his word against Bill's. Undoubtedly, Danny would believe Max's lie over his enemy's truth.

LIKE A scene from a Stephen King movie, Max watched as the vintage black Mercedes-Benz slowly circled the cul-de-sac outside the Cavanaughs' house on Telegraph Hill. Polished to perfection, the ebony surface and polished chrome momentarily blinded him with the reflection of sunlight. Shielding his eyes from the glare, Max managed to identify the driver as the car passed by. With her hands locked on the ten-and-two position on the steering wheel, Florence Woodside was "Miss Daisy," without the chauffeur, as she retraced her route back down the road toward her home.

Max forced back a feeling of panic from the matriarch's unscheduled appearance as he entered the office through the side door and dumped the stack of library books on his cluttered desk. A Styrofoam container with Michael's breakfast sat untouched next to his morning tea. Max was just about to head upstairs to the family kitchen to find Danny when the pocket doors to his boss's private office slid open.

"There you are!" Michael exclaimed, beaming with a smile as he pulled the gold foil and metal cage off the neck of an expensive bottle of champagne. "Now, we just need to find my son so I can tell you both the good news."

"I'm right here," Danny said, suddenly appearing in the doorway to the back deck, wearing a scowl. "But maybe we should speak in private, first."

"Don't be silly. Max has given his blood and sweat to the Foundation. He deserves to hear this news as much as anyone. Bill Woodside has pulled the chapel from his development plans and the town council has unanimously voted to give the Foundation the first option to buy it. If all goes as planned, we can close on the property and start renovations next month."

"Isn't that great?"

Danny answered his boyfriend's question by abruptly turning around and disappearing back outside. Max quickly followed, but by the time he reached the spiral staircase, his runaway boyfriend was already up on the roof. Grabbing on to the metal railing, Max slowly climbed to the top of the house.

"What's going on, Danny?" Max asked as he gingerly stepped out onto the roof. A sinking feeling warned him that he wasn't going to be happy with the answer.

"Why don't you tell me? Florence Woodside just dropped by to return my college ring. She found it on the porch of her guest cottage when she was out gardening this morning and noticed it was engraved with my name. Fortunately, my dad was in the kitchen and missed the whole thing."

"I can explain..."

"It took me a minute, but I connected the dots. I was too stubborn to talk to Bill one-on-one, but you knew he might be more reasonable if you went alone and met him on his own turf. I don't know what you said to get him to change his mind about the chapel, but it worked. Somehow you came through for my dad and saved the day."

"I just went through our talking points again." Max said as his mouth suddenly went dry. "After I explained how much time and money it would take to develop the land, he must have decided it wasn't worth it."

"Damn it! Why couldn't you just leave well enough alone?" Danny asked as he turned away and looked out at the vast expanse of sea grass swaying in breeze. "This morning, I had the chance to go back to Lisbon and do something important. Now, I'm right back where I was at the beginning of summer – stuck in this shitty little town, working under my father's watchful eye."

"So much for not forgetting about me. It doesn't sound like I'm even part of the equation anymore."

"That's not what I meant."

"I thought that you might actually *want* to stay in Provincetown so we could be together. But I guess the whole promise ring and 'I love you' shtick was just a tidy ending to your gay summer romcom."

Danny swiftly closed the distance between them and took Max firmly by the arm.

"That isn't true and you know it. Look, I'm sorry about what I said. Right now, I don't know if I'm coming or going, but I do know how I feel about you. Just give me some time to process this, okay?"

Like a breeze off the water, the heat of their argument had started to cool. The worst of it was already over. Max stepped closer and leaned his head into Danny's shoulder. He'd never wanted anyone to find out anything about what happened last night, but the best way to cover up a lie was to hide it behind some truth. Now that Danny knew about the lost ring and Max's clandestine meeting with Bill, there was only one awful secret left to keep.

"How about I take you into town for a romantic dinner?" Max asked as he mentally tried to calculate how much money he had left in his wallet. "Afterward, we can catch Angel's final show of the season at the Crown."

"That sounds great, Maxie," Danny said, exhaling slowly as he melted into his boyfriend's chiseled arms. "There's nowhere else I'd rather be."

THE LADIES of the Crown were determined to pack the audience for their farewell performance. Canvassing Commercial Street in micro mini-skirts and thigh-high boots, the color and cut of their stylish bobbed wigs epitomized the "girl power" mantra. Hand in hand, Danny and Max walked right into the center of what felt like a Spice Girls music video and into Angel's open arms.

"*Zig-a-zig-ah!*" Angel exclaimed as she spread her arms wide and offered up her most dazzling smile. "Part the sea, ladies, and make way for my two favorite men!"

Since she was out of glossy fliers for the show, Max was about to suggest they take her into the restaurant for a cold, pink drink when Liam came stumbling out the front door, screaming at the bouncer and stinking of Planter's Punch.

"Well, well, well. If it isn't The Prince of Provincetown, Danny Cavanaugh, painting the town red with his Evil Queen."

"Cheers, Liam," Max said, flashing his most disarming smile as he raised his hands in a gesture of mock surrender. "It looks like you've really been enjoying yourself tonight."

"I dare say I deserve a bit of harmless reverie. Why should you and Bill Woodside be the only ones who get to have a good time?"

"Let's get out of here," Max said under his breath. "Liam's kind of a mess tonight."

"A mess?" Liam asked, with his hand cocked to his ear to show he was listening. "Like the one you made at Billy's place? That's right, Max. I was there to see the whole torrid scene. He was supposed to be buggering *me* last night, but when I showed up for our date, I found the two of you on the front porch, going at it like rabbits. I was half tempted to strip down and join in on the fun, but you know what they say – two's company, three's a crowd."

Max tried to squeeze Danny's hand tighter, but he'd already pulled it away. Ready to disappear into the nearest crowd, Danny took three long strides down the street, then abruptly turned and charged back toward Max.

"You cheating bastard!"

A single punch connected with Max's solar plexus, knocking the wind from his diaphragm and bringing him down to his knees. Alone on the sidewalk, Max held his stomach and sucked in air. When he finally lifted his head, he saw one of the tall, blond drag queens holding Danny back by the shoulders as she whispered into his ear. When Max stood up and staggered toward them, it was Angel who stepped forward to block his way. It would have been easy enough to push past, but the look on her face warned him it would be a mistake to try.

"I just need to talk to Danny. Please, let me do something, before it's too late."

"Honey, you've done enough already," Angel said, in a way that made it clear she'd already chosen sides. "Go home."

The jarring finality of her words was like the explosion of a starter pistol. Running as fast as his legs would carry him, Max took off down the street and didn't look back.

"HEY, BIG bro." Josie waved to him from the couch without even looking up from her trashy magazine. "Mom is still at work, but there a bunch of leftovers from the dinner in the refrigerator. There's also something for you on the counter. I think it's from your school."

Max grabbed a butter knife from the silverware drawer and slit open the letter. With shaking hands, he pulled out the single sheaf of paper and scanned the typed the words on the page.

Dear Mr. Balais,

The Admissions Committee has carefully reviewed your application for the Berklee School of Music.

After much consideration, we regret to inform you that we are unable to offer you a place in the Class of 2004. This year's application pool was the strongest in the university's history. In light of this, we were unable to offer admission to every worthy applicant.

We appreciate your interest in the Berklee School of Music and wish you the very best in your future endeavors.

Sincerely,
Charles J. Mapletoft, Ed.D.
Dean of Admissions

Max slumped into a chair and slammed the letter down on the table. All the work and effort he'd put into chasing his dream had all been a colossal waste of time.

With calm detachment, Josie watched her brother suffer a crushing disappointment. She expected to feel empathy, or even regret, about what she'd done. After all, Max had always been good to her, even when she didn't deserve it. But she had lived too long in her brother's cold shadow. Seeing the bright glimmer in his eyes dim gave her hope that the light he'd been basking in all summer would finally be reflected her way.

Although he'd never mentioned the missing mouthpiece, the story of his trip to Boston confirmed that her efforts to sabotage his audition had failed. Josie had assumed her brother would be too busy sightseeing with Danny to notice she'd tampered with his trumpet case; by the time Max realized his predicament, it would be too late.

No one could have anticipated that Danny Cavanaugh would come running to the rescue.

The competition for admission to Berklee was stiff, but Josie had heard Max play. The admissions committee would undoubtedly recognize his talent. Ironically, the only way to ensure her brother's defeat was to orchestrate it.

It was easy enough to plagiarize the wording from one of the many rejections she'd received when she applied for nursing school last year. Once the real letter from Berklee arrived, she'd steamed open the envelope, and waited for Max to slip away for his early morning breakfast with Danny. Using a thick sheet of white paper, Josie covered up all the magic words of acceptance, and ran the redacted page through the Xerox machine at the library. It took a couple tries to get it right, but in the end she had a stack of Berklee letterhead. She'd just gotten done printing out the final forgery when Max had unexpectedly shown up. Still half-asleep and obviously in a hurry, he was too busy asking the librarian about books to notice his sister slip past him.

Max was devastated, but he still had Danny and a great job working at the Foundation. This would be a setback, but her brother was strong enough come back from this and dream new dreams. At least that's what she told herself as she watched him crumple up the counterfeit letter and throw it into the trash. Without saying where he was going, Max quickly changed into his favorite Red Sox t-shirt and headed out the door.

Once she was sure he was gone, Josie reached under the couch and pulled out a stack of color brochures. As long as she aced the SATs in October, her admission to one of her fallback schools was virtually guaranteed. It would take some begging and pleading to get Max to lend her enough for the first year's tuition, but he'd inevitably believe her empty promises to pay him back.

This time, Josie Balais was going to succeed. No one, not even her big brother, was going to stand in her way.

BY THE time Max climbed the winding metal staircase up to the roof, he was too tired and winded to even think about his fear of heights. Downstairs, the lights of the main house were already dark.

The moon wasn't as bright as it had been a week before, but there was enough light to see two bodies lying together on one of the chaise lounge chairs. Danny's strong arms were wrapped around Angel and his face was pressed up against her smooth, black hair. Danny's shirt was unbuttoned down to his navel, but otherwise they were both fully dressed. Max knew nothing sexual had had happened between them, but the closeness of their friendship felt like something worse than betrayal.

The smart thing to do was to call it a night, but it was still early and he was too wound up to sleep. Back at the apartment, Max grabbed his trumpet case and headed up Commercial Street toward the center of town. Instead of retreating to the safety of his usual performance space on the sidewalk outside the town hall, he purposely stopped in the middle of the street, right in front of The Crown & Anchor.

Max pulled his trumpet from the case and shoved one of the borrowed mouthpieces into the neck. The first blast from his horn got the crowd's attention. There were a few curious looks from passersby, but the gaggles of gays staggering on to the next venue only had one thing on their mind, and it wasn't music. Max was tired of waiting around for people to notice him. If sex was what the people wanted, that was what they were going to get.

Throwing his inhibitions to the wind, he pulled off his t-shirt and casually tossed it to the ground. That definitely got the crowds' attention. Determined not to leave his audience wanting more, he unfastened the top button of his shorts and pulled them down an inch onto his hips. Starvation and countless hours at the gym had produced a nearly perfect physique of toned muscle and v-cut abs. Right then and there, Max made himself a promise to spend less time practicing runs and more time pumping iron.

By the end of the first set, his lips were numb and his trumpet case was full of money. Paper bills, like a bed of green leaves, blanketed the dark velvet lining. Max had scored more cash in thirty minutes than he'd make playing all weekend. As usual, the crowd quickly dispersed as soon as he stopped playing and put on his shirt. This time, however, there were more than just a few casual admirers waiting for a chance to chat him up. Taking more time than he needed to, Max blew the excess saliva out of the drain valve and unscrewed the mouthpiece from the neck of the horn.

"Hey. I'm Zachary."

Max felt the raw hurt in his belly melt into heat. The guy standing in front of him was lean, with a swimmer's build and a head of thick, jet-black hair that had been buzzed short for summer. Gazing into his eyes, Max was sure this "ten" was the hottest he'd seen all summer.

"I've been around all week, but this is the first time I've heard you play. Lucky for me I decided to skip the A-House and talk a walk. You're amazing! Any chance you might want to join me for a nightcap?"

Max couldn't tell whether the guy was genuinely interested in his music or just saying what he thought Max what he wanted to hear. Either way, his smile made it clear he was offering Max more than a cold drink and some clever conversation. The last thing Max was looking for was another empty one-night stand, but going home with a handsome stranger was better sleeping alone. Maybe Danny had been right all along; it was time to move forward and leave the past behind.

"Well, Zack," Max said, as he picked up his trumpet case and slid a muscled hand into the small of his new friend's back. "It looks like tonight really *is* your lucky night."

"Good morning, Mr. C," Max said, trying his best to act like nothing was wrong. "Is Danny around?"

"No, I'm sorry he isn't."

Sunbirds usually stayed in Provincetown until Labor Day, but the grounds crew was already outside, pulling back the canopy awnings and covering the patio furniture. By the look of it, the Cavanaughs were closing up the house early and heading back to Boston.

"I don't know why you boys had a falling out last night, but whatever happened hit Danny hard. He went straight upstairs when he got home and didn't even stop back down to say goodnight to his mother. This morning, Sam came down for breakfast and ceremoniously announced that his brother had snuck a girl up to his bedroom. When we asked Danny about it, he lost his temper and told us it was none of our business. We spent most of the day arguing before he left in a huff."

Max sucked in a deep breath and held it in his abdomen. Danny was way too smart to slip up and get caught in a compromising position with Angel. All summer, he'd been leading his parents to the inevitable conclusion that he was hiding a secret. The only way to throw them off the trail was to give them a plausible alternative to the truth. Any suspicions they may have had about Danny and Max would have instantly vanished the moment he got caught with a girl. Sometimes, the best way to hide a major indiscretion was to expose a minor one.

Max stopped ruminating on his predicament long enough to notice the desks in the office had been cleaned off. Waiting in a box by the door, his library books and coffee mug had already been packed up as a clear signal that his summer internship at the Foundation had come to an end. Unfortunately, Danny had told his dad all about Max's secret meeting with Bill. Michael didn't know the details of the transaction, but he'd done enough backroom deals to know that whatever bargain Max had made put the reputation of the family at risk. Eager to cut ties before the subterfuge became public, he decided to put the chapel project on hold and move his work back to Boston. Although Michael knew Max would be grateful for the opportunity and experience, the hefty severance check that came with the pink slip felt too much like a cheap payoff.

Trying hard to hide his anger and disappointment, Max watched everything he'd ever wanted disappear. Maybe, just maybe, there was still a chance for Max to salvage his relationship with Danny, but first he had to find him.

"Do you have any idea when he'll be back?"

"He called Cape Air this morning and booked the jump seat on the noon flight to Boston. Jeffrey is already packing up Danny's things for his trip to Lisbon. He leaves on the red-eye tonight."

THE AFTERNOON ferry to Boston was late. Even longer than usual, the line of anxious tourists snaked all the way down MacMillan Pier. Max stopped at the ticket stand to confirm what he'd already guessed – both of the afternoon boats were completely sold out. He'd just turned to leave when he noticed a familiar face standing in the crowd. Even from a distance, he could see his ginger's red hair blazing in the afternoon sun.

Max should have been angry about the way Liam so callously stabbed him in the back, but they both knew he'd had it coming. To his credit, Liam had never held himself out to be any better or worse than he actually was. Of all the people Max had met over the summer, he was the least apologetic and the most authentic.

"Well, look what the cat dragged in," Liam asked, as he removed his sunglasses and squinted into the sun. "It's hard to believe you're the same shy bloke I met back in June."

"I guess we both got a little older and wiser this summer."

"I haven't the foggiest notion of what you're talking about," Liam said as he put his sunglasses back on and pretended to study the unmoving line. "I'm the love child of Dorian Gray and Narcissus— eternal and unchanged."

Smiling in spite of himself, Max leaned forward and kissed Liam tenderly on the lips. Although Liam had ended up as a secondary character in his story, Max could relate. Liam had spent the summer acting out the role of "scoundrel," but he'd played his part perfectly nonetheless.

"Take care, you gorgeous egomaniac."

"I will."

"And don't even think about looking me up if you ever get to Boston."

"Darling, I wouldn't dream of it."

DOWN AT the *La Benedita*, Captain Avellar delivered yet more bad news. Jasper had held Max's spot open for as long as he could, but after three days and no word from Danny, he'd had no choice but to offer it to someone else. Max would be at the top of the crew list next year, but he was done for the season. Luckily, the extra money he'd gotten from his job at the Foundation would make up the difference.

Max was just about to head down to the hold of *La Benedita* to clean out his locker when Angelo appeared on deck. Wearing a blue baseball cap and a simple t-shirt and shorts, anyone who didn't know any better would've mistaken him for a tourist. Max wasn't particularly interested in hearing about Angel's last night with Danny, but curiosity was like itching a scab. Even though it would undoubtedly leave a scar, Max couldn't help but scratch.

"Hey, *mijo. Cómo estás?*"

Max could only bring himself to shrug as a reply.

"I'm heading back to Puerto Rico tomorrow, so I guess this is goodbye."

"I'll see you next summer." Max tried to make it sound like a statement, not a question, but there was something about the look on Angelo's face that already told him the answer.

"I'm afraid not. I promised my mama that I'd get a real job at the rum plant with my brother Gino. I keep trying to think of a fun performance name that I can make from 'Bacardi,' but nothing comes to mind."

"I'm sure you'll come up with something absolutely fabulous," Max said, feeling the first tears welling up in the back of his eyes. Of all the costumes he'd seen Angel wear, this was the one he wouldn't forget.

Max lifted Angelo's heavy suitcase and turned to take it toward the ferry when he felt a hand reach out and grab the oversized bag by its canvas handles.

"This one's really stuffed. You sure you can handle such a big package?"

Max wasn't sure if he heard a chuckle or a muffled sob in response to the familiar taunt, but Angelo's smirk confirmed he was more than up to the task. Arms locked and knees bent, he managed to take the whole load without breaking eye contact.

"Suit yourself."

Max watched the last of his posse walk away and climb the long metal gangplank that connected the jetty to the pier. Just before Angelo passed out of sight, Max called out to him, one last time.

"Hey, *hermana*! *Mucho gusto*."

Pausing only to adjust his grip on his bag, Angelo kept his eyes forward and kept on walking. He knew that if turned around and revealed his longing for that other, worldly life, he'd turn into something harder and more bitter than a pillar of salt. It was safer to just savor the memories than to risk looking back.

THE CHILL of a sunless afternoon had driven the few tourists left in town back indoors. The empty streets reminded Max of a time, not so long ago, when the prospect of summer had filled him with anticipation. Now, all he had to show for the past three months was a lingering suntan and a belly full of regrets.

It seemed fitting to stop at Spiritus for a final slice to mark the end of the season.

Max pushed open the door and walked up to the counter. He didn't need to look at the chalkboard of specials or peruse the menu to know what he wanted. His order, like his future, was already chosen.

"Just give me a plain slice," he said, without even bothering to look Gus in the eye. "And can you wrap it to go?"

"Sure, kid. Hey, you wouldn't happen to know anyone who's looking for a job, would you? Two of my guys just quit and we're really in a bind."

Max laughed out loud at his stupid luck. As usual, Destiny brought him an opportunity when he needed it the most. Unfortunately, taking the job meant staying in Provincetown and living with his mother and sister. Still, nothing was forever.

Next year, he'd reapply for school and compose an even better audition piece. One more year was all it would take. After that, he'd be ready to conquer the world.

EPILOGUE

MAX KNEW the warm weather wouldn't last. The cold would return, as it always did, forcing everyone back inside for at least another month.

Up on Telegraph Hill, the houses were all still dark. Like Rip Van Winkle, the largest one slept on through the passing seasons, donning its familiar cupola like a sleeping cap. It had been over a year since anyone had seen a light on in any of the windows. Perhaps the stately home was destined to become one of the historic properties that had fallen into disrepair. Lost to folklore and memory, it would become just another colorful strand of thread in the tapestry of Provincetown.

The ding of the copper bell above the front door to Spiritus took Max by surprise. Another customer, right before close, was a good sign. Business was picking up.

The man looking back at him was familiar, but changed. His face was unshaven and he was wearing a red baseball cap to control his tangle of curls. The passing of a decade had brought his handsome features more into focus, sharpening the contour lines of his face, and deepening the distinctive cleft in his chin. His eyes were still the color of the ocean, but the smile that had always danced across his face had been wiped clean.

"Hey, Max. How you doing?"

"I'm great, Danny, thanks."

And just like that, they were just two old friends catching up with one another. Still, the simple exchange of civilities was like walking on broken glass; one wrong step could leave them both cut and bleeding.

"How's your mom? And Josie?"

"Josie just finished her master's in nursing. Mom went to their house in Somerville at Christmas and decided to stay for a while to help out. Josie's husband Emilio is doing his residency at Mass General and they have two boys, Tommy and Michael."

"It's hard to imagine Josie working in Boston with a family of her own."

"Yeah. At least one of us made it out of here alive. Shit. I'm sorry, Danny. That just slipped out. I called and left a couple messages for you after the accident, but...."

"I know," Danny quickly interrupted to stop Max from saying more. "I never got around to checking the voicemail at the house. Byron told me you spoke at the public memorial service. Thanks for doing that."

"I know they weren't my real family, but I loved them too. So, I guess you heard about Bill Woodside?"

"Yeah. I'm sorry." Danny said, taking off his hat to run a hand through his hair. "It's no secret how I felt about him, but I know he was pretty important to you."

"We were just friends, but it was hard to see him suffer, especially toward the end. Cancer sucks. We all tried to help out with his care, but Florence just shut down and locked him away. She wouldn't even let anyone attend the funeral service."

"That's rough. I'm sorry."

"You keep apologizing for stuff that had nothing to do with you."

"I guess what I'm trying to say is that I think you deserved better."

"Let's just agree I got as good as I gave."

"Fair enough."

There were so many things Max wanted to tell to Danny, but the words were stuck in his throat. Too much had happened for them to pick up where they'd left off. Still, the history that had connected them to each other was like the jetty. The massive, granite stones were swallowed up by the rising tide, but the bridge that connected Long Point to the mainland was always there, hiding just below the surface, waiting to be crossed when the water subsided.

Nearly ten years had passed since Max had last spoken to the Cavanaughs. Somehow, it felt like yesterday. Sam would have been twenty now, the same age Max had been that last summer. The memories of his time with Danny's family were bittersweet; painful to remember, but too precious to forget. Stored away like his dad's painting, Max would bring them back out someday, when the time was right.

"I heard you were back in Provincetown last August, right before the accident, but I didn't see you around?"

Danny adjusted his stance and pulled inside himself before he gave his answer. There was a time, a lifetime ago, when he would have been stoked to tell his best friend about the guy he'd met last summer.

"I ended up renting my own place up in the East End. Actually, it was only a couple doors down from Liam's parents. He decided to go check out Ibiza, but I spent most of my evenings hanging out with his family. I got really close with his brother Kyle."

Danny stopped to collect his thoughts. When he continued, his voice was quieter.

"He's actually the reason why I wasn't on the plane with my family. My dad decided to fly us all back to the city in his Cessna, but at the last minute, Kyle asked me to stay and go with him to a party. I told my parents I'd take the morning ferry instead of going back with them at night. They were almost back to Boston when a short in the electrical system blew out the instruments. Dad managed to fly by sight for a while, but he misjudged the altitude in the dark and...."

"So Kyle's the reason you're still alive?"

"I guess you could say that."

"Then I guess I owe him a drink."

"Yeah. Me too."

The silence that followed made it clear that Max finally understood everything about Danny's sudden disappearance. Now he was back in Provincetown, haunting Max like the ghost of a past he'd spent a decade trying to forget.

"Take care, Maxie. It was really good to see you again."

Max was just about to offer Danny some free food to try to get him to stay and talk when the bell above the door rang again and his spectre disappeared back into the cold.

"So, how was the pizza?"

Max stepped out of the shadows hefting two loaded trashcans. The hooded sweatshirt he was wearing barely covered his broad frame. Despite Peter's initial antipathy, the idea of going home to an empty bed tempered the tone of his response.

"It was good. Thanks for not sending me away hungry."

It was getting late and neither man seemed particularly interested in small talk. Lonely enough to spend yet another night in bed with a stranger, Peter let Max lead him back to his studio apartment. There was no logical order to what happened next: strong hands tugged and pulled at Peter's belt before they'd even exchanged a single kiss. Max was more than just a player; he was captain of the varsity. Scoring with the new guy was all that mattered.

"Wait a minute," Peter said, trying to pull away. He realized what he was about to do would make him feel even worse. Suddenly, going home alone didn't seem like such a bad idea.

"Wait for what? Come on, man. Just loosen up."

Powerful arms snaked around Peter's torso and sharp teeth nipped at his ear; those muscles under his jacket weren't just for show. Max could easily force Peter to stay, but for someone like him, the chase was half the fun.

"No? You sure?"

Peter answered with a stone-cold stare.

"Not tonight, huh? That's cool. No worries."

Defiantly, Max gave him one last hard kiss and disappeared down the nearest alley.

Peter waited until he was out of sight before wiping his mouth with the back of his hand. A momentary lapse of judgment had almost led to another colossal mistake; at least he'd stopped before it was too late.

Max watched his last chance for company retreat into the night. For a split second, he thought about chasing after him, but experience had taught Max not to go after things he couldn't have. Pulling a keychain from his pocket, he climbed the wooded stairs to his apartment and slipped the key into the lock.

Too late, Max found his missing words. Telling Danny "I love you" probably wouldn't have changed anything. Still, after replaying that last night in his head for so long, it would have been nice to get the chance to finally say it out loud.

Maybe tomorrow he'd dust off his trumpet and play. Just this morning, his mom had emailed him an article from the Boston Globe about a new musical ensemble that was holding open auditions for summer stock. The pay would be shit, but at least it would be a step forward, in the right direction.

Turning his head, Max looked back over his shoulder at the empty alley as a familiar voice told him to forget about music and spend more time at the gym.

"If only..." Max whispered as he squeezed the outline of the gold ring hidden beneath his hoodie and stepped through the open door. There was no point finishing his sentence. There was no one inside to hear.

Born into a blue-collar family, John Wells beat the odds and came out a winner. As chief of staff to Patrick Donovan, a US senator and aspiring presidential candidate, he enjoys all the power and privilege of a DC insider. But while riding high on a wave of success, he's blindsided by a series of betrayals from the people he trusts the most. In the space of a single day, John's perfect life unexpectedly unravels when his career falters and his marriage implodes. Following a final, devastating blow, John assumes a new identity as "Peter" and flees to Provincetown, where a tight-knit community of eclectic characters slowly transforms him.

Peter finds himself drawn to Danny Cavanaugh, an enigmatic carpenter who is struggling to come to terms with his own troubled past. As they work together to renovate a local landmark, the two men forge an unlikely friendship that blossoms into love and becomes the foundation for a new life they hope to build together. But when a reversal of fortune pulls John back to DC, the treacherous world of politics he thought he'd left behind threatens to destroy his chance at true happiness.

ABOUT THE
AUTHOR

WILL FRESHWATER was born and raised in a small steel town outside Pittsburgh. He graduated cum laude from Boston College and was awarded a Juris Doctorate from the University of Pittsburgh School of Law. Will has lived and worked in Boston, Philadelphia, Washington, DC, and Tampa. Although he enjoyed a successful career as a corporate attorney, Will can happily confirm that his true vocation is writing. He currently resides in Rehoboth Beach, Delaware, with his husband, Stephen, and Daisy, their golden retriever.

You can contact Will at www.willfreshwater.com.

Made in the USA
Middletown, DE
15 February 2024